PRAISE FOR OF STRANGERS AND BEES

'Learned, strange and charming, *Of Strangers and Bees* enriched my understanding of history.' — Marcel Theroux, *Guardian* (Book of the Day)

'An alluring, disjointed novel of parables and allegories [...] In many ways, *Of Strangers and Bees* feels like the culmination of all of Ismailov's works, experiences, and philosophies.' — Will Harris, *Books and Bao*

'Any reader might find themselves with a pen and paper handy, ready to take down tokens of wisdom [...] For all its depth and complexity, *Of Strangers and Bees* remains a page-turner, driven by Sheikhov's captivating inner monologue.' — Hannah Weber, *Calvert Journal*

'It is Ismailov's skill to keep us fascinated by the story or, rather, the stories, which are both deadly serious but, in some cases, very funny, as well as to educate us about his culture, his faith and the very real problems of exiles, particularly those coming from a culture that threatens them, their family and their well-being.' — *The Modern Novel*

'I am extremely excited to see this "modern Sufi parable" being published in the UK. This is a magnificent epic [...] a must-read for anyone who likes reading diverse literature.' — Rabeea Saleem, *BookRiot*

'Many of the episodes are beguiling. One could characterise the overall effect as *Master and Margarita* comes to the Uzbek Cultural Center of Queens, NY.' —David Chaffetz, *Asian Review of Books*

PRAISE FOR THE DEVILS' DANCE

'A mesmerising – and terrifying – novel of tremendous range, energy and potency. This brilliant translation establishes Ismailov as a major literary figure on the international scene.' — William Boyd

'A beguiling tale of khans, commissars, spies and poet-queens [...] in a rare English translation of modern Uzbek fiction.' — *Economist*

'Captivating. A rare example of Uzbek literature translated into the English language – in this case admirably so by Donald Rayfield.' — *Times Literary Supplement*

'Might Hamid Ismailov's *The Devils' Dance* open Central Asian literature to the world as Gabriel García Márquez's novels did for Latin America? It deserves to' — *Asian Review of Books*

'Ismailov shows that even under extreme duress, a writer's mind will still swim with ideas and inspiration [...] Rebellious, ironic, witty and lyrical [...] A work that both honours and renews that rich tradition [of Central Asian literature]' — *Financial Times*

'[Ismailov is] a writer of immense poetic power.' — *Guardian*

MANASCHI

TRANSLATED BY

MANASCHI

HAMID ISMAILOV

DONALD RAYFIELD

TILTED AXIS PRESS

dedicated to the Manaschi Saparbek Qasmambet

TRANSLATOR'S INTRODUCTION

WHAT IS THE MANAS AND WHO IS A MANASCHI?

The oral Kyrgyz folk epic, *Manas*, is as important to the Kyrgyz nation as Shakespeare is to the English-speaking world. It was not recorded in writing until the 1870s, and only very recently have full editions been published. Depending on the reciter, the *Manas* can comprise from 250,000 to 900,000 verses, and is longer than the Finnish *Kalevala* or Sanskrit *Mahabharata*. Each reciter adds, deletes or varies the verse, so that the epic has constantly evolved. Researchers date it to the eighteenth century, but believe that it incorporates earlier folk episodes, possibly from the tenth. The eponymous hero Manas may well be as historical as he is legendary: the son magically born to the elderly cattle herder Jakyp, Manas unites and leads the Kyrgyz in the battles they fight over the centuries to overthrow Chinese and Mongol domination and to return from the Altai Mountains to their original (and present) homeland in the Tien Shan. Manas acquires allies, enemies, wives and magical powers, and survives assassination attempts in a series of struggles with virtually every nation of Central Asia.

The epic itself varies from lyrical and mystical episodes to evocations of battles, betrayals and intrigues – from heroic grandeur to, on occasion, shockingly patriarchal lewdness. The *Manas* is usually linked to epic poems of Manas's successors, the *Semetey* and *Seytek*. It is not only a retelling of centuries of history in legendary, sometimes mythical form, it is a moral work that dictates codes of behaviour for Kyrgyz men and women. Translations have been attempted, but few succeed in rendering the quality of a poem that demands a musicality and stamina lost to modern cultures. For an English-speaking reader by far the best experience comes from the translation, with original text and extensive commentaries, by A. T. Hatto of a particularly fine episode, *The Memorial Feast for Kökötöy-Khan*, Oxford University Press, 1977.

The epic's performer, the Manaschi, was (and still is) a special individual in Kyrgyzstan: he has to be endowed with a phenomenal memory, an ability to induce a trance-like state, and with musicality (the *Manas* can be chanted or accompanied by a stringed instrument). Almost always, the Manaschi inherits his knowledge and his genius from a close male relative or mentor: frequently the Manaschi is credited with shamanistic powers (which is why Islamic clerics often regard the poem and the Manaschi with suspicion) and magical abilities to move through time and space, even to prophesy. In this novel the hero Bekesh inherits from his Kyrgyz uncle and foster-father Baisal not just a horse and an eagle (as important as any human family member to a traditional Kyrgyz), but the vocation and knowledge of a Manaschi, which he is reluctant to realise. At the same time, Baisal's schoolboy grandson, Dapan, also has a miraculous memory of the *Manas*, a gift that is to prove disastrous. To be born a *Manaschi* can have a tragic outcome.

ETHNIC CONFLICT

One main thread in this novel is the complex web of ethnic relations and conflicts in what used to be Turkestan and then Soviet Central Asia. Ever since Turkic tribes started migrating from Siberia in the fifth century AD to a Central Asia dominated by Iranian peoples, an uneasy symbiosis has developed: the Kyrgyz and Kazakhs remained nomads and cattle herders, while the Uzbeks integrated more closely with neighbouring Tajiks, who are Farsi speakers. Bekesh, the hero of Hamid Ismailov's novel, has a Kyrgyz father and foster-father, but a Tajik mother. After a period of Mongol domination, Turkestan split into Emirates and Khanates, sometimes at peace, sometimes warring with one another; under Russian and Soviet rule, new borders were established. Today's republics (the 'stans') have old borders which leave Uzbeks stranded in Kyrgyzstan, Kyrgyz in Tajikistan, Kazakhs in Uzbekistan: an endless source of violent clashes. People are aware of a common identity, and many remain bilingual in an Iranian dialect and a Turkic language, but ambitious local politicians, as well as 'alien' influences – Russian, Islamic (Central Asia traditionally has a tolerant version of Islam, which Wahhabi clerics militate against) and Chinese – disrupt what was once an enduring, albeit uneasy symbiosis. In Hamid Ismailov's novel there are good people and bad people of all nationalities, but sudden incursions arouse ancient enmities: the Chinese, now arriving with bulldozers instead of swords, building 'belts and roads' instead of (or as well as) a multi-ethnic empire, remind the Kyrgyz of the Imperial China that oppressed the Turkic 'barbarians' with such ferocity centuries ago, in a resurgence of hostility which leads the *Manaschi* to a violent end. Hamid Ismailov's novel is not just an evocation of a traditional culture, but an alert to an unfolding disaster.

ON THE TRANSLATION

Hamid Ismailov has, one might think perversely, written a novel in his native Uzbek about Kyrgyz and Tajiks (Uzbeks have only a marginal presence), and the novel sometimes reads as if written in an Uzbek that a Kyrgyz would write. The two languages are closely enough related to be, with care, mutually intelligible. But Uzbek has lost half the Turkic vowels preserved in Kyrgyz, and Kyrgyz has lost four guttural consonants preserved in Uzbek, which gives the translator a challenge in identifying from the Uzbek form the Kyrgyz word that should be consulted in the dictionary. Whereas Uzbek borrows unstintingly from Iranian and Arab vocabulary, Kyrgyz is much more homogeneous, just now and again admitting Mongolian or Chinese words into its lexicon. Fortunately, the Soviet tradition of lexicography has left us with superb dictionaries of Uzbek and Kyrgyz. But the linguistic wealth and diversity has made an English rendering a kind of linguistic triathlon that strains the translator's every muscle, an experience which I do not complain of, but look back on, dazzled and grateful.

Donald Rayfield

PART ONE

On the last day of the third twelve-year cycle, Bekesh had a dream which might have been a hallucination. He dreamt that he had crossed many rocks and hills to see his Uncle Baisal's yurt on the highland pastures. In one gauntleted or gloved hand, his uncle was holding Tumor the hunting eagle, while in his other hand was a bowl full of fresh or sour milk. When the fierce Tumor saw Bekesh, who had not been very cautious in his approach, the creature grew alert, as if he were about to fly off to hunt; then he flapped his thickly feathered wings and crashed against the door through which Bekesh had just entered. Bekesh greeted his uncle and sat down across from him, his face pallid with anxiety. His uncle proffered the bowl he was holding and said, 'Drink!'

The drink in the bowl was white, but neither fresh nor sour milk. If it was salt, it didn't taste salty; if it was snow, it hadn't melted; if it was sand, it wasn't grainy. When he was a child, in pioneer camp, Bekesh had had to down a liquid slurry called 'gulvata', and this was what he was reminded of in the dream. If he had to sip it, he couldn't have; if he'd been told to chew it, his teeth wouldn't have coped with it. As he sat there, his head spinning and his mouth parched, the sharp-eyed Baisal stared at his nephew and ordered him again, 'Try it!' Bekesh made an effort and took a gulp of the stuff: he felt a heavy weight in his stomach. The tape recorder he held in his hand and the desire he had had for a heart-to-heart interview were now forgotten.

Just then a loud noise rang out. It was as loud as if hordes of horsemen were bursting in, turning everything upside down. Alarmed, Bekesh looked all around him. The panic-stricken eagle flew through the wind back into the yurt. Together with the stinging cold of the snow, like myriads of sparks, there came what may have been foot soldiers or perhaps horsemen. Something like ice penetrated Bekesh's heart, it was some strange force that seized his whole being. The lordly Baisal, who was sitting by his side now, instantly had his eyebrows and beard turned white; he dissolved into spinning whirls of snow dust and wormwood. And with a rumbling roar, together with the yurts and everything in sight which was swallowed up in a white blizzard, he vanished...

In a cold sweat Bekesh awoke from this dream. He vigorously rubbed his swollen eyelids. He worshipped a God whom he had never once recalled in his life. He looked all around him. Utterly alone, he saw his walls still standing, calmed down a little and became settled.

—

In the morning, when Bekesh looked in the mirror to shave his thin beard, his face had turned into a piece of hide, stretched over his skull. Had it always been like this, or had the flesh on his cheeks and jaw thinned? This was how aliens were de-

picted: had he now turned into one too? Had his Kyrgyz heritage come to the fore now that he was ageing, and had every
trace of his Tajik mother been lost? As he was shaving his wispy
beard, recalling his dream the fear he had felt the night before,
there was a knock at the door. Bekesh took a slightly dirty
towel, wiped his face perfunctorily and went to answer it: a
postman in a black gown stood at the threshold, holding a sin-
gle-sheet telegram in his hand. 'Sign for it,' he said as he offered it to Bekesh. Bekesh signed for it, took the letter, and
without saying even a word of farewell to this black shade, set
off downstairs.

'Your Uncle Baisal has died. Come!' read the telegram.

Staring through the door after the departing black crow,
Bekesh shivered violently, stark naked but for his dirty towel,
the flesh on his shoulders sticking to his bones.

—

That day, when he got to the local radio station where he
worked, Bekesh asked for indefinite leave of absence. His boss
was uncooperative initially. When he heard of the death of
Baisal, the famous *Manas* reciter, he had his underlings run to
the archives to search for dialogues recorded at one time by
Bekesh himself. Only after these were recovered did he finally
sign off on Bekesh's request. Bekesh now took the opportunity
to retrieve for himself copies of some conversations that had
slipped his memory. Then he borrowed a small sum of money
from his Jewish colleague Yashka, and went on his way.

It was a long time ago that Bekesh had arrived in this town,
which was an intricate patchwork of ethnicities. After leaving
the army, he had turned to his studies, and then this radio

work. He was tethered to a stake here, as the Kyrgyz say, 'Whomever my elder brother marries, she's my sister-in-law.' This place kept him on an even keel, it kept him calm. He'd licked its salt and grazed its grass. He was used to the people, he was recognised by the locals.

So now, as the snow fell, his loneliness hidden under the broad brim of his felt tricorne hat, and as he dashed off towards the bus stop together with the flow of the town's anxious citizens, he heard on one side a joyful shout, 'Hey-y-y, Bekesh, man!', and on the other side, a question, 'Is that you, Bekesh?', and elsewhere 'Hey there, did you see that?', spoken by yet another voice from a truck passing as softly as if it was wearing felt boots, too.

But Bekesh's mood was sombre. There's no dawn for an old maid, as they say, and he remembered a village in the distant mountains: the very village where death had struck his uncle. In this snow, as thick as sawdust, would any bus be going to the mountains? It was just as well that he'd borrowed money from Yashka: if the bus didn't come, he would simply stop a car or lorry and pay the driver.

Chekbel, the village where Bekesh was born and raised, was in the same Pamir ravine as Chong Alay, in the mountains that straddled the borders of two countries. Half of the villagers were Kyrgyz, half Tajik. This division went right through Bekesh's family. Those born on his father's side of the family were pure Kyrgyz from Alay, whereas the relatives on his mother's side were Pamiri Tajiks. Probably it was because of this split that, inclined to be neither Kyrgyz or Tajik in his village, Bekesh had gone to live in this town as an adult, a place so alien to him and so mercenary. True, Bekesh's mother, the red-head Zarina, had died when he was a child, so Bekesh was more or less left in the care of his Granny and, after his father remarried, he had remained dependent on her. When his father passed away, he grew up under the supervision of his Uncle Baisal. So now, Bekesh, who had become a townsman, was in effect journeying through the snow to bury his father. Hadn't the dream which came to him last night been about this? Or did his dream have some other meaning?

—

There was indeed no bus going to the mountains. Bekesh caught a lorry that was travelling halfway there. He was the third passenger crammed into the cab. Once they left the town, the road became hilly; the snow had covered the road, and by now it was dark. If it weren't for the chains on the wheels, no force could have kept them from skidding on the slippery tarmac. The half-drunk driver, who was aware of this, constantly engaged his passengers in conversation as if to distract himself, and the passenger next to him seemed to be equally loquacious. Nobody else could get a word in, which suited Bekesh. Ignoring the unending flow of the conversation between a bird-brain and a chatterbox, he remembered his uncle, recalling his pleasant figure and noble turn of phrase.

Once the lorry had climbed the first pass and had begun the easy section downhill, which wasn't so steep, the driver had had an earful of all this chatter. 'Now, man, let's hear from you too!' he addressed Bekesh. Bekesh was reluctant to be torn from his inner thoughts. 'What can I say, then?' he mulled, and the passenger sitting next to the driver suddenly blurted out, 'A thousand flowers!' Bekesh unexpectedly cracked a smile. For nearly ten years Bekesh had been broadcasting a programme on the local radio called 'A Thousand Flowers'. These lovely people had recognised him from just five words he had spoken. Bekesh unburdened himself in all sincerity, explaining that he was going to Chekbel and that his Uncle Baisal had just died. There was a general expression of sorrow, as everyone touched their faces with their hands in prayer.

This was something which his interlocutor couldn't let pass: 'Do you mean the great Baisal?' he asked, showing off his knowledge again. Without waiting for an answer, he continued deferentially, 'They say he stopped reciting the *Manas*, but why?' Bekesh had always shunned such questions. But, as it happened, the lorry screeched, and suddenly swerved on its path, the load in the back compartment rumbling loudly with a bang. With one wheel completely jammed in a great pothole in the middle of the road, they came to an abrupt halt.

For all the talk about the lorry's getting stuck, thank God it hadn't overturned. In the blink of an eye the bewildered driver sobered up; and the trembling passengers, including that idiot of a chatterbox, all got out of the back of the vehicle onto the side of the road. The engine had stalled and there was absolute silence all around. The only audible sound was of snowflakes falling gently onto their faces. There was not a star in the heavens, nor a glimmer of light on the ground: just a deep blue darkness. For a moment everyone was stunned, then the driver switched on a Chinese torch and inspected the wheel that had plunged into a pothole. Fortunately, there was no sign of any puncture. Stretching their limbs, the passengers all followed the torch and walked round the lorry. Everything seemed to be all right. 'Let's get a move on!' said the chatterbox; the driver agreed and dived into the cab. After a call of 'One, two, three!' they pushed the lorry. The wheel sent out a flurry of snow, which had turned into muddy slush: the vehicle was still stuck in the deep pothole.

The driver got down again. 'Put some juniper branches under it,' he said. But while searching for his hatchet, he came across his dinner, which he'd tied into a bundle. 'It's dark now, let's have a bite to eat!' he said, inviting everyone round the lorry's headlights. The others now took their bags and sacks out of the cab: some had doughnuts, some sweets, some bottles. Bekesh filled his chest with a deep breath of the mountain air; the day was now virtually over but he felt neither hungry nor thirsty. Besides, he hadn't taken any provisions for his sudden journey. So he did the decent thing by grabbing hold of the axe in the lorry's ladder-rungs and announcing that he'd cut some juniper while the others ate. His fellow passengers wouldn't agree to this, 'Let's each cut a hundred, that will be something to do!' There was no alternative: Bekesh joined in with the rest of them.

It was a special pleasure to be lit up by two columns of light from the headlamps in the nocturnal darkness, to gaze out at the gradually fading shadows of the mountains around, the heavy clouds pouring down on the land their load of snow, the peace and quiet not broken by a single sound... The driver passed some vodka for Bekesh and a piece of Kyrgyz sausage to bite on. Out of a kind of forgetfulness, Bekesh swallowed the food and drink he'd been offered without being aware of doing so, so distracted was he, and he once more recalled that he was in fact in mourning when his lips felt the sweetness of sustenance. Trying to wipe away the fat with a greasy hand, he said grace, grabbed the hatchet and hurried off into the pitch darkness.

—

One part of the route followed a bottomless abyss: it ran along a rapid, burbling stream that now crackled under ice and snow; on the other side was a mountain which seemed to have eroded to a mere hill. If you strained your eyes in the dark, the snow which had turned blue seemed to be mixed with blackish patches. Bekesh took note of one of these patches and began to climb towards it. His spirits were beginning to rise. Perhaps the vodka he'd drunk had got into his blood: he couldn't feel the snow getting into his socks, nor was he afraid of slipping in his city shoes and tumbling down over hillocks and rocks. Finally, he reached that black spot underneath the snow and was satisfied that he could feel the crooked branches of a juniper bush. Sitting sideways, holding on to its craggy trunk, he regained his senses.

Life was like this journey, he unexpectedly thought to himself. After passing smoothly, it's broken up with a thump, and you never know who you are, where you are, or why. As Uncle Baisal used to say, when one's mouth touched the plov, the nose hit a stone.

Bekesh remembered his uncle and shuddered. He needed to move a bit faster. He grabbed the drooping juniper trunk with one hand, and with the hatchet in the other he aimed a downward blow at the bush. The tree shook and shed its load of snow, the axe bounced off its trunk and struck Bekesh's knee. In the pitch darkness Bekesh howled and swore. When the pain abated, he stood back a little and once more struck the juniper with the axe. The juniper's core, as hard as a leather strap, threw the axe back again. Bekesh grabbed the axe with both hands, stood with his legs apart, and struck its core at an angle, rather than straight. The axe now penetrated the juniper trunk. As if hacking with a pickaxe, Bekesh swung the tool from the shoulder and once more slashed the juniper's open wound. He struck again, again he hit it!

Bekesh's head was spinning – perhaps because the inner sap of this unsightly juniper, rigid in the cold, perfumed the air. Apart from the wind, coming from the mountains and rocks, the juniper had to endure the snow and rain, and risking a rush of water or an avalanche, it had to use all its strength to cling to its little patch of earth and to life itself. Bekesh's hands were covered with blisters, all the worse now they were lacerated. The juniper's resistance roused Bekesh to a drunken fury, seething and unbridled and wordless.

—

After crushing the juniper and forcing it under the wheel, they set off again on their uneventful travels and reached the small town, their destination, at midnight. The mountain Kyrgyz are good-natured folk, and the driver was suddenly concerned for Bekesh. 'I'll take you to your village, I can relax there too,' he said, after he'd unloaded his lorry in three different places, taking care in the darkness. Treating Bekesh as a bosom friend, he set off over the ruts and potholes towards Chekbel. Night passed, so did early morning, and they reached the village before noon.

Bekesh was wondering whether they would keep his Uncle Baisal's body for three days, as the Kyrgyz do, waiting for kith and kin to come down from the mountain pastures so as to hold a wake for the departed. Walking sticks would be propped at the threshold of the house so that when the mourners came, they might lean on their sticks and emit loud wails. But because his uncle's family was descended from mullahs, they may well have been in a rush to bury him before sunset.

When Bekesh got to the house, he noted the absence of any sticks, and he caught the sound of his uncle's widow Rabiga reciting verses of the Qur'an. So they had buried his uncle without waiting for him. Bekesh's heart was filled both by resentment and regret. In his bewilderment, he had even forgotten to wail for the dead at the threshold before coming inside. Leaving his lorry on the road, the driver followed Bekesh in, too. In the living room were Auntie Rabiga and, sitting next to her, around a tablecloth modestly laid for dinner, three elderly Kyrgyz and two Tajik women.

When his aunt spotted Bekesh, she hurriedly closed the book she was holding, said a brief final prayer, stood up and began to weep:

My true moon in moonlight,
You're as beautiful as the moon,
We couldn't stay together in the world,
God has separated us, alas.

If an eagle should flutter in the net,
There are scissors for that.
You set off for the other world,
Who, then, will stay with me?

When Bekesh heard this lament, he couldn't help but hug his aunt. To his surprise, he himself suddenly howled out:

My father gave me a horse to ride,
My father gave me an eagle to hunt with.
How sad! My father is no more,
Father, there isn't enough to shoe even one horse.
How sad! My father is no more,
Father, there's nobody to care for the eagle.

Quite unexpectedly, these words had burst forth from within as Bekesh was wiping tears of misery from his eyes with Aunt Rabiga's black-dyed handkerchief. After the sobbing and weeping, the old women ceded the place of honour to Bekesh and the driver, and Bekesh recited the Qur'an's first sura, the Fatihah, and the 112th, Qul huwa Allahu ahadun (He is Allah, the One), which he had learnt only recently. Everyone said Amen.

'This is our townsman,' said Rabiga, introducing Bekesh to everybody, then looking inquisitively at the driver.

'He's my travelling companion...' said Bekesh, giving the driver an apologetic look. They'd had such a great journey together, and he hadn't had the foresight to ask the man his name!

'Joomart,' said the driver, to put an end to the embarrassment.

'Yes, Joomart,' Bekesh repeated after him.

The hostess moved the pieces of bread closer to them. The youngish Tajik lady next to her poured the men bowls of lukewarm tea, while Rabiga began the conversation: 'He's the favourite son of my husband.

'My Bekesh, when he was a child, he slept right through when Baisal was reciting the *Manas* to the people. I shook him awake, but my husband made a sign to say, "Stop, don't touch him!" He was allowed to lie there sleeping. When he finished reciting the *Manas* the people slaughtered a sheep, and Baisal gave the "sleepy boy" the sleeping side of mutton. He was so utterly fond of this child,' she said, and began to weep again. Hearing this story for the first time made Bekesh tremble. No, not at the thought of a greasy slice of mutton at this early morning hour, but because for some reason his dream from two nights ago came back to his memory.

—

Bekesh was like a much-indulged son of his foster-father Baisal, and he considered Baisal's other three sons as his younger brothers. None of them could find work locally, so they had left for Russia. Baisal and Rabiga were left in sole charge of Bekesh's sisters-in-law and the infants in their care. Although Bekesh stayed away, every month he posted some of his earnings to his uncle and to a certain extent he compensated his younger cousins for his own failure to find them work in his town.

After suddenly ceasing to recite the *Manas* about ten years ago, Baisal had followed in the footsteps of his own father, living as a hunter and mullah. But once Shavvol, the offspring of one of Bekesh's paternal uncles, had come to these parts after pursuing his Islamic studies in foreign countries, Baisal's simple daily life as a mullah pretty well came to an end too, and he had only the hunting eagle Tumor and the trotting horse Topon to care for.

As he swallowed his cold tea Bekesh wondered what would become of them all.

'How did my father die?' he asked his aunt.

'He was as sound as a bell. In the night the eagle was suddenly restless, it started vaulting off its perch. Then the horse started whinnying. They must have woken him: he said, "I feel thirsty." I got up and brought him a bowl of sour milk from the larder, he took a mouthful and for some reason he called for you and fell back onto the pillow with a thump. The sour milk was spilt...' After beginning to tell this story so grimly, Auntie again lost control of herself and, once more she began to sob, clutching the end of her handkerchief to her swollen eyes:

If there is no moon in the sky,
Then what is there in the darkness?
If Baisal is not coming back,
What is there for me on earth?

Early the next morning his aunt gave Bekesh a slice from the sleeping side of the sheep they had slaughtered. Together with Joomart the driver, Bekesh went to the cemetery and once again recited the Fatihah and Qul huwa Allahu for his foster-father Baisal and for his own mother and father. Stepmother Rabiga put the same slices of mutton in dough for Bekesh to eat.

'He kept asking for you these last days,' his aunt told Bekesh. 'The others were a long way away, you were not far, but did you come?' she said regretfully. 'He was about to go hunting. It was the season for foxes, you could have flown the eagle together.' Bekesh was chewing the tender meat, when his heart felt a pang.

'Where is Tumor?' he asked.

'He hasn't let anyone come close since yesterday,' said the

lady of the house, pointing over her left shoulder to the next room. 'He won't eat a thing now,' she complained.

Bekesh hurriedly wiped his hand on the edge of the table-cloth, thanked God for the meal, took a piece of the meat he had been eating, and went off to the next room. If Baisal needed anything for hunting at any time, it was all was laid out for him here, beginning with an iron horseshoe and ending with leather jesses, from a quiver of arrows on a belt to an Izhevsk 58 double-barrelled shotgun. Every time Bekesh came to the village, he was sure to spend whole hours in this room with Baisal, listening to his uncle's stories of his past life while the older man wove hemp bird nets by hand and fashioned whip handles from sticks.

Very gingerly, Bekesh opened the door to the hunting room and entered. Tumor, who was tied by a leather strap to his perch in the corner, ruffled his feathers and fixed his sharp eyes on the interloper. Bekesh had known the bird since it was a fledgling. But that was another story. As he did every time he came, he greeted the eagle in a sweet voice by its name, 'Tu-um! Tu-um!' The bird shook its ruffled wings and averted its rolling eyes from Bekesh, as if to say, 'No, no!', twisting its head sharply right to left. Bekesh considered throwing the bird a piece of meat, but he knew this might only scare it. He held back. Once again he drawled in a soft voice, lamely, as if in apology, 'Tu-u-um! Tu-u-um!', tentatively stretching out his hand towards the bird. Thereupon the bird suddenly flapped a wing and hurled itself in Bekesh's direction. After being an ur-banite for so long, Bekesh had perhaps lost his courage around animals! He flung the meat at the bird and rushed out.

—

Bekesh recalled how they had come to keep Tumor. It was not so long ago, when spring was turning into summer. Bekesh was fed up with work and had come to the village to drink kumys and unwind just as his foster-father Baisal was getting ready to go on an excursion with his hunter friends. They had taken Bekesh along, mounting him on Topon, as he was skinny and agile, stopping at the nearby summer pastures on their way to Asqarqoya, which was also not far away. Baisal had suspected there might be an eagle's nest in the area and, judging by the behaviour of the parent eagles, by the way they swooped up and down, he'd realised that there must be fledglings in the nest, on the point of flying off. As they had enough time to get to Asqarqoya just before noon, they dismounted, tethered their horses and discussed what to do. Baisal pointed out a patch of twisted juniper on a mountain slope that he knew well. On top of the juniper-covered hill was a passable gap, and it was through this gap that the hunter's piercing eyes spotted a nest that looked like a woven basket.

Above the nest a stepped rock, the size of a two-storey building, rose vertically, and Baisal and the sharpshooters Janish and Topoldi would find a way up over it. A man called Chokmor would fling a goat carcase on his horse and, with the help of a tame gyrfalcon, they had planned to lure the eagles to leave their nest. Heading for the river that went around the rock, Chokmor would fling the goat into an open space and take cover himself, leaving the gyrfalcon to hover over the carcase. The eagles, taking flight and seeing both the carcase and the gyrfalcon, would hurl themselves down, challenging the gyrfalcon for this sought-after carrion, and the latter would let the eagles rob him of it. Meanwhile Baisal would climb down to the nest, put the fledglings in a thick hemp saddlebag, after which Janish and Topoldi would pull him back up onto the crag.

Had this sleight of hand worked, even if the eagles returned to their young, Jiparbek and Sattor the Tajik would scare them off by firing their rifles. If the eagles took no notice of that, then Janish, Topoldi and Baisal would use their guns. Bekesh, however, was standing by, watching over the horses who were tethered to rocks. Everyone had a job to do.

Now Chokmor galloped on his horse towards the ravine, while the three strongmen slung their rifles across their backs, and then crawled on all fours towards the crag and the nest. His rifle by his side, Baisal tied a four-metre-long stick to his waist to act as a balancing rod. Jiparbek and Sattor the Tajik now picked up their guns and headed off on foot for two sides of the crag.

On the left, the sun broke over the mountain slope, so that the snow on the summit was dazzling. Nevertheless, the three men crawling towards the nest were clearly visible, appearing to Bekesh like a line of ants. They took a detour round the ledge where the nest had been built, and made for the top of the hill, where they took cover. When the pair of eagles flew off to hunt, however long it took, the men would be ready to strike.

Perhaps the sun's rays had agitated the eagles, or they sensed the commotion all round them: the great birds, first one, then the other, now suddenly rose up into the sky. The trio of hunters on the crag froze. One after the other, the eagles swooped over the ledge and started to veer, not to the some-what distant mountain and the three hunters, who were now utterly motionless, but towards where Bekesh and the horses stood. Bekesh was anxious, and on the verge of panic. He had neither gun nor stick. He hurriedly glanced around him: there was nothing he could use to defend himself—no stones apart from the huge rocks, which were too heavy to lift. The eagles were getting closer and closer to him. Bekesh unbuttoned the leather jacket he was wearing and waved it around his head, making as much commotion and noise as he could to frighten the birds off. The eagles retreated, apparently put off by the screaming, but then rose up to the skies again, surveying the horizon. Sweating and feverish, Bekesh emitted a groan.

Once the eagles had become just two black points in the sky, they had apparently spotted the carcase, which Chokmor had laid down, and the gyrfalcon over it. Passing through Asqarqoya, the bird had flown to a ravine some distance away and was by now out of sight. The three hunters scurried like spiders to the ledge around the nest. In a minute they had gathered at a clearing over the ledge. Bekesh couldn't take his eyes off them, his heart pounding; he was aware that the eagles had just now gone behind the mountain. Uncle Baisal, with one end of a lasso tied to his waist, was about to descend. Janish and the strongman Topoldi had twisted the rope two or three times and tied the other end to a rock, and they were holding on to the remaining twists.

If the eagle came back, which hand would they use to shoot? Bekesh worried. Perhaps one man could hold onto the rope and the other could shoot: after all, the rope was tied to a rock. Baisal put a foot onto the narrow ledges on the rock, hanging on by one hand, and began to descend towards the nest, using the rope to help him down. At this point Bekesh understood the secret of the four-metre rod. Baisal had tied this rod diagonally to his waist, and it stopped one end of the rope from twisting at any time, so that the other end struck the vertical side of the crag, and held Baisal in place.

In no time at all Baisal covered the height of two storeys, reached the nest and, with the saddle-bag in one hand and a gauntlet in the other, he took something whitish from the nest. The eagle-eyed Bekesh had recognised it immediately, 'A fledgling!' At this point Baisal's horse Topon began neighing for some reason. Bekesh's heart had been reasonably calm, but now it was fit to burst. He shifted his gaze from the nest, he searched the sky. But his eyes, after being trained for so long on another distant object, warily searching far off, began to fill with tears. Bekesh rubbed his eyelids hard. As if crucified to the ledge on the crag overhanging the nest, a blurry figure was very calmly emerging upward, then he vanished, so that his being there was just a memory to be turned into a story. And the story turned into this memory.

After this, Baisal slaughtered a horse for his friends to celebrate capturing Tumor in this way.

—

Separated by force from his father, mother and siblings, for the first few days Tumor had tempered his stubbornness and defiance. Baisal showed Tumor an extraordinary tenderness, such as he had never shown any other bird. Bekesh was a witness, for he was studying the secrets of caring for this summer bird. The eaglet's obstinacy and resistance, however, had not dimmed, even now. So Bekesh tried his hand at a trick from those past times. He went out onto the veranda, took from his aunt a piece of raw meat from the slaughtered sheep, stuck it on the end of that very same four-metre stick and quietly opened the door to the hunting room.

Tumor's mood had not improved: he was sitting, his feathers ruffled, on the perch. Under it was the slice of meat which Bekesh had flung at him earlier and which the bird had left uneaten and ignored. Bekesh retreated to the door and proffered the eagle the raw meat on the end of the stick. The bird ruffled its feathers, clenching its big talons, prepared to attack. It stabbed towards Bekesh, narrowing its two cherry-like eyes. Bekesh felt he detected in those eyes some kind of demonstration, a cry for help.

'The king of the eagles can rip a wild boar to shreds,' Baisal used to say when caressing Tumor. Sticking his head through a crack in the door, from a place the eagle could not expect, Bekesh now repeated those same words. Tumor was still very distrustful, he would not look at the bait he was offered, nor was he assuaged by the familiar affectionate words. Bekesh kept repeating the words, and moved the meat on the stick nearer to the eagle's talons. Tumor made not one move. So Bekesh bent over, and propped the other end of the stick against the bottom of the wall. Once the bird's wings had started to stir, Bekesh again jumped back, expecting to be attacked, but this time Tumor folded and relaxed his wings. Bekesh silently expressed his gratitude for this. Once more he spoke affectionately to the bird; he said, 'An all-black eagle's wings have a wide reach,' and closed the door.

—

By now Bekesh's nephews had returned from their schools, his sisters-in-law had come out of their rooms, and the house was full of noise and shouting. Bekesh forgot about the eagle. Meanwhile, once Joomart the driver found out that he had a friend, a Kyrgyz or a Tajik, who lived nearby, he took his leave and drove his lorry to the far end of the village. Together with the great number of nieces and nephews Bekesh had, there was a nine-year-old boy whom he was especially fond of, his cousin once removed. The child's name was Sapar, but right from the start, since he was a toddler, Baisal had called him Dapan because he was so fearless, and the name stuck to him like glue. When this Dapan heard that Uncle Bekesh had arrived, he would go straight to his Grandfather Baisal's house.[1]

Seeing Dapan, Bekesh's eyes shone with pleasure. Baisal had made Dapan a fox-fur hat, and he wore a fur waistcoat over his school uniform, girded with a soldier's belt; in his kersey boots he was a real highlander child. He had red hair, and bright red cheeks, so full they seemed about to crack, and his mischievous eyes looked at you like a knife blade: if you had a camera in your hand, you'd photograph him in this exact position. Chatting non-stop, he was like a bird singing in the elaeagnus bushes, 'My father said, he said you're coming! Granddad Baisal has closed his eyes, he's shed tears, he's said farewell to the whole wide world. We heard you on the radio! As they say, you can think a man famous at a distance, if you come close, he's just ordinary!'

Baisal could have spat in this child's mouth, to judge by all the gifts he had passed on to this boy. The boy uttered his words very precisely, as if they had been blown by the wind in successive waves. When he heard about Tumor's terrible mood, he made for Bekesh's uncle's hunting room: without the least hesitation he went in straight away to see the eagle, and now he picked up with one hand the piece of meat which the bird's beak had not touched and put it in both hands, very calmly

1. Translator's note: from Chinese dà bān, 'big boss'.

saying, 'Here you are!' For a moment Tumor tried to work out what was going on, turned his head away, and, dismayed, lowered one wing towards Dapan's arm. The child deliberately gripped the perch with one hand and offered the raw meat in his other hand to the eagle's beak. 'Take it!' he said. The bird was stunned, turning its head towards the meat, then pecking, as if he'd never been sore at heart. The meat's reddish juice dripped from his sharp beak, and Dapan wiped it gently. Bekesh stood by the door, his jaw slack, watching eagle and child.

—

Once he had fed the eagle, Dapan spread out a prayer rug there and then for his midday prayers. Bekesh stood there in amazement. When had the child managed to learn the namaz? Had Uncle Baisal bequeathed him not just the prayer rug, but this knowledge, too? A hidden regret, almost annoyance came over Bekesh at that moment. But his feelings of affection and pride in his nephew were loftier.

Once Dapan had finished reciting the namaz, he folded up the prayer rug, took a hunk of meat that was lying on the ground, blew on both sides of it and put it in his mouth, 'My stomach is empty,' he said. He chewed and swallowed, then cleared his throat:

> The days pass one after the other,
> It's time now to stretch the stomach,
> In a village at Great Mount Talas,
> Over the extent of broad Lake Ota,
> In the black eye of the spring,

In the green plane tree itself,
He had a fat colt slaughtered,
Yellow sausage meat, chopped mane,
Cut it crosswise, scorched it,
Old man or young ones,
Every newcomer
Gets down to the meat with open mouth...

Thus he recited from the *Manas*. Not fully sated, he was carried away by verse and seemed to want to finish his tale, but then suddenly stopped: 'Uncle, I have to go and start studying the Qur'an,' he explained apologetically. 'At Uncle Shavvol's place.' And the two of them left the room and went outside.

Dapan was a child and he could play all day long: he spent his time on an isolated mud brick wall like a man on horseback. Bekesh now took the opportunity to provoke Dapan by teasing him. 'In town the Kyrgyz say you are either a follower of *Manas* or a Muslim, so say which side are you on?' Dapan said without hesitation, 'Our forefather Manas was a Muslim, he converted everyone he conquered to Islam. Our forefather Manas made the heroes Shavruk and Akhun Muslims!' Jumping off the wall, throwing his skull-cap into the air, he left the yard and vanished.

Judge a child by his age, a woman by her head: Bekesh pondered with pleasure that this saying must be right.

Once upon a time Bekesh himself had recited various excerpts of the *Manas* epic, but he had never claimed to be a *Manas* bard. It was simply that as a member of a Manaschi's family, he had learnt various episodes by heart, had recited them not particularly well, as it were, for his own amusement. But a moment ago, whilst his little nephew was versifying, scenes and words of the *Manas* seemed to spill over from Bekesh's innermost soul. Scenes which he had never memorised now seemed of their own accord to manifest themselves to him visibly, scenes whose sources were unknown to him. Naturally at first this made him afraid; yet here he was sitting alone, not out of his mind, he told himself warily. And as soon as Dapan had left for Shavvol's house, these scenes, which came to mind so easily and disappeared just as easily, were like a mountain breeze blowing a gust and then vanishing.

Or was it that his dream had infected him with the idea of becoming a *Manas* bard?

This was not the first time that the idea had occurred to Bekesh. Starting with last night's journey in the dark, if he thought about it, this feeling had become almost palpable. If Uncle Baisal were alive, he would have cleared up Bekesh's doubts and confusion, but whom now could he ask? Who would tell him, 'You may be a *Manas* bard, or you may have fallen victim to Satan,' and distinguish truth from falsehood?

—

Bekesh was exhausted after travelling all night, and his aunt, noticing his eyes were closing, offered him a mattress in one of the girls' rooms. 'Have a little nap!' she said. Bekesh lay there staring at the ceiling. He recalled Dapan's words, and the scene that had burst forth from within him. Where had it come from? Was it the episode where Manas marries Kanikey? Bekesh had loved that story with all his heart: for some reason it reminded him of his mother Zarina. It went something like this: when Manas wanted to find a wife for his friend Almambet, his own father, Jakyp, journeyed in search of a girl for him and, not finding a suitable match in Samarkand or Bukhara, he went to Tajik country, a city called Keyin. Here he came across a Kyrgyz khan called Alym-Mirza.

Alym-Mirza told him there was a girls' school in this city and that there studied Temur-khan's daughter, the beautiful Soniyrabiy. When Jakyp saw the girl, he was struck dumb, and he realised that he had found himself a young daughter-in-law, a wife for Manas. This story wove its way into Bekesh's sleepy mind and set off a whole flow of verses. He couldn't differentiate between a recital of the *Manas* and a recall of his own life, his own grandfather Jakyp who, in his own words, had found a daughter-in-law for himself and a wife for his son Bakit, 'not in a medrese, a religious school, but in a medsestra, a nursing school'.

When Bekesh went to sleep his blue eyes saw his beautiful mother Zarina with her red hair: she was wearing a white gown, and had a white kerchief wrapped round her head. She went up to her son, who was reciting a poem, and offered him what might have been ayran, milk or sour milk. 'Here, drink this, while I recite you something,' she said in her own language, in the falak, the heavenly style:

There came from China a man of eloquence,
Whose peer in painting earth will not behold,
By which accomplishment he gained his ends.
He was a man of might by name Mani.
He said: 'I prove my mission by my painting,
And am the greatest of evangelists.'

Bekesh recognised these words, which were wrapped like cotton wool around his mind, but he'd forgotten what the Farsi meant: gulping down the white liquid, he suddenly began to weep bitterly.

—

Bekesh was woken by the sharp sound of a child crying. When he opened his eyes and looked, his new-born nephew's mattress was hanging from the cradle by Bekesh's side, and the baby was yelling: he had freed his arm from the cradle strap holding him in. Bekesh got up and rubbed his swollen eyes, approaching the cradle; just then, the baby's mother came rushing in with freshly baked bread in her waistband. Bekesh went to wash himself in the household ewer. Still weighed down by his dream, he spoke to his aunt about his desire to pay a visit to their Tajik relatives.

Historically, this oasis had been a Tajik settlement, for the Kyrgyz had mostly lived on their summer pastures, but in Soviet times, when a school had been opened and a hospital and government offices were set up, the Kyrgyz had begun to camp on an elevated spot on the banks of a nameless mountain stream. It was not yet dark now as Bekesh crossed the stream's Kyrgyz bank towards the Tajik shore. Here, there was a pond where the Tajiks reared perch. You could call this village of a hundred households by its Tajik name *kishlak*, a winter camp, or by its Kyrgyz name, an *ayyl*. Towards the end of Soviet times, as a result of intermarriages, the community was becoming ethnically mixed, so that Bekesh's father's side was from the left bank, and his mother's from the right. But once the Soviet Union fell apart, the bad side of disintegration was now affecting this kishlak and ayyl. Finally it was decreed that a line along this nameless stream would mark the boundary between two neighbouring countries! This was laughable: a Kyrgyz bank going to a Tajik country, a Tajik shore supposed to belong to the Kyrgyz homeland. All right then, because the administration of neither country could deal with this isolated kishlak or ayyl that was hidden between mountains, or because there was no will to put a Chinese wall over the stream or lay mines on the periphery, as was done elsewhere, Bekesh could still, quite casually, quite without concern, pass from one sovereign country to another.

He looked at a new mosque raising its minaret at a bare spot by the water's edge, as he entered one neighbourhood. Bekesh was thinking that first of all he would go and see either Nigina his maternal aunt, or Sattor his maternal uncle. Probably at the former's he would be detained by a hundred different offerings of food until evening, at the other's house there would be in addition a poetry recital until dawn… Bekesh's Kyrgyz stubbornness was redoubled: he set off for his Uncle Sattor's place, which was nearer.

—

Uncle Sattor turned out to be cleaning the lower part of his cattle shed. When he laid eyes on his nephew Bekesh, he hurriedly washed his hands in water from the tea kettle, and wiping them on a kerchief, he rushed towards Bekesh. 'Alas, we've lost your Father Baisal,' he said in Tajik, visibly downcast, and pressed Bekesh to his chest. Because Uncle Sattor had no children of his own, he felt affection for his nephews, and of all these nephews he singled out Bekesh, and so he was much closer to Bekesh's Kyrgyz relatives than to his Tajik kith and kin. Didn't Bekesh remember a while ago how Sattor had taken part in capturing an eagle with Baisal. 'We buried him ourselves! May he have his place in paradise!' said his uncle, kneeling down at this point to recite a prayer from the Qur'an. Bekesh knelt down beside him.

After reciting the prayer, Uncle Sattor took Bekesh indoors. Men usually summon their wives by their eldest daughter's name: 'so-and-so's mother,' they might say. But Uncle Sattor lacked such possibility and therefore exclaimed, looking indoors, 'Wife!' Mutriba, Bekesh's aunt by marriage, came out. When she saw Bekesh she tapped his shoulders in a violent fit of joy, kissed him on the forehead and went off to lay the tablecloth, still smiling in delight. Mutriba was an Uzbek who had migrated to the mountains, and on seeing Bekesh, for some reason would always switch to her mother tongue: 'Dear boy, my treasure, I'm so glad you've decided to come and see us! I'm so glad, you're well, are you? You're not tired, are you? Now let's lay things for lunch!' The tablecloth had been spread out, the roast meat was brought promptly, the rice was now being cooked for plov.

Bekesh and Uncle Sattor were involved in a conversation, about the town and about the kishlak. Sattor talked about the kishlak's problems and worries. About Shavvol, who had studied Islam with the Arabs, and was now dismissing everyone else as unbelievers and renegades, or else about the rise of drug and opium dealers. They also spoke of recent times when a lot of Chinese and Afghans had started to settle here. Bekesh reported with much regret and pain that in the city nationalism was on the increase, and that everyone worried only about money now, and was desperate enough to nibble at one another.

The plov was served during this bitter conversation, and

now they were drinking tea. 'Let's talk about good things,' said Sattor. So saying, he picked a book off the shelf. As he leafed through the pages, Bekesh uttered a few brief words about Tumor the eagle's agitated state. Uncle Sattor said, 'Here we are!' and recited a quatrain from the *Masnawi* by Rumi in Farsi:

The falcon is he that comes back to the Shah
He that has lost the way is the blind falcon.
It lost its way and fell into some ruins;
then in that wilderness it fell amongst owls.

Bekesh knew his mother's tongue perfectly, but since he had moved away he had begun to find the meaning of even fairly familiar words vague; he mostly followed the general direction of the narrative, and would sit enchanted by the harmonies and rhythms of the couplets that he recalled. This particular fable was in fact about the owls in the ruins finding themselves invaded by a falcon. When the falcon says that he belongs to the Shah, the screech owls don't believe it, 'He's trying to take over our ruins,' they say, suspicious and panicked. Bekesh tried to apply this story to himself, then to Tumor, then to Uncle Baisal and Uncle Sattor, they each fitted the story amazingly well; he attempted to make sense of this part of the tale's secret:

Since my genus is not the genus of my Shah,
my ego has passed away for the sake of Our ego.
As Our ego passed away, He has remained alone:
I roll at the feet of His horse, like dust.

Hadn't Bekesh known that the poetry session would have to go on until dawn? In fact, first Uncle Sattor extracted the inner meaning of this fable by Maulana Rumi, then before his nephew Bekesh could recount his recent couple of dreams, Sattor picked up another book. He brought up the Prophet Daniel and Ibn Sirin's interpretation, and expounded them both. Thereafter he recited the couplets from the *Shah-nama* about the eagle and the storms.

Shone mid the dust – dust like a rainy cloud,
which through vermilion droppeth from the sun

and

For the world this rain is useful,
For preparing a journey this knowledge is befitting

It was finally the crack of dawn when Bekesh, thoroughly saturated with poetry, revealed his deepest secret to Uncle Sattor.

Explaining the dreams that had gripped his imagination, he said, 'Baisal offered to pass on to me the full chalice of being a *Manas* reciter, the words are seething inside me, I've got a lot to say. I don't know, it all makes me tremble inwardly.' He was trying to express his doubts and hesitations. What should I do?' he asked. Sattor gave it a moment's thought and, instead of offering a direct response, picked up another book and began reading about a journey taken by a pupil to see his master.

As far as Bekesh understood the story, the apprentice had seen his master shedding tears, and had joined in and himself begun to weep. Then the master overcame his tearfulness and looked at his pupil. 'I don't see any good reason for weeping,' he said. 'This would not be genuine, only simulated. Simulated tears are like rain, shed by a cloud to no purpose: they are not the same as when tears pour from the heart.'.

But Bekesh couldn't make sense of the fable. He would get no support in this house, he thought to himself, and felt disappointed: he could find no resolution to his doubts and suspicions, but all the same, at first cockcrow, Sattor made a bed up for Bekesh, went ahead and opened the door to a separate room, saying, 'From now on this room is yours.' Then he left Bekesh to his own deliberations.

—

Bekesh didn't sleep for very long on the five-layered mattress. He lay there, his mind turning; a man won't be sated by thoughts, nor a wolf by sheep, as they say. If being a *Manas* reciter was to be his fate, he was assessing the weight and the permanence of this calling. He remembered an occasion from a long time before. Bekesh had just begun working at the radio station then, and on his first return back to the village, he had brought with him a present, a beautiful light, fashioned out of Bohemian crystal, which he had purchased with the money he had saved, thanks to his knowledge and skills. Aunt Rabiga's joy was indescribable: 'If you have a good horse, you can travel far; if you have a good son, you have the light of your heart's desire!' she said, completely overcome, not knowing where she could find a proper base to stand this crystal light on. Finally, she took all the tea bowls and pots off the new shelf, and reaching as high as she could, arranged this precious present on that very shelf.

That morning, before recording the interview with Uncle Baisal about being a *Manas* reciter, Bekesh had sat preparing his questions in his own room. He leafed through a small book he'd grabbed off his editors, and began reading about the *Manas* reciters' extraordinary abilities: how they could establish relations with ghosts, how they could have information about the absent, easily travel in spirit to the past and to the future and, if necessary, when travelling in the guise of someone else, transform the atmosphere with the help of magic gallstones. On a blazing hot day, these folk singers could summon clouds and send rain pouring down, they could melt the ice in the bitterest of winters and were capable of getting rid of it entirely. Bekesh knew that Uncle Baisal had a magic gallstone among his possessions, but his uncle had never actually spoken of it, nor had Bekesh himself taken any interest in it. Judging by what was said in the book, the magic gallstone's miraculous powers had no limits. Suddenly, a crackling sound came from the neighbouring room. Bekesh leapt up, but when he went into the room, he saw that the Bohemian crystal lamp which had been left untouched on the shelf was now smashed to smithereens.

—

Not wanting to make too much of a fuss, but inevitably tired by these thoughts, Bekesh didn't wake up for breakfast, and even slept through the midday meal: he slept right through the night without dreaming. After midday his cousin Dapan had come looking for him; his mission was urgent and desperate. 'Wake up! Tumor is having a tantrum and won't let anyone calm him down,' he said, crying and sobbing.

Bekesh couldn't quite make sense of this, hurriedly got dressed and washed his face and hands. 'Hey, have you had anything to eat?' Aunt Mutriba asked him; but he rushed after Dapan, who was jittery with impatience. Bekesh skidded as he headed for the bridge over the mingling icy waters and the stream, and fell two or three times. But, like a mountain horse, he moved from a trot to a steady pace as he reached Uncle Baisal's house.

His Aunt Rabiga, a rather wiry woman, had seen off all her fellow mourners; she was sitting alone, not knowing what to do. 'All this time the eagle has been restless: it seems to be raving mad,' she complained.

'Did you go in?' Bekesh asked Dapan.

'Yes, he attacked and was going to stab me in the face!' Dapan replied, his heart in his mouth.

Then Bekesh thought of a cunning ploy, and asked Rabiga, 'Why don't you give me Uncle's everyday clothes?'

His aunt instantly understood her nephew's meaning and brought out her husband's things, not just his fur coat and boots, but also a fox-fur cap for his head, and for his arms two Kyrgyz hunter's gauntlets.

Bekesh very cautiously put these garments on. They were a little too big for him, so they seemed rather heavy, nevertheless the smell was familiar even now: the clothes exuded Baisal's scent. Bekesh experienced an amazing feeling at this moment, but his gestures gave nothing away. He pressed the fur cap's ear flaps against his eyes and brows; the fur coat's collar hid the rest of his face. 'In the name of God,' he said, deciding to enter the hunting room backwards, rather than facing the bird head-on. He caught the sound of Tumor's vicious rage – a domineering sound, a shaking and flapping of wings – as it clattered its long, pointed talons, as if to sharpen them. 'I'm a dead man,' Bekesh thought, and he shut his eyes tight. The eagle's heart and lungs

were swollen with blood and malice: it crashed noisily onto
one perch, then bounced off onto a saddle which was hanging
by the wall; then suddenly it stretched out its full wingspan and
hurled itself at the door, while Bekesh froze in horror, for he
felt as if a heavy rock had been split apart on his shoulder. Naturally, Tumor's powerful claws could not have penetrated him
while he was wrapped in the fur coat. But now its wings,
which had been whooshing noisily through the air, were
folded; and what had been a prolonged defiant shriek of anger
had turned into disgruntled croaking. His mind and heart
numbed, Bekesh could understand how the bird felt.

> My eagle, your grief
> I've noticed but not understood.
> So your coming to my hand
> Is for me a gracious visit.

—

When Aunt Rabiga found out that Sattor the Tajik had set
aside a room especially for Bekesh, she took great offence:
'How can you be apart, when you have a cooking pot in your
father's house? Your father should be everything to you!' But
Bekesh's first thoughts were for Tumor the eagle and Topon
the horse; only then did he think of his aunt's resentment, and
he now recalled a pile of papers which she had earlier taken
out of the chest of drawers. 'Your father should be everything
to you!' his aunt had said. But she hadn't remembered the
magic gallstones, nor could Bekesh find the courage to remind
her. All very well, as far as his father's being everything went,
they had wakes to hold in seven and in forty days' time. Some-

how, he had to please Uncle Sattor's heart, and then he would find an opportunity to talk about the magic gallstones, too.

It was cold now, so Bekesh went outdoors to chop wood, stacking it for a fire on the cast-iron hearth. Gradually, the house warmed up. Meanwhile, his aunt had gone to the stream to wash the dirty linen, and consequently perhaps he could read the documents that had been saved for him?

He picked up the package, which was wrapped in muslin and must have weighed over a kilo. What could it be? Perhaps it was the *Manas* reciter's lore. Didn't a person have the right to confide these secrets to paper? The package was very grubby and stained with smoke; Bekesh's fingers trembled with excitement as he undid the string holding it together. Inside the muslin was a glued packet, and inside the glued packet a thick yellow paper packet, and from inside that emerged a thick paper file which had lost its colour. On the right-hand corner of the file the Russian words 'Top Secret' had been written, and lower down, also in Russian, was printed 'Ministry of State Security of the USSR' and then, written by hand, 'Investigative section for especially serious cases'. In the centre was stamped in gigantic black letters, 'Case No.', the digits having been scratched out with black ink. All that was left on the spine was Uncle Baisal's first name, spelled slightly differently.

His heart pounding, Bekesh undid the binding, and in a somewhat disturbed state, he began leafing through the documents. He picked up a summary of the papers, then a statement of charges, then an interrogation questionnaire, then a search warrant, some more official records, then a decision to terminate an interrogation linked to a criminal case, and then the sentencing papers. It was curious that Bekesh had not found the secrets that he expected and was probably searching for at first, that there was no full-face or profile photograph within. He rummaged through the file one more time: no pictures. Probably, there was a set of papers outside the case file, and he began ruffling through the papers beneath it. His eye alighted on a pamphlet inscribed in Latin characters 'National Turkestan'. Judging by the dates, it was from the wartime years: a couple of photographs fell out, but they were of soldiers, one in Soviet uniform, and the other in apparently German uniform, but what Bekesh was seeking was not to be found.

Meanwhile, Dapan's cheerful voice could be heard in the courtyard; he was returning from his Qu'ran lesson, humming as he approached, so Bekesh hastily gathered up the papers.

—

By the time Dapan had come into the room, Bekesh had tied the papers back in their muslin and hidden them between the quilts stored in the niche. Like a racing colt, accompanied by the chill of the mountains and the wind of the ravines, Dapan began with frank sincerity by giving his news: 'Uncle, I told the Imam, he'd like to pay you a visit.'

'What, now!?' asked Bekesh, somewhat taken aback.

'No, any time you'd like!'

'Have you forgotten, we have to attend to Tumor, he seems to be a bit restless again…' said Bekesh. Dapan nodded at this. 'But before that there's another job to be done. I've brought some tapes from town, of my father talking. We'll listen to them.' Dapan nodded at this, too.

Bekesh took his cassette player and the tapes out of his leather shoulder bag and sorted them out roughly. They sat closer to the iron hearth, and Bekesh inserted a tape and pressed the recorder's play button. There was a crackle, then you could hear Bekesh's voice saying, 'One, two... Is it recording?' The sound cut out at that point, then came a joyful, 'It is. Let's start! If it's not too much, Uncle Baisal, begin with your childhood. In what kind of a family were you born, what were your early years like?'

Again, the sound seemed crackly, then came Baisal's rather hoarse, muffled voice: 'Should I speak?' he asked, then he coughed briefly and cleared his throat. 'In the name of God. If you ask where I come from, from which Kyrgyz tribe, we descend from the wolf tribe of the Chong Alay mountains. "A wolf's offspring will never be a dog," all our seven forefathers, who were mullahs, used to say. "I'll turn an orphan into a mullah with my zeal," it is said in the Semetey epic. Likewise, when I was a child, I was left an orphan: in the 1916 rebellion my father lost his life, so I was sent to Kokand to study in a medrese.' At this point Dapan coughed meaningfully. Bekesh looked at his nephew and, across a single moment, Baisal's entire life as a fatherless orphan made itself visible.

There was more about Baisal's childhood: at that time, in order to return from Kokand to Chong Alay, he had to wait for mounted Kyrgyz at the markets. They had brought him to Kokand, too, and he had travelled with one of the horsemen to the rider's destination, then begged someone local to take him further. In order to get further, he'd said a prayer for someone, written out a talisman for someone else. When it was summer, things were okay, but in winter travelling was especially slow. He was speaking at length about the ordeal of his travels as if describing a fantastic journey of roughly a week or so, at most a fortnight.

'One summer I went by horse and cart from Kokand to

Kyzyl-Kyya, and from there I managed to get to Eski Nookat. At that place, there was an important mullah called Abu-Kari, he was from our tribe, and I told myself, "Anyone who doesn't have a father and relatives will be an outcast and never gain respect." I decided to visit him and get his blessing. Abu-Kari asked all about me in detail, then he slaughtered a sheep. I was treated like an honoured guest for three days, and when I set off on my journey, I had a colt, and they blessed me with a good journey.

'The blessing's power may have been at work: in no time I reached Kök Bel, the Blue Pass. On a summer pasture here, on the banks of a spring, I tethered my horse to a rock, I shut my eyes, and went to sleep on the green grass. In a dream, the distant snow seemed to come down from the mountains in a thick downpour, and an enormous bird of prey – a white-tailed eagle – was flying noisily towards me, its talons pressing into my shoulders like rods, swooping me up into the heavens like a hurricane. It was as if my ears and nose had been cut off, my tongue stuck to my throat, my heart was trembling, yet my young eyes were taking it all in as they observed those talons. The bird's feathers were thick, its eyelids like cracks, its head a white blaze, its eyes as white as milk, its beak thin. Wherever it's taking me, I thought to myself, I must say the words on the tip of my tongue, "There is none like Allah!" as one starts to say one's creed.

'It carried me off and put me down near a dazzling white yurt in mountain pastures by the white glaciers. There were about forty men in the yurt, all with completely white eyebrows and beards, but their eyes were as piercing as the eagle's. Among them, right in front of their master, who was also dressed in white, the eagle perched, its talons relaxed. I flopped down and fell on the floor. I greeted the master. He didn't acknowledge my salutation, but merely nodded his head: "Did Abu-Kari send you?" he asked, and offered me a bowl he was holding. "Drink!" he said. "It's kumys, isn't it?" I said, as I sipped: it was so icy a drink that it made all my thirty-two teeth ache. I forced myself to down it. Although the kumys had been frozen, it thawed as I drank, the drink warmed up as if on fire, and in an instant, without uttering a sound, I was asleep. I've no idea how long I slept, but I was awakened by my horse whinnying. The white snow on the hill slope was sheltering the eagle's beautiful body from the mountain wind, but on my green hill the snow was hiding the sun, which was fixed motionless in the sky. When I opened my eyes, an object fell from the bird's talons: it made a clattering noise; if I hadn't averted my face, it would have cracked my head open, but it fell onto the spring grass, and straight away, when I looked to my side, I turned my eye from the eagle, which veered towards the Chong Alay mountains, and I saw a bright green, heart-shaped magic stone...'

———

At this point the tape stopped with a click. Bekesh and Dapan seemed to have woken from a pleasant dream with a shudder: that's it, gentlemen, it's over! Bekesh recalled bit by bit Baisal's meaningful dream, he compared it to his own: taken on the whole, the dreams were similar, but his uncle's seemed more extensive, whereas his was relatively helpless and hopeless. If you haven't ordered any food, you've nothing to look forward to, as they say when dismissing something out of hand: Bekesh put the cassette player back on the shelf and reminded Dapan,

'We have to feed Tumor.' Baisal had fed Tumor twice a day, but because the eagle had eaten almost nothing for two days since his master's death and its crop – the muscular tract under its throat where it stored food – was now empty, it was absolutely essential to attend to it again.

Bekesh thought he would resort to his former ploy, and once again deliberately put on Baisal's outer garments as he went back to see the bird in its room. Again, he wrapped himself up under the fur cap's ear flaps and the leather collar of the fur coat. Meanwhile Dapan cut a piece of meat weighing just under two pounds and, when it was ready, passed it to Bekesh's gauntlet. This time Bekesh did not tremble as he entered the hunting room, and moving across towards the great bird his hands were steady while Dapan looked on, observing him through a crack in the door.

On this occasion the bird didn't fling itself in a frenzy, but it still sat nervously on its perch, wary, its neck feathers slightly ruffled. All the while Bekesh was observing it through the narrow gap between his ear flaps and the fur on his collar. Holding the meat with his gauntlet, he offered it to the bird and, very quietly, imitating Baisal's voice, his words muffled, he said invitingly, 'Tu-um'. For an instant the bird seemed to be in two minds: 'Kee', it cried in a rather plaintive voice, then, flapping both wings, it struck out at Bekesh's hand. Its wings, or rather the gust of air blown by them, hit Bekesh's face. Bekesh felt as if his hand had been struck by a hundredweight, but his heart filled with pride at the thought that he had won Tumor's trust. Now the eagle would readily peck at the meat, and Bekesh could use his other hand to stroke and smooth its wing, speaking affectionate words into its ear.

As if to put an end to these fancies, the eagle raised its long head and with a sudden stab of its beak plucked the fur hat off Bekesh's head and hurled it into the hay on the floor. Bekesh felt as if his heart had been snapped: he was a dead man, he thought! The eagle's blood-filled eyes fixed on Bekesh. Bekesh's jugular vein bulged and began to pulse. If the enormous eagle sank its steel beak into that treacherous vein, it would all be over. Bekesh may have thought this, or the bird's red eyes may have suggested it: 'Allahu akbar...' he recited. The bird raised its pitiless head once more, then with all the strength it could muster it plunged its murderous beak into the hunk of meat.

—

Dripping with sweat, Bekesh came out of the hunting room, where calm now reigned. He hurriedly took Baisal's garments off his shoulders and threw them down; the feeling he had had a minute ago of utter nakedness was growing and showed no signs of diminishing. Again, worms were devouring his innards; again, the bird seemed to have exposed his deceitful ambitions, the stupidity of a man who proudly steps into a pit! It was just as well that Dapan now cheered him up by going into the hunting room, so that through the slanting door Bekesh could hear the boy talking to Tumor. Judging by the sounds, the boy had bent down and picked up Baisal's fur hat, shook off the hay and straw sticking to it, then approaching Tumor, had begun stroking the feathers on his full crop, now shiny. This was a trick to put a leather and felt hood over Tumor's head: once the bird was in darkness, Dapan gently approached it again and tied the soft leather jesses to its leg.

Bekesh only vaguely sensed all of these things while he

managed to change his clothes and headgear, but he couldn't put aside his feeling of total self-exposure in the bird's presence. 'Oh what an idiot you were to think you could deceive an eagle!' he thought, squirming at the thought of the belated demand he had made. 'And were you trying to deceive yourself, too?' And then, it was as if Tumor's inarticulate voice asked: 'Did you think that you would become Baisal just by putting on Baisal's clothes?' Bekesh's head was spinning.

Meanwhile the hunting room door was shut tight, and Dapan came back to join Bekesh. 'Tumor recognised you!' he said, standing tall. 'He let me know, too, what he was feeling,' Dapan added, pleased with himself. Then he said, 'Let's listen to more of Father Baisal!' as if he had suddenly noticed an awkwardness in the air. Bekesh was thinking exactly the same thing: he took the tape recorder, chose one of the tapes from the bag and inserted it into the cassette player. Baisal's gruff voice spoke. 'No,' said Bekesh and pressed the recorder's button, fast-forwarding then rewinding. After one or two more attempts, he reckoned he had got to the part that he wanted, and pressed play.

'Tumor has become famous in every part of the country. I can hunt a wolf, hunt a fox with him. Only a hunter called Kalcha looks down on my eagle and belittles him. "When that eagle gets old, he'll only be good for catching mice," this was the rumour he was spreading. He was getting on my nerves, and I publicly laid a bet against him. Putting a hood over Tumor's head, Chokmor was going to take him off behind the hill, while I sat some distance away, taking my place among all the other witnesses. As soon as Chokmor came back, Tumor instantly leapt about, couldn't sit still, he shuffled about, excited by the journey across the steppe. Hurling himself in all directions, he got near to the crowd, struck against one person, kicked another, after which, perhaps thanks to my actions and movements, he recognised my smell, and he leapt onto my knee in front of everyone.'

> You have given joy to this man
> Your tameness is special,
> You sat there, even-tempered and calm
> If I took off your hood and sent you flying...

———

In the morning, as he had no lessons, Dapan took his Uncle Bekesh to see Mullah Shavvol. Shavvol was one of Bekesh's younger cousins, in fact, but since Bekesh had moved away, he didn't know him well. It was only from a few conversations relating to Shavvol's father's and grandfather's profession that Bekesh had gathered Shavvol had come back after studying under some Pakistani or Arab mullahs.

The house was in the hills, it sheltered on the side slopes on the edge of the mountain range. Halfway along the baked mud walls, this palatial residence stuck out like a sore thumb after other Kyrgyz houses: it had a green sheet-iron roof and window frames which were painted blue; overlooking the buildings below, it rose to its full height with a sneer. Dapan, seemingly a familiar person to this house, yelled out three times in succession from below as if this was the custom, 'Shavvol sir, Shavvol sir, Shavvol sir!' and stood with his head bowed below the door. Almost immediately a forced cough could be heard from behind the door and a gate within a metal wall opened with a slow creak.

When he saw Bekesh, Shavvol said politely, 'Salam aleikum and God's mercy and favour be with you.' Bekesh was a little embarrassed by this formal greeting. 'Are you all right?' he asked, stretching out his hand to shake his, though Shavvol barely grazed his palm. Shavvol was at most thirty years old with a thin beard, a thick nose, and though his narrow eyes were quite youthful, his bearing and manners had the aura of an elderly man of around sixty.

Standing proud and upright, he held the door open, and invited them to follow him. He wore a shiny velvet gown and a plush skull-cap wound round his head like a short turban. His walk was a gentle jogtrot. Once inside, Shavvol himself took the place of honour and showed the visitors to their places. When they'd sat down, facing each other, Shavvol closed his narrow eyes, recited a prayer in Arabic and broke the bread. At that moment the door behind them swung open, and Shavvol made a sign to Dapan. Bekesh kept his head on Dapan: out of the corner of his eye he saw a woman's hand offering a tea tray through an opening in the door. Dapan said, 'In God's name' and rearranged the bowls as they clattered on the tea tray: he offered one to his master and passed one to Bekesh.

'Have you come as a man of faith?' Shavvol asked with pointed significance. Bekesh seemed to have heard the words, but not understood their meaning.

'Please forgive me...' he begged.

'Do you say your prayers?' asked Shavvol, clarifying.

'No,' Bekesh replied, taking the burden on himself. Then, as if trying to justify himself, he said, 'We have kept our forefathers' Muslim faith, we were brought up on the *Manas*...' Then he added somewhat inappropriately, 'I know by heart both Al-Fatihah, and Qul huwa Allahu ahad.'

Shavvol laughed, and did little to conceal the fact. 'Your *Manas* is utterly heretical and erroneous,' he said, making his feelings perfectly clear to Bekesh. Bekesh leapt up from where he was sitting. If Dapan hadn't pressed his hand, which was clenched in anguish into a fist, Bekesh might well have started a fight with their host. '"Al yawma akmaltu lakum diynakum wa atmamatu alaykum ni'mati wa radiatu lakumu al islama diynan." In other words: This day, I have perfected your religion for you, completed My Favour upon you, and have chosen for you Islam as your religion,' explained Shavvol, interpreting the Arabic.

'These days, when Muslims are making holy war against unbelievers,' he continued, 'no Muslim can stand aside.' But somehow Bekesh was obstinate and recalcitrant, full of inward defiance; he lost patience, refused to listen to these childish and boastful words and, quickly gulping down his tea, he made haste to get away. Not because Shavvol's words weren't true: his resentment arose because the milksop was so exalted that Bekesh lost all desire to speak his own mind.

———

'Your *Manas* is erroneous and deviant,' he mimicked as he walked later to Uncle Sattor in the distant part of the village, to be rid of the dirt filling his heart. 'Would you fashion a boy full of arrogance and air out of my Dapan, then?' he grumbled to himself, and then quickly and boldly added, 'As if I'd let you have him!' He felt ruthless and jealous. Tripping and falling on his way, he blamed Shavvol for his own clumsiness and the pain in his bruised limbs. Finally, he reached Uncle Sattor's house. Even though it was the depths of winter, Uncle Sattor was looking after the cattle and the cattle shed. 'Your mother's sister has just made dumplings, and we've been waiting for you,' he said, immediately showing Bekesh into the house.

As Bekesh was of Kyrgyz descent, keeping a secret was an inner torment for him. Uncle Sattor seemed to have known everything in advance in any case and to have taken it seriously, but he heard Bekesh out and, as was his custom, he picked up one of his thick books. He began to recite in Farsi:

A maidservant let an ass cover her
Because of strong lust and extreme recklessness.

This time, being a little gentle with Bekesh, he stopped at every quatrain to render it into Kyrgyz. The story went like this: a maidservant went to have sex with a donkey in order to satisfy her lust, but she took a cunning precaution: she put a carved gourd on the donkey's penis, so that it only entered halfway up her body. Although she kept this a secret, one day her mistress saw through a crack in the door and watched the maidservant under the donkey:

When she went to check on the ass's condition,
She saw that little flower girl lying under it.

'The mistress felt envious. "If this is possible, then why shouldn't I do so?" she thought. She shouted demandingly through the door, "Hey, you, how many rooms have you swept?" When the maidservant heard her mistress's voice, she hid her depraved paraphernalia and picked up the brooms.

She made a sour face, her eyes filled with tears,

Rubbed her lips together, as if to say, 'I'm fasting.'

'As for the donkey, it stood there, its prick hanging down. The mistress sent her maidservant off with a message to give to some faraway stranger and, after the girl had departed, she quickly made haste in her eager lust and hunger, taking with her a stool she'd seen the maidservant put under the donkey. Donkeys will be donkeys, won't they?

> She raised her feet, the ass thrust into her,
> A fire was kindled in her by the ass's penis.
> The ass was trained; it pressed into the lady
> Up to its testicles: the lady died at once.

'Her innards and her liver were torn apart, the stool fell to one side, the lady to the other, the room was flooded with blood.' At this point Uncle Sattor roared with laughter, and recited the same verse three or four times.

'"Have you ever seen anyone pass away after sex with a donkey?" said Rumi.' (Sattor said the line first in Farsi, then in Kyrgyz.) Again and again, Sattor held his index finger up. 'If you said these words to today's religious interpreters, you'd be publicly disgraced.' Then he went on with the rest of the parable.

'When the maidservant returned, she saw what had happened. She looked at the corpse and cried, "O madam, you went ahead without anyone to guide you, you died because of ignorance. You stole from me precious knowledge, but you didn't use it properly. Oh, stupid lady, if an expert had shown you his engraving, you would have seen the outward appearance, or the superficial, but the main thing would be hidden from you, in other words it would remain unrevealed."

You saw the penis, as obvious as baked dates:
Why did you not see the gourd, O greedy one?

'Maulana Rumi summed up this tale to say we are like parrots or pet starlings, imitators, unable to see the sense or the
essence: we are content with the superficial, we limit ourselves
to seeing the exterior only. What you get from the words of
those blind bats, those religious teachers, makes you like the
lady who saw the penis, but not the gourd. It was because of
such people that Maulana deliberately made this fable explicit
in his writings. If you gave this to the pious hypocrites who
can only see what's on the surface, then, God forgive me, it
wouldn't be surprising if the Maulana himself were to be declared a renegade because of this parable!'

—

After eating Aunt Mutriba's dumplings, all the while chewing
over his conversation with Uncle Sattor, Bekesh left the house.
Uncle Sattor's observation that all people were imitators, like
parrots or tame starlings, had lifted a weight from Bekesh's
heart, and his spirits were raised. Still, mud sticks, and the
memory of Shavvol's words trailed behind. Again he had to
make himself feel welcome in another man's house. He had not
hung about earlier, because Dapan was being given a lesson by
the mullah, but by now Dapan must be free, so he could be
taken for a session of the *Manas*. Bekesh set off towards Dapan's
family home. This time, crossing from the kishlak to the ayyl
did not involve the big bridge: there was a rope bridge on the

hill leading towards the mountains, to the Kyrgyz side.

Dapan's family's cob house was on the mountainside of the village, directly opposite Mullah Shavvol's. Dapan's father Bukar had fought with some Chinese in Siberia, and after he died, Dapan's mother, Sairake, not wanting to remain a widow with two children to care for, entrusted the family to her younger brother-in-law and married him. What was his name? However much Bekesh tried, he could in no way remember the name of Dapan's stepfather. There was nothing good in what people said about this young man: truth be told, it was more in Baisal's house that Dapan felt the true presence of a father's joy, so that is where the boy usually went and got under everyone's feet.

Soon, Bekesh spotted from afar the brother-in-law sitting on the veranda. Whatever he was called, Bekesh still could not recall it. 'Hello!' he said, as he came onto the veranda. The young man probably thought Bekesh was a stranger who had got lost, he didn't bother to get up. Bekesh saw at a glance that the brother-in-law was using both palms to rub down Indian cannabis – devil's weed – busy making hashish out of the fine dust of the leaves and twigs. Bekesh automatically asked, 'How are things? What might you be doing?' but this man with no name didn't care in the slightest.

Bekesh looked at his spotty baby-faced features, and sensed that he was high. He put a hand on his shoulder, which the brother-in-law now acknowledged and, without a greeting or a response, he cried, 'Poverty forces me...' As he began to sob openly Bekesh didn't know whether to console him or make him stop: he was dumbstruck. The brother-in-law suddenly stopped weeping, pointing to the cannabis stalks under Bekesh's feet. 'Pick them up!' he ordered.

'Where's Dapan? Where's Sairake?' Bekesh yelled out, frantic now.

'I told him to clear off,' the brother-in-law said calmly. Then he became frank and added: 'If you're sending off your driver Joomart, I'll crush some weed for him.' His words were so unexpected that Bekesh was utterly unable to reply: but he came within inches of his brother-in-law, then hit him as hard as he could right in his gaping jaws. Without looking back, he left.

—

Both Dapan and his mother Sairake, with her new baby, still being breastfed, were already at Baisal's house. Bekesh pretended that, as family members, they were here to visit Granny Rabiga. So they all got together for a series of evening meals. After roast meat, they had milky tea, then chatted; the wooden board was taken off the shelves and they got down to a game of nine pebbles, Kyrgyz drafts. Everyone, young and old, took part. But nobody spoke about Dapan's stepfather, and Bekesh didn't mention that he had gone to their house. They were wary of hurting Uncle Bekesh's feelings; Bekesh, too, tread cautiously: secrets were not to be blurted out.

It was getting late. The game was over. As was their habit, Bekesh and Dapan decided to see to Tumor. Wearing his own clothes, Bekesh opened the door to the hunting room: the bird took fright and tried to get out. Bekesh retreated. 'Put on your father's clothes!' the child cried, catching on immediately. Bekesh was in two minds: he put Uncle Baisal's garments over his own clothes, but he did not cover his face. Quietly, he entered the hunting room. Tumor gave him a look that seemed

gap in the door: so, still perched, Tumor flapped a wing and
made a contented sound. The two of them entered. They fed
the bird. They tidied the hunting room. Shutting the door behind him, greatly relieved, Bekesh passed into his own room.
'Let's listen to Father!' said Dapan now. Bekesh didn't refuse: he
went along with the child's wish, took a tape at random from
his bag and inserted it into the cassette player.

Uncle Baisal's rather muffled, hoarse voice resumed:

> If a giggling is heard,
> A bird makes a different sound.
> The fan is resplendent,
> Its fleece is whiter than a swan's...

Bekesh instantly understood that this was the dream that
Jakyp had after the birth of his son, Manas. Dapan seemed to
have understood his thought: 'It's Father Jakyp's dream!' In this
fabled dream, the aged childless Kyrgyz khan Jakyp sees a mon-
strous bird. He is struck with amazement by the sight, at the
bird's talons which are like daggers, at its harness which is
washed in silver and silk. Jakyp takes a good look at the bird,
and ties on the jesses.

> On heavenly wings
> Too grand to fly,
> When my feet touch the ground,
> I'm unable to move, leave or run,
> Here I'll make my nest.
> (The cotton-neck white gyrfalcon
> I shall tie down to it.)

I knew goodness in the past,
Only when it was the past
Not knowing my bitter days would seethe.

Bekesh and Dapan, Jakyp-khan and his foster father Baisal
seemed to have had the same dream, in which exactly the same
Manas reciter, and a bird the same as Tumor had manifested,
moving from side to side, sitting there flapping its wings
drowsily.

—

Baisal talked about Manas's birth and how he grew up. Manas
was a naughty child; in order to discipline him a little, his parents apprenticed him to the shepherd Oshpur. At this point the
tape broke off. Bekesh switched off the cassette player, using
nightfall as a pretext, or perhaps he had had no luck rummag-
ing about in the bag for the next part of the epic. But it was
clear from Dapan's blazing eyes that he wasn't going to bed for
a while. 'Tomorrow is market day!' the child begged.

'Then you recite the next bit!' Bekesh said to test him.

'Whatever you say!' Dapan responded readily, and as serious
as an old man, frowning surlily, he got down to recite:

It was all chaos, confusion and dust,
Head and eyes were daubed in blood,
Rocks crashed through with a roar,
There were head-splitting shrieks,
The Kalmak Mongol went on his way.
The chief shepherd lord Oshpur
Went out to the hill to look

In search of the forty children.
Smoke blew from the heavens,
Burning people's eyes,
Blue-maned is the panther Manas
When he is seen to enter the fray.

Bekesh sat in wonder, enchanted by Dapan's uninterrupted narration. Had he learnt it from Baisal, or worked the story out for himself, or had these words and scenes come out of the blue? Didn't Dapan's birth match the date at which Baisal had stopped reciting the *Manas* in public? Or was there a secret, esoteric way that he could have recited it to Dapan in the form of fairy tales and riddles? This, Bekesh sensed, was how the boy had stitched together stories of Baisal's childhood, of the visit to the mountain pastures to see the sheep belonging to Manas's foster-father Oshpur... Bekesh was delighted, and these words and scenes began to come back to his imagination. His mind took on renewed strength and a freshness of perception.

Perhaps it was this sudden need to prove himself that brought Bekesh to say: 'Now, Dapan, stop at this point, let me recite the ending...' Dapan immediately understood the suggestion, and, as if accepting a dare, stared him in the eyes and prepared to listen. Now Bekesh, with a certain amount of tension and anxiety, took up the epic from the point where Dapan had broken off his recital.

At first Manas had listened to Oshpur, minding his sheep (this was where Bekesh had perhaps deliberately, perhaps superstitiously, had Manas go, just as Dapan himself did, off to gather a few dried cow pats). But, gathering together other child shepherds and slaughtering a lamb for them, Manas proposed holding a feast. (Even if Dapan had a lot of friends, he would never in his life have slaughtered a sheep, so he was transfixed by this turn in the story, his eyes ablaze.) Oshpur was perturbed to see his flock was depleted, instead of increased, and went to see Jakyp: 'Make your son come back home, I can't control him any more!' he complained. Feeling very embarrassed, Jakyp made to do so, but as he travelled, nine or so Kalmaks appeared. (Bekesh was taking the epic to a point where, he thought, if he made Dapan a part of it, he would find it trickier to pick the narrative up. He continued in the usual way.)

They learnt that these Kalmaks struck at Jakyp's horse herder, Iyman, and mounting Jakyp's nine fiery horses, the rogues turned back in their tracks. Recognising his horses, Manas brought out his lasso and threw it at the Kalmaks. He hit one, knocked another off the saddle, made another one spur his horse and another flee in panic. At this point Jakyp exclaimed to his son, 'What's this you're doing? Do you know what evil will come of this? You're waking a snake with its head bashed in, lurking in wait: you will have brought down the Kalmaks' dragon-like horde upon us.' Here, with great feeling, Bekesh wanted to imitate the scene when Baisal and Dapan had talked to each other. But looking at Dapan, he saw he was fast asleep, his head propped against a pillow!

Bekesh wrinkled his brow like an anxious dog that doesn't know whether to be affectionate or to take offence, and finally lay down on his side next to Dapan.

—

In the morning Bekesh was woken by Dapan's desperate, hopeless wail. 'He's come, he's come,' he sobbed with all his strength. 'Who's come?' asked Bekesh, leaping to his feet.

Looking at Dapan's hand pointing excitedly to the door, he threw Baisal's fur coat over his shoulder and went out. There was a rowdy group in the yard: accompanied by about ten men, Sairake's foul husband was lashing out at her with a whip, while she was shrieking. 'Damn your black head!' she cried.

Bekesh yelled with all his strength. Distracted by Bekesh's voice, Sairake's husband looked at him, angrily flung his whip and signalled to his companions, who hid their faces behind balaclavas. As they threw themselves at Bekesh, he saw that the ruffians were armed with cudgels and crowbars, with a wolfhound pulling on a lead. Was this all a dream? The dog was barking ferociously, but moving ahead of the dog, Sairake's husband was challenging Bekesh.

Although the wretched young man's blows turned out to be feeble, his fist struck Bekesh straight in his aquiline nose, and there was bright red blood dripping onto the newly fallen snow under his feet. Bekesh took a hold of himself. He retaliated, hitting the man in the face as hard as he could, so that the latter flopped to the ground and onto the dog behind him, inadvertently crushing the dog's leg. The dog groaned and leapt aside. Violent confusion ensued. They would now start hitting out with their cudgels, Bekesh thought with lightning speed: it was kill or be killed. After rolling one of them over, he had to grab a cudgel, and then... then Bekesh was suddenly hit from behind. But his shoulder seemed to have taken the force, and then the blow glanced off him. It was, in fact, Tumor! Flying out of the hunting room, the eagle had perched on his shoulder. In the background Dapan shrieked, 'Get him! Get him!'

The masked men were transfixed. When the dog spotted the eagle, it tucked its tail between its legs and began to whine. The brother-in-law leapt up determinedly from where he had

been lying, grabbing hold of his now bare head, and, not looking ahead or behind, he ran off in panic. Perhaps Tumor was
bored sitting on his perch this wintry morning, and had
thought it a good idea to direct his eye and beak at the clear
white light. Now, sinking his talons into the thick fur coat, and
flapping his wings two or three times, he soared up into the sky
and then fell upon the ruffians' wolfhound, like a meteor
plunging from the heavens. His talons, thick as rods, penetrated
the dog's shaggy neck; and the dog, with just a whimper, collapsed onto the snow. Tumor's beak, as strong as a pickaxe,
struck once, and sent the dog's blood pouring onto the pure
white snow: the dog gave up the ghost.

Upon seeing this, or perhaps because their leader had run
away, the remaining nine or so men tore off their masks. But
just as they were about to make a run for it, Topon broke free
of his tether and came galloping into the yard. Without waiting
to be told, he hurled himself after the fleeing men, and managed to trample one or two of the thugs.

Bekesh's bloody nose remained badly swollen, but he wasn't
too badly hurt, despite his vile brother-in-law's clumsy fist. It
was more his heart and mind that had been smashed. At first he
had shouted to Tumor, who was pecking and stabbing at the
dog's guts! The bird heard his appeal and flew to Bekesh's
shoulder, its beak smeared with blood. Topon had travelled
some distance after those shitty-nosed thugs. Yet when Bekesh
yelled 'Topon! Topon!' , he understood why his heart ached.

Ten days had passed since he arrived in the village: he had
been busy with the bird, with Dapan, with Uncle Sattor, and
had even gone to see that thin-bearded Mullah Shavvol whom
he thoroughly disliked. The only soul he hadn't asked after was
the meek Topon. His face flushed with shame. 'A man's horse

is equal to the man.' Hadn't Baisal said this in every other sentence? Wouldn't Bekesh himself add to this: 'A man's horse is like a wing for him.' So why had he not thought of Topon? After all, if he had stroked Topon, if he had taken him to the hunting room, Tumor would not have got up to any of his tricks. Did he then need this uproar and conflict to revive his memory of the dear horse? Living in the city, he neglected his Kyrgyz origins. Indeed, he had turned into a wishy-washy Kyrgyz.

Topon responded to his call and trotted back into the yard. Seeing Tumor on Bekesh's shoulder and Dapan standing behind him, he snorted once, and came up to join them. Taking care not to frightening the eagle on his shoulder, Bekesh slowly went up to Topon and, approaching from his left side, put his hand on his mane. He combed it with his fingers, stroking and caressing the great steed. The horse looked at him with its left eye, lowered its head, and pranced playfully.

'Are we all at peace now? Calm again, Topon?' Bekesh asked, rubbing his tearful eye against the horse's smooth skin. The eagle's mood must have softened, for Tumor now tucked his beak into his feathers, and hid his eyes. Dapan went in to see his mother. And as if now agreeing to make peace, Topon whinnied just once.

———

Although everyone was now peaceful and calm, the kishlak was all astir by the next morning. Sairake's husband gathered all the thuggish Tajik teenagers he had recruited around the mosque and told them, 'A Kyrgyz wolfhound has killed our dog.' This time, some took up a rifle, some a pickaxe and they made themselves look vicious and serious. Mullah Shavvol found it very hard to restrain them. But now, his face pale, he spoke up for Bekesh. And before he could arrive at Baisal's house as an intermediary, rumours about the gathering around the Tajiks' mosque had spread to the Kyrgyz ayyl, and five or six young ruffians had apparently set off to rouse the Kyrgyz to action.

'Now what are we going to do?' asked Shavvol, seeking advice from Bekesh: yesterday he had known no more than a louse. At first, Bekesh didn't take things seriously. If anything came of it, they would end up with Kyrgyz beer, that was his guess. But to judge by Shavvol's tone, these idiots weren't going to listen to anybody: they would work up their petty resentment and start a riot, the whole kishlak and ayyl would catch fire.

'You must get out of here!' Mullah Shavvol begged Bekesh, in a tone that implied that thanks to his coming here their people's peace has been destroyed. At any other time Bekesh might have listened to this sort of thing without getting worked up. But he thought about what could happen to Tumor and Topon, Dapan and Sairake, and suddenly exclaimed: 'Should I pay them blood money for their dog, then?' Mullah Shavvol was lost for words, then he remembered the men who had no prospect of work in the kishlak and the harsh winter they faced. 'How much?' he asked. Bekesh went indoors to collect the money he'd saved for Baisal's twenty-day and forty-day wakes: he also brought out the money he had borrowed.

'That mangy wolfhound cur!' he mocked, as he handed over the money. Mullah Shavvol accepted the money, shuffling the notes awkwardly, and set off to see those who'd run away or scattered the previous day.

In the early evening Uncle Sattor came to see Bekesh. He had heard about the rabble and Shavvol's coming to see Bekesh's people, he said; he reported that he had heard the ruffians egging each other on, saying, 'Let's go, don't let the trace get cold, we'll follow him, and have our revenge on the eagle that killed our dog!' A dog close to home has a long tail, it's true, but seeing the Kyrgyz forewarned on the other side of the mountain stream, they became slightly more inhibited. Meanwhile, once he heard about the clash, Uncle Sattor had gone off to the mosque, sworn at some of the youths, and remonstrated with others.

'I'd prepared a legend of mine for you, it came in handy for putting them down,' said Sattor apologetically. Noticing that Bekesh was nodding, he went ahead and recited the legend he had been saving up.

A snake-catcher went to the mountains
To catch a snake by his incantations.

'The snake-hunter headed for the mountains, where he intended to catch snakes. On this occasion there was a white blizzard on the mountain, and snow carpeted the slopes. When the man looked, he saw a dead dragon lying along a narrow passageway. Intending to amaze people, he tied the dragon with a rope and, dripping with sweat, dragged it to Baghdad. "If work affects your head, water gets into your boots," was the saying, wasn't it, and dripping black sweat, he got this dragon to Baghdad. You can imagine the spectacle! Some came again and again to see the great dragon, some for the first time.

'The next day was sunny and the snow began to thaw. The great heat of the sun thawed the dragon too, and it began to come to life. The spectators, like dogs that had swallowed needles, fled in various directions. The snake-catcher clutched at his head in great consternation, and he was the first to be devoured by the dragon, now it had awoken...

By his dragon hundreds of thousands of people
Were killed in the rout that he had designed.

'That's what I said to those damned people, brother!' said Uncle Sattor, as he finished the parable. 'Then that rotten Mullah Shavvol came along. Even with that blood money handed out, we've still hardly got anywhere. Now, brother, you'd better not leave your house, let me come and get news from you,' said Uncle Sattor, as he went back to his place.

———

Uncle Sattor had a big heart, Bekesh thought. Thanks to those contemptible people, he had recited to Bekesh the fable which he had been saving up. Whom was this parable directed at? If at Bekesh, did he mean, 'Stop, don't touch any of them, in case you awake a dragon'? Or had he prepared this fable well ahead of the violent incident? Was it in fact meant for their conversations about the *Manas* from two days earlier? If that was the meaning, perhaps he was asking, 'Do you know what a burden you're taking upon yourself?' Once again, Bekesh didn't know what to do, it was as if a sinking feeling had struck his belly and was pulling him down. This must be what it's like to be pregnant, it suddenly occurred to him. What was he pregnant with? Was it the *Manas* or an empty nutshell?

Uncle Sattor was so subtle that he could have given a louse a blood transfusion. That was why Baisal, whether at home or out hunting, used to keep him close. Maybe that was why those shitty dirty dogs with their rusty rifles hadn't actually come here. Bekesh couldn't even show his shadow on the street: there was no place for him to go now. Dapan was with him, and Tumor and Topon were safe now. 'I've left my footprints behind me, because there's no way I'm going to see you bastards!' he grumbled, angry with his loutish brother-in-law and the dope-smokers he had hired.

After the previous night's disorders Dapan was still sleeping. Bekesh didn't wake him up. He dressed as warmly as he could and went to the stable. He combed Topon's mane and cleaned his flanks and hips; he scrubbed his lower parts. He poured oats into his manger. He chatted to him for a long time. He constantly gave vent to his thoughts about the kishlak and the ayyl. 'When spring comes, let's all go off to the summer pastures,' he coaxed the horse. Topon took it all in and seemed to agree to everything. 'Like my master Baisal, I've lived my years and drunk my fill,' he seemed to be saying, but, trying not to break Bekesh's heart, still desolate, he sniffed at him once, then stuck his head in the manger. Tears welled up in Bekesh's eyes; he wiped away a tear with his sleeve, and, giving Topon a friendly pat on the neck, opened the door and went out.

—

'When I was sent off to fight in the war, I was just nineteen,' Baisal's voice began. 'In the city I was put into a railway carriage, it only took a week, and we were dropped right into a forest. People had been rounded up like cattle from the kishlaks and ayyls, whether they knew any Russian or not. "Those who don't know will drink poison," as they say. This was our Day of Judgement, poison instead of food, and off we went. Whatever we said, the Russians beat us, thrashed us, you wouldn't believe it. Our people were lying in the trenches, it was damp, we were soaked through; at night we used each other's body heat to thaw the ice and the snow around us. Water poured from the holes in the roof, our people were lying there as the place filled with muddy water. We were freezing cold, so we couldn't get any sleep, all of us were coughing and coughing, and sores were breaking out on our skin. "Anyone who hasn't got a brother to look after him gets no respect, he is a stranger to everyone!" We were ready to eat each other's flesh, "Any lad who says he isn't starving will starve one dark night." One day they put a gun in our hands and told us in Russian, "Come on, for Stalin!" they said, and made us face tanks.

'Armed with rifles, we snipers fired continuously, at anything alive, but how could we stop tanks with bullets? "Yoghurt drinkers escape, bucket lickers get caught," they say: those of us who weren't killed were taken prisoner. "White dog, black dog — all dogs are the same," they say. However much we didn't understand the Russians, we had no idea at all what the Germans were saying. They were just chasing ewes and lambs, but they could have split rocks with their conceited ideas: they were herding us like cattle into a pen, locking us up in a place called a lager. Once a day they gave us food. They boiled some wheat in a cauldron, and gave us a ladleful each. And a lump of barley cake. We didn't know if we were dead or alive: "A man's mind doesn't work when he's starving."

'How much time passed, how many black-eyed men died, God knows. One moment a lad is walking about, the next the young man is on a camel's back. One day a black-browed, shaggy-haired Uzbek came and questioned us all: "Are there any Turkestani Muslims here among you?" We didn't understand what he meant by Turkestan, but we did understand Muslims. The steel knife didn't stay in its scabbard: some of us responded. There was a man called Vali Kayum-khan: he said, "Kyrgyz, Kazakh, Uzbek, Turkmen, Tajik, you're all Turkestanis! He's come to liberate Turkestan from the infidel Russians!" Then they got me to recite the *Manas* to the people. Again we were given rifles, and dressed in German uniform, saying, "If your name is unknown, burn the earth!" Again, like our forefather Manas, we exchanged one fight for another.'

This was a tape that Bekesh had hidden from Dapan: he listened to it now on his own. True, he had been searching for a different one, about the half-forgotten magic stones and the peculiarities of the *Manas* reciters. Baisal never ever actually let anyone catch sight of his miraculous powers: Bekesh had once heard second-hand about his foster-father's magic stone helping Chekbel one time. He had had to journey to a ravine that had been hit by a mountain landslide, and had used his whip to expel demons from some senseless newcomers. At the time, Bekesh had tried to ask about these things and keep up the conversation. Now he was searching to test a conjecture.

In any case, however, anything he got from the tape enthralled him; as Aunt Rabiga said, he was enchanted by any beautiful speech. Until now he hadn't paid attention to Baisal's going off to war: he had supposed he'd joined up of his own free will. Now that he was listening with his full attention, he saw that Baisal's experience of war, fighting on both sides of the front line, affected the way in which he recited the *Manas*. Further on in the tape, Baisal said with some feeling about his life as a soldier, 'War: there's no fixed point in a war! A colt is a frog in a dried-up pond. Storytellers recite the *Manas* when they've never in their life experienced war. If you've seen only a single mountain, you haven't got far! If you've actually seen something, you've got lots to say; if you haven't, then say no more.'

Baisal's narrative broke off at this point, and he started reciting Manas's first battle, part of the war against King Neskara.

> He set off on a long journey,
> Neskara was there, prepared...

With Neskara's six devils to teach him how, the Chinese king had wanted to kill Manas ever since he was a child. With six thousand soldiers, Neskara set off towards the Altai Mountains. On his way, as he ravaged and pillaged, a noble old man came over to Manas's side, and sent Neskara's devils so far away that they couldn't come back. Now Neskara, deprived of his devils, reached the Altai, and the fourteen-year-old Manas sent out his four-hundred-strong army against Neskara's six thousand. A fierce hand-to hand cold-steel battle ensued:

> Manas smashed two, speared three,
> Slipped his foot out of the stirrup,
> 'Let my people be at peace,' he said.
> 'My loins are wounded,' he said.
> Chasing the pain to this place,
> He said, 'This is why I came.'

So he did battle.

Bekesh was listening to Baisal's tale and at the same time looking through the Soviet case file. His eye caught one of the photographs, showing a young man in German uniform on horseback, raising the Turkestan banner (yak tail and crescent). It was Baisal. Suddenly, Bekesh felt he understood a lot of things that now seemed self-evident.

—

Towards evening, Bekesh tidied and packed the papers and tapes, then sat down with Rabiga to discuss Baisal's memorial feast. Dapan had taken to Muslim customs, and, upon waking, wouldn't utter a sound to them until he'd gone home and done his ablutions. Once he had washed, he greeted them, grinned and waited for a gap in their conversation, to say, 'I dreamt I saw my father!' The aunt stopped mid-sentence: with great interest she asked Dapan what he had seen in his dream.

Dapan began, relating his dream scene by scene, bit by bit:

My father was extremely young,
Then he went off on horseback to war.
His horse was a thoroughbred charger,
It had a tiger-skin saddlecloth,
Qur'anic writing woven into the saddle;
The horse was throwing off its beaver-skin saddle cushion,
It was rearing, trying to throw its rider,
Eager to be off, playful, you'd say, as a white snake...

(Was Dapan describing a dream, or was he dreaming now? Bekesh suddenly wondered.)

He was champing at the bit, his eyes were bright,
My father was mounted on him. The battle was over.
Many corpses lay on the battlefield.
There'd been no end of shooting in this battle,
The fighting was merciless, people met their hour of death,
Red blood was spilt, many battle horses were killed,
A whole race of fine soldiers was killed,
My father calmly rode his horse among them.
He said, 'Suddenly dismounting, to sacrifice my charger for them,
Not wanting to drink my own blood,
Let me drink my charger's blood; swallowing blood,
Let me bleed, taking the horse by the neck,
Slaughtering it on the spot, cutting its throat like a sheep.'
Suddenly the heavens opened, and a proud warrior
From heaven descended, all ready to fight.
He took my father by the hand, and set off for the blue sky...

'That was a good dream you had!' said Rabiga and made an Amen with her hand, 'Our forefather Manas himself took your father's ghost as a guide to lead you along the right path.'

'When your father,' the aunt told Bekesh this time, 'left for faraway places in Russian times, he was a cavalryman, and he was surrounded. About five of them fled to the forests for twenty days: they didn't have a bite to eat. When your father wanted to slaughter his horse to feed himself and the others, his horse made a break for it, ran off, stumbled and fell into a pit. When he looked, he saw there was food left by the Russians or the Germans in that very same pit.'

Then she spoke very quietly into Bekesh's ear, 'Dapan has heard about this.' She said no more.

—

Bekesh was well aware of the wartime story his aunt had told him, about young Baisal being taken off to fight. Rabiga was then an adolescent girl with uniformly excellent school marks. Ever since school Bekesh and Rabiga had agreed to marry, and this mutual agreement was something amazing. Young boys and girls from the mountain ayyls and kishlaks were rounded up, boarding schools were opened, one for girls, one for boys, and the girls' hostel was guarded by an old man with a wispy beard who was always utterly drowsy. Getting above themselves, coarse boys poked their heads in, sneaking into the girls' dormitory and hiding in the rooms, telling some a riddle, singing others a song, trying to win the girls' affection. Baisal had been attached to a medrese, but since medreses were closed, he was now registered with this boarding school at least for a time. He was utterly absorbed with reciting the *Manas*, and this is why he made the highland girls' hearts melt like butter – they all thought of themselves as the epic's main heroines, with their hair in plaits, either Kanikey or Aychurek.

One day, the young Baisal was, as they say, 'overwhelmed by work': he was sitting consoling some of the girls, when the door to the dormitory suddenly opened and the girls were paralysed. 'What's he doing here? What a crowd!' the tiny girl who'd just entered said, fixing Baisal with a stare. Baisal, as mentioned, was not at all embarrassed by the opposite sex, but when he looked at this tiny invigilator assessing him with her eyes, he felt at a loss, and his courage wilted. The other girls whispered, 'Our class monitor's nasty...' 'What group do you come from?' she pursued her relentless line of questioning, and

Baisal seemed to take the blame on himself and told her his group. Following a nonplussed Baisal on his way out, as they passed the sleepy guard, she just about smoothed things over: 'You're a *Manas* reciter, let's have you give a concert in the club so everyone can listen.'

When this concert was put on, the pair were instantly enthralled by each other.

—

'Granny, tell me a story about the war,' red-haired Dapan pestered Rabiga.

'Oh, do stop,' she snapped dismissively, but her eyes narrowed. 'Which one should I tell you?' she asked.

'The one about you being abducted!' Dapan replied hurriedly. Bekesh had never heard this story, so he listened and watched attentively.

'When your father went off to war, my heart froze with grief,' Rabiga began. Her half-closed eyelids again drooped. She shut her narrowed eyes, and plunged into the depths of her memories. 'I just flopped, like sorrel lashed by the rain. I looked like a beggar taking shelter, I couldn't go out anywhere, I couldn't see anyone. We had a house cow, and I took care of it so that it took care of us. Oh, the wartime was bad. Before the war, you wore as many dresses as you liked, but in wartime you were left stark naked. We wore homespun cotton, we ate maize flour pancakes.

'We heard that in Ashun, a neighbouring village, there was an "administration" run by a relative of ours. My mother was elderly, she couldn't get there, and we couldn't leave the cow in her care, all she could do was to lie on a felt rug in the yurt.

Finally I abandoned my mother to the care of a local tramp's small child, and I attached the cow by a rope that I held, and, carrying all my household goods, I set off. I climbed hills and mountains, I crossed a mountain stream, the days were scorching hot, but the two of us, me and the cow, lumbered on. All I hoped was that our relative in the administration would have some respect for my mother, and all being well would give us two saddlebagfuls of ground meal.

'Nothing can be expected from someone travelling like a magpie: when the day ended and night fell, I arrived at the district office. After a lot of asking and a lot of honeyed talk, I found our relative's house. Being in need makes you open your eyes wide: the "boss" relative wasn't at home, and his son, who was too lame to be recruited, took me and the cow in. His name was Damir or Dayor, he gave me a dirty look. He was as happy as a dog pissing on a pine tree, he staggered past me, circling one side, then the other. When I asked "Where's your mother?" he said she had died. "My father and I, the two of us are alone. We need someone very caring to look after us," he said, grinning.

'I couldn't sit there twiddling my thumbs while I waited for his father to come back from work. I tethered my cow to a stake, I tidied up their house, I beat their felt rugs. "If a frog pisses, then it's a dowry for the lake," I told myself. At least I'd been hiding from the young man's greedy eye. Finally, his father arrived, and I told him of my ordeals. His father was probably in the administration, so he looked down his nose at me: he barely recognised us as relatives. "War is equally painful for everybody," he said. "There's no tolerance for idlers!" But because he saw the house had been tidied up, or because my feelings were so palpable, he came out with a promise, "Probably you should sleep here today, and in the morning we'll see."

'When night fell, feeling anxious for myself and my cow, I couldn't sleep. Early the next morning, the admin gave me a saddlebagful of maize. "Tie it from the bottom of your skirt to your waist, so that anyone who sees you will just think you're pregnant," the relative said, before he himself went off to work.

'So, holding its tether, I led my cow off, and went into the street with the load attached to my waist. Carrying the bag of maize was so very hard, I had no strength left, it was all I could do to walk out of the village. I let my cow graze at the top of the first hill we came to. I collapsed onto my knees and undid the sack. Because I was on my way home, I took my time, but then I sensed behind me the clip-clop of a galloping horse's hooves. I felt a brief moment of relief, and wanted to sing at the top of my voice!

'But then the dishevelled man galloping up on horseback was that Damir, Dayor or Dinor. My instincts about him were spot on, he was hot on my traces. It was obvious that his horse was sweating and foaming, its nostrils flared and snorting. "Hey, young woman, you look rough!" he said, while his horse pranced. He stuck out his chest. I was a woman who looked like a trophy, a girl on her way to a festival, so it seemed. "You think I'm yours!" I thought to myself. "I shan't give in to you!"

'"I've come to take you away," he said, still on his horse. Then, he added, "I love you!" My mind and my heart seethed, I could see my hero Baisal. "Have I become a mattress anyone can piss on?" I asked myself. I decided to act the simpleton. I tossed my hair, and told myself I'd make a fool of this idiot on his horse. "Gallop off with me, but you've got to take my baggage and my cow!" I said. "Here's a rope. Put it round its neck, then tie it to your horse, and then put me on the horse!" I told him. The man didn't suspect a thing, he took the bait and fell into my trap. He got off his horse, handed me the whip and bridle, took the tether from my hand, and hobbled over towards my cow, which was some distance away. I picked up my bag and rushed over to mount the horse, lashed it with the whip, and, swaying in the saddle, made the horse gallop! We reached the village by noon. I put my mother next to me on the horse and we left for the mountain pastures.

'So we had lost our cow, but found a horse. The horse, it turned out, came with another two saddlebags of ground meal. So you see, a dog can piss on your dead: the cripple had hoped to buy me from Baisal in exchange for two saddle-bags of ground meal.'

———

'Oh dear, I've been sitting here telling you all these stories and mysteries,' said Rabiga, gathering her skirts suddenly. She went out with the young women of the house to cook doughnuts for the seventh-day remembrance meal. Bekesh and Dapan sat quietly for a short while. Bekesh was thinking that it was not Baisal, but more likely Rabiga who had told Dapan the mysteries and the legends, including the *Manas*. He asked Dapan, 'Does Sairake tell you stories?'

'Always!' replied Dapan without hesitating.

'Come, even if she doesn't, let's recite *Manas*,' Bekesh quietly pondered, as if he were repeatedly testing not Dapan, but his own memory. 'From the story of Kanikey,' he added, for some reason, and gave Dapan a searching look. Dapan responded, 'In God's name!', cleared his throat and, as if he had

been expecting this, began at exactly the same point which
Bekesh was turning over in his mind:

> Oh my hero Temir-khan, father of Kanikey,
> Listen to what I have to say.
> Take the lion left by his father
> And make him your son-in-law...

When Jakyp came to betroth his son to Kanikey, he settled
the dowry: Manas himself went to Bukhara with a gift of thirty
thousand sheep and three thousand horses, taking forty thousand soldiers with him. Seeing this great mass, Temir-khan was
afraid that the cattle would trample Bukhara down, and so he
kept the matchmakers waiting in yurts on the outskirts of the
city. This infuriated Manas. At night he went to see his future
bride in the palace. Sanirabiga saw the young man, and instantly fell in love with him, but she hid her love. Instead, she
tried to threaten him: 'Why are you going against holy laws by
coming at night into my chamber?' she demanded. 'I am
Manas, I've come to elope with you!' said the young man, as
he tried to embrace the girl. She leapt back: 'I call Manas my
dog!' she said. Manas felt bitterly ashamed. He felt like hitting
the girl, but she deftly stepped aside and tried to strike Manas's
hand with her sabre. Raging, Manas kicked her until she was
unconscious, then left the palace, vowing to seek vengeance.

At this point Bekesh cleared his throat and continued with
the poem. No, he didn't hesitate, nor did he interject: deliberately and without hurrying, he continued smoothly.

> From then on a quarrel broke out among the people,
> This Sanirabiga, Kanikey, is my little foal,

Eighty soldiers have abducted the girl,
The people are celebrating the spring festival...

Manas in his fury was thinking that only bitterness would
defeat bitterness: he wanted to raze Bukhara to the ground.
'May Bukhara be struck by the dust of accursed horse herds!'
he cried, and prepared his army for conflict. Temir-khan was so
afraid that for two days and two nights he wouldn't let anyone
come to see him, he simply lay there, not eating a morsel of
food. (At this point Bekesh felt like comparing Temir-khan to
the contemporary bullying yet cowardly authorities, but he
held his tongue.) Temir-khan put a woman, his wife Akmama,
to work, and she shouted out, summoning their unhappy
daughter: 'Because of you these people are going to raze
Bukhara to the ground!'

Sanirabiga then took leave of her mother and galloped off
on her own: she would manage to get past the thousands of
Manas's warriors by waving her white headscarf. The army that
was full of wrath came to a halt, like blood flowing in veins
that have been tied...

Bekesh stopped at this point too, because he did not know,
like a swimmer halfway across a river, whether he had the
strength to turn back, or enough remaining power to carry on.
He took a deep, deep breath.

—

Sairake seemed to have heard this episode from the neighbouring room. The next morning she invited her short-tempered
husband to come out of hiding, to make peace and to come to
Baisal's seventh-day remembrance feast. Bekesh, who was

greeting the male guests that afternoon, pretended not to notice him, on the pretext of having business to attend to. One could see that Dapan, the child of the house, had wrapped his face, upon which downy hairs were already sprouting, in a three-cornered hat to hide from his step-father, as if to protect himself from the cold. Doubtless, he was recalling Kökötöy's feast from the *Manas*.

Baisal the father crossed the pass,
Threw a rock at the feast,
Pressing forward, in urgent haste,
At the top of his voice, he yelled at his horse,
Having chosen a thoroughbred charger.
Dressed in a blue gown,
He mounted a dappled thoroughbred,
The people came and they set off,
They were like a lake with no visible boundary.

If Bekesh was truly glad to see anyone, it was Uncle Sattor, who had brought his red-bearded neighbours with him. These people were special, although they arrived rather late: Bekesh had great pleasure in bringing his mother's side of the family into separate quarters, and, following behind, he settled down alongside them. He sat next to his uncle and let off a little steam. Sattor recited the Qur'an in a chant, and everyone said 'Amen'.

'Oh, I feel distressed – old age, you've taken my strength away,' speaking in Kyrgyz, he repeated regretfully. The meal was served. Meat and dumpling soup and doughnuts were there to eat, and milky tea to drink. Then the tablecloth was taken away. 'We're all one people,' said Sattor, now speaking

Tajik, introducing everyone to Bekesh. 'We all knew Father Baisal virtually as our spiritual guide, let's honour his memory by holding a commemorative prayer, a zikr!' Bekesh shook his head. Uncle Sattor moved around and settled down among the seated guests, and after saying 'in God's name' began to recite the first sura, Al-Fatihah. Then, his frown disappearing, his eyes half-closed, he recited Rumi's verse in Farsi:

> Listen to this reed flute's story,
> Making a complaint about separation,
> Saying, "Ever since I was parted from the reed bed,
> Men and women have moaned along with my lament."

Sattor raised his voice, setting the verse to music, while the other men moved their hands in strict time, still seated, swaying their heads and bodies, calling out, 'Allah! Allah!' As the verse was reaching its climax, their movements speeded up; joining in, Bekesh was more and more intoxicated by the melody's power and the people's ecstatic state, until he had neither strength nor desire to accompany them. Without being aware of it, he was being carried away by the mood circulating in this circle.

And he remembered his childhood, when the women sat in the yard, beating a handful of wool, and a certain amount went flying off in a gust of wind from the mountains. Then his aunt would say, 'If a new bride lets the wool fly off, the wind's beauty is shown all over the plain.' And he himself could now feel the lightness, like wool blown away by a breeze.

———

The guests were parting. Bekesh and Dapan went to see to the horse and the eagle to show the beasts some affection. Now the whole house was full with members of the family, everyone came together to sit down. Bekesh was somehow feeling ill at ease, sitting face to face with his brother-in-law, who only two days ago was a dyed-in-the-wool enemy. Sairake sat between them, looking first at one, then the other, chatting away nervously, as if she were trying to broker the peace.

'I couldn't get Dapan off the breast from babyhood until he was four years old,' Sairake said, yakking away. 'That was when some Americans came to Chekbel, to teach the women about family matters. Even if your husband has watery sperm, there's a way of getting pregnant!' she said (at this point her eyes flashed at her husband, who sat there hunched and sullen). 'They showed us how to use artificial sperm, taught us a few words of English, and a bit of the alphabet. I took my Dapan to all the classes, I nursed him on my knees and breastfed him,' she continued.

'One day we were revising the letters we had been taught, and our teacher Carol showed us a letter that looked like a comb. "What's this?" she was asking. Well, if only I could remember. Then Dapan takes a look with his great bright eyes, purses his lips, tears himself from my breast and, believe it or not, comes out with "Double-u!" Carol's mouth gaped like a pit.'

Here, rolling his eyes at each utterance, Dapan grinned.

As if stripping every covering or decorum from the two embarrassed men, Sairake once more launched straight into another story, throwing her words straight into the space between them.

'That was the year my first husband died in Siberia, and Dapan had to start going to school. I cut his tangled hair, but left two plaits at the back of his head. "One for your father, one for your mother," I said. He cried at first, then he got used to wearing a skull-cap. That was for this side: when we got to the other side, the children in the school ripped off his skull-cap; if he tried to play football, the two plaits came out from under his skull-cap. "Red face, thin waist!" they said, making a girl out of him, pulling and tugging him by the hair. Dapan cried buckets when he came home from school. I sent my second husband off to the school.' (Sairake again flashed a look at her husband who, irritated, was sitting in the honoured guests' place.) 'He got things off his chest, left blood on the carpet, he beat up innocent children so that even the ones who didn't know anything would learn. After that Dapan wouldn't go to school for a month.'

'Even close relatives don't like being told the truth,' Sairake recited the saying. Her words were taken by everyone as an end to any harmonious conversation. 'My husband then cut off both plaits, he didn't leave even a tiny tuft, and he took Dapan back to school.' Then she seemed to get everyone bustling again with these casual words: 'We've spent a whole day lying here, we haven't had much to drink,' and she bent over, laying the tablecloth.

—

That evening, the brother-in-law and his chatterbox of a wife were, in one sense at least, on good terms with the family, and they left for their own house. Dapan and his Uncle Bekesh had been sitting with their feet warming under the table.

'Granddad Baisal used to forbid me to recite the *Manas*,'

Dapan said. 'If he'd known I was reciting it, he would have been quite ruthless,' he furrowed his brow just like Baisal.

'Then who taught you the *Manas*?' Bekesh asked in amazement.

'My mother told it to me as a story,' Dapan replied.

That was, in fact, the way Bekesh had heard some scenes, in part from Baisal, when he recited publicly. He'd heard the narrative in full, whereas Aunt Rabiga had given him fairy tales and riddles to study. While Bekesh was pondering these thoughts, Dapan seemed to say, if you've got a blind tune, play it, and changed the subject to something lighter. 'One day I went to see to my calf, and I lost consciousness when I was reciting from the *Manas* Almambet's quarrel with Chubak. When I looked, my calf had wandered off and was missing. Everywhere was quiet, bare, there wasn't even enough wind to rustle the grass! "Come, come," I yelled out, but it wouldn't even bleat.' Bekesh was listening to Dapan chat, perceiving that the child's eloquence sometimes echoed Sairake's tones, sometimes his Aunt Rabiga's.

'The tune I'd been reciting just then somehow irritated me. I grew angry, I was stumbling and shaking, leaping about to one side, then to the other. When I looked, some way away, on the left, an old man was trying to load two bundles of firewood onto a donkey – he was so weak he couldn't lift just one bundle, any more than a nit could crush a louse. I went over to say hello. I braced myself and loaded the firewood onto the donkey. "Two eyes are what a blind man wants," said the old man, making a long face, and he shook his snow-white goatee and gave me his blessing. I felt that this remark was something he'd been meaning to say to me. "I've lost my calf," I said. "I'll go and look for it."

"'It's getting dark and misty, my child, let's not wander about, you don't want a devil grabbing you, you'd best go with me," he said, heading for the mountains, along a single-track donkey path. I stuck close to him. While we were making our way there, the village was hidden in a cloud of dust. The old man's house was in a sheer, rocky ravine, and you got to it by climbing down steep slippery steps. I couldn't actually see, that wasn't the direction we'd come by. We went into a rough, cavernous house. By the fire on the hearth, an old woman was sitting. "My wife is blind, I lead a quiet life," said the old man by way of introduction, screwing up his eyes, and he told his wife: "Woman, we have a guest! Look after him!" His old wife then really did look after me, first embracing me and sniffing me as she would a guest.

"'We can't possibly fail to kill an animal for a guest," the old man said as he unloaded the donkey and tethered it to a stake: he chose one of the three rather skinny goats he kept in a corner. He rubbed a shepherd's crook against the doomed goat, and the wretched animal bleated loudly. The old man slit its throat in the doorway. He skinned it and gave the meat to the old woman, who put the meat into a cauldron. It was as if everything were normal, as if I hadn't been grieving for my lost calf, I sat there calmly, like the unknown goat who had suffered a sheep's fate.

'The goat meat needed a lot of cooking, so the old man and his wife left time to do its work and asked: "Who might you be, whose seed, whose tribe?" "I'm Baisal's grandson, and Sairake's son," I said. When I mentioned my forefather, I became as pliant as a willow wand: seeing this, or hearing my forefather's name, the old man nodded his skull-capped head, and exclaimed 'Good heavens!' I felt proud. "I recite the *Manas*

too," I boasted. "Recite, then," said the old man. I continued
from the point from which I had recited not long before, in the
fields and hills:

> After Almambet had gone,
> Akbolta's Chubak followed him.
> Seeing Chubak's anger,
> Almambet learnt his place.
> Seeing Chubak was following after him,
> Stirring the people into action,
> Almambet now knew...

Bekesh was especially fond of this episode, and hearing it
now played on his most tender heartstrings. Before the 'Great
Raid' that Manas made on Beijing, the capital of China, he
had sent as a spy his closest friend, the hero Almambet, who
was himself originally a Chinese prince, but who, upon con-
verting to Islam, had then sided with the Kyrgyz. To travel to
Beijing Almambet had to take what he knew to be the safest of
five routes. A certain Chubak, a jealous Kyrgyz prince, thought
to himself, 'I've been in Manas's service since I was thirteen
years old: I have many times saved him from death, yet he has
given a Chinaman the upper hand over me!' This man chased
after Almambet. A discussion and then an argument ensued.
Chubak said one thing, Almambet another. Chubak stressed his
Kyrgyz origins; Almambet boasted that, despite his Chinese
descent, he had renounced all those connections and now
served the Kyrgyz. Manas came in a rush on his horse Akkula
to listen and resolve this dispute, and stood between the two
men who had drawn their swords.

'I thought that if Almambet were on my side, I could take

control of the whole world,' he said. 'I thought that if Chubak were on my side, I could add eighteen thousand men to my kingdom,' he said. 'But, to judge by appearances, you are both deceiving me; the two of you are capable of shattering my army to pieces. If I were to call you lions, you'd both run away from the Great Raid like hares.' The two men couldn't take such criticism. So Manas grabbed with one hand the bridle of Almambet's horse Sarala, and with the other hand the bridle of Chubak's Köktaka, then shook and dropped both bridles. 'I am no longer a mediator between you!' he announced.

> On his right side was Almam
> and he shook him off to the right,
> On his left hand was Chubak
> and he shook him off to the left...

Then Dapan said, 'At this point the old man stopped me, and, saying, "Let me recite this part of it," the old man continued:

> "Akbolta's Chubak
> Now pale-faced, turned around.
> Almambet the great conqueror
> Was now disgraced and shamed...

"'After they had been made to tremble by Manas's words and his wrath, Chubak asked for Almambet's forgiveness and submitted to him, and in response Almambet too submitted to Chubak, and handed his horse over to him. As the two of them departed, they bowed their heads to Manas."

'The old man cleared things up by saying, "I'm a *Manas* reciter, too. Your father must have known me: I am Shapak the *Manas* bard," he added apologetically. When I left the next morning and emerged from the ravines, my calf was standing at the threshold, its neck lowered.'

———

'To a Kyrgyz, even flying an eagle after a snowfall seems interesting,' Baisal used to say. From nightfall on, snowflakes had started to fall. Tired after their conversation, Dapan had lain down to sleep on his Uncle Bekesh's lap and was snoring. When dawn, the early morning bandit, broke, Bekesh suddenly awoke and spoke into Dapan's ear, 'Shall we go out hunting?' Dapan leapt to his feet. 'Sh ... sh! Don't wake up the whole house!' Bekesh urged. His eyes still not fully open, Dapan remarked with painful restraint, 'There's no dawn for an old maid.'

They quietly got dressed. Bekesh brought an excitable Tumor out of the hunting room, then they saddled Topon. By now the clouds had cleared; so much snow had fallen that the dawn was bright, and the stars, by the time they emerged, were becoming faint. Bekesh, Dapan and Tumor mounted the horse and set off towards Kökbel. Topon had been hobbled for too long, or perhaps the air outside was too cold: he blindly looked for the path and failed to find it, trying to locate a cattle track leading from rocks to grass. The ground was blanketed with freshly fallen snow, and they trampled on it with a crunching sound that was pleasing to the ear.

Bekesh strapped a hood to Tumor's head, so that the eagle wouldn't be aware of its surroundings during the journey; listening to the horse's hooves' rhythmic clopping, the bird dozed off on Bekesh's shoulder, undisturbed by Bekesh and Dapan's conversation. Along this blind, single-track path they rounded Askarkaya and found themselves in a wide plain. It was here that, once upon a time, Chokmor had tricked Tumor's parents, though Tumor couldn't possibly be aware of this.

Daylight began to show blue and green first over their left shoulders, then like a ripening fruit it turned yellow, and then red and grey once they had arrived at Kökbel. Their eyes were dazzled by the pure white snow that had covered the entire oasis and by the bright sunlight they were bathed in. In the distance a pair of scrawny crows were cawing, and Tumor seemed to shake off his drowsiness, so that Bekesh stopped his horse. 'There's no peace in turbid water, we've reached where we need to be,' he said, and he began to observe the flanks and the bare ground that lay beneath the mountain ridge. 'If crows are cawing, then a fox is about to come out,' he recalled the hunter's saying. Dapan was now shading his brow against the sun, wrinkling his face, using his hand as a screen, and peering deep into the oasis. Not the tiniest thing could be seen. The horse had been overexcited; it was now cooling down, but still losing patience, and it began pawing with its hooves.

They made the horse follow one more small mountain ridge. 'Make your red tongue say something,' Bekesh tried to rouse Dapan. Dapan opened his mouth and prepared to speak: he was about to say something appropriate, but suddenly he blurted out in an explosive whisper, 'Jackal! Jackal!' And Bekesh spotted below him – barely visible in the clumps of tamarisk – a crooked, scraggy gully, and an emaciated jackal emerging from it. Bekesh could see it trotting towards them, completely unaware.

'If this is the day he meets his end, who can escape the

grave?' Bekesh spoke the conclusion of a delighted hunter's saying. The eagle's talons and feathered breast were shaking with excitement, though his hood stopped him from seeing anything. From where he was perched, he suddenly flapped his wings twice. The jackal was making its way through the snow, it was obvious that it had no blood or juices running through it. Perhaps it was infected by some disease, there was no disputing that. The idea flitted through Bekesh's mind, then vanished.

They hurriedly dismounted, then hung back a kilometre away. Bekesh removed the hood from Tumor's eyes, and ran towards the jackal, saying: 'After him! After him!' The eagle freed itself from its jesses, and plunged off the leather gauntlet: it launched towards the oasis. The bird immediately spotted the quarry, its enormous wings circled into the cold heavens, and it filled its breast with air; three or four flaps of its wings brought it over the jackal, but now the jackal had caught sight of the eagle and suddenly turned back on its tracks. Either because Tumor had not been flown for some time, or because he had filled his breast with cold air, for some reason he landed on the snow, and started looking in a desultory way for the jackal, which was hiding in the tamarisk copse. However loudly Bekesh and Dapan yelled from the mountain ridge, the eagle was unable to fly up from the soft, friable snow, which it tried pathetically to shake off its wings.

Bekesh was heartbroken. He left Dapan with the horse at the hillock; he himself was sinking to his knees in the snow, as he ran down to try to retrieve Tumor, whose beak was stuck in the ground.

—

'If you've left your horse behind, you're flirting with death,' old men used to say. Bekesh could have fallen into a snowy crevasse on his way to rescue Tumor. Fortunately, he wasn't all that far from Dapan and Topon: Dapan forced the horse on until it was over the crevasse, and, throwing one end of Tumor's straps to his uncle, he tied the other end around the horse's haunches. So Dapan got the horse, all in a sweat, to pull Bekesh out of the crevasse.

It was lucky that all four of Bekesh's limbs were intact. They now proceeded cautiously on horseback; Tumor flew alongside and settled on Bekesh's wrist. If they didn't get any game to eat, at least they had some slush to drink; so they came out to the mountain ridge, when Dapan's sharp eyes spotted not one, but two foxes. 'You're a fine lad!' Bekesh, now his old self, praised the boy. 'You can make cream out of muddy water!' The pair of foxes were scouting the area, heading for the tamarisk bushes below the slopes of the oasis. The beasts were not just cunning: one went running off, the other froze, as if it were a rock. Bekesh had a heavy bird on his wrist and a leather helmet on his head, so he couldn't see a thing; after his recent near-disaster, he was as droopy as a leather strap, thoroughly soaked in slush.

After failing to deal with a single jackal, how could they cope with two foxes? Bekesh thought to himself, didn't they say when an eagle gets too old, he becomes a mouser? Tumor was an old bird now, perhaps the game was not worth the candle. While Bekesh was mulling this over, the eagle suddenly livened up and began to fuss and stir. 'Uncle, let him fly!' Dapan drummed at Bekesh, pointing his hand from behind at the foxes. 'Right, let's see if he can't get them!' said Bekesh, tearing off the eagle's felt hood. At a glance, Tumor's two eyes had

aimed at both foxes, his crop jerked up and down, and he
shook all over. Bekesh undid the eagle's jesses: saying, 'Get
him! Get him! Off you go! Off you go!' he launched Tumor
into the air.

This time the eagle dropped down into the air, as leisurely
as a lord's bride. It gently stretched out both wings, and using
the wind's strength to descend to the oasis, in an instant fell like
a meteor onto the foxes. The animals froze to the hillside. One
fox, confused and angry, raised its head to the heavens and was
tossed over by the eagle's talons. The other fox immediately
scampered off in panic.

Bekesh and Dapan rode up until they were level with the
fox that the eagle was holding on to. Bekesh dismounted and
slit the fox's throat with his knife, as the animal was trembling
in its death throes; when the blood had poured, making a red
channel in the snow, he gave the innards of the quarry to the
bloodthirsty eagle, and when the fluids were drained he handed
the fox to Dapan. It was now well into the evening, and their
arms and legs were flagging when they returned to the ayyl.

PART TWO

Some time passed. In spring, tulips and edelweiss sprouted on the mountain slopes; then the melons ripened and it was summer and things were good everywhere. Exasperated and fed up with his pointless work at the radio station, Bekesh resigned, and went to stay in the country. He hunted with Dapan, he looked after the cattle, he completely forgot about the magic stone, and he went to the summer pastures and enjoyed reciting the *Manas* at the top of his lungs. Tumor and Topon recognised him and obeyed him. But even though he dressed just like Baisal in gown and leather coat, at heart he felt there was something not quite right. He was searching for himself, wondering if this was how he ought to be living. He imagined a voice inside him saying he was a melon when sweet melons were being picked, but forgotten once the bitter beer is poured.

In any case, he was upset by the hostility in a story by Sheikh Sa'diy that he was given to read one night by Uncle Sattor. It went like this: a young man was travelling the world and arrived at one of Anatolia's main ports. Since he couldn't find anywhere to stay in this unfamiliar place, he set off for a dervishes' teahouse. The dervishes gave him a warm welcome, and took him to see their elders, who made an exhortation to cleanliness: they said it would be good for the young man if he cleaned the prayer room and swept it out. The young man bowed, and took his leave. An hour passed, then two, then night fell, but there was no sign of the youth. The dervishes assumed he was too lazy to get down to manual work.

Early the next morning one of the dervishes, on his way to the market, came across the young man by the outside door and told him off: 'You idler: you're no good as an apprentice, because you don't know the first things about the path of cleanliness, nor about service without expecting reward.'

Immediately the youth began to weep. He said to the master dervish, 'I couldn't see any dirt or any dust that I could get rid of in the prayer room, apart from myself. Because I didn't want to sully its cleanliness, I brushed myself down and, being a specimen of dirt, I freed the prayer room of my presence.'

Bekesh gave a lot of thought to the sense of this parable and applied it to himself, looking at his foster-father Baisal as a dervish saint; and although it seemed a heresy to juxtapose the world of the *Manas* with a prayer house, he could not put an end to these thoughts. He was spending the evening in the yard, sitting at a grindstone sharpening a scythe, before the hay had to be cut the next morning. His heart leapt when he saw Dapan come running in from the fields, and as soon as the boy had filled his mouth with something, he started jabbering away about all the recent incidents.

He told Bekesh that while he was taking care of his calf, angling for fish by one of the dams made in a gully where a mountain stream ran down, a man dressed in red had appeared by his side and sat down on a big mountain rock. Showing curiosity, the man said, 'Do you know that fish talk with their tails?' In fact, the rod that Dapan was holding had begun to shake violently. Then the man cast a glance, 'There, now you can pull in your fish, you can hear it yourself.' Throwing down his rod and line, Dapan ran away in fright.

'Where did you leave your calf?' asked Bekesh. Dapan pointed to the mountain stream. 'Well then, let's go off together,' said Bekesh, but Dapan absolutely refused. So, clutching his scythe, Bekesh went off to the stream's bank: the calf had been grazing and got itself wet, and was happily lying under an overhanging rock. By its side was the handle of the fishing rod. Of the man dressed in red there was not a trace.

—

The next morning Bekesh asked around and learnt that some forty Chinese builders had come to the village. They had a contract with the Tajik government to tunnel through Mount Asqar as part of a road-building project. As we have said, Chekbel had its own peculiar qualities. Bekesh had now lived in the village for quite a time, and was discovering quite a few things that he had not known about. For instance, until very recently he didn't know that Dapan was a pupil at the Tajik-language school. He knew now that their documents would be issued by the Tajik authorities, because they were actually situated in Tajikistan, and, as Tajik citizens, they would not be accepted in a Kyrgyz school situated in the Tajik kishlak.

Basically, all this portended trouble for Chekbel: the Kyrgyz children were being forced to study Tajik, the Tajik children to study Kyrgyz. Though others found this either ridiculous or deplorable, for some reason Bekesh was secretly pleased by the idea that the children would grow up bilingual. But there was one thing that did affect him, and which he found both ridiculous and deplorable. Now that he had resigned from his job at the radio station, he had to sort out one or two documents; and he discovered that in Chekbel not one, but two village administrations existed, each belonging to one country. The Kyrgyzstan administration was in a Tajik kishlak, and the Tajik officials were situated in the Kyrgyz ayyl. The police station, of course, and the post and all the rest were likewise all randomly scattered, higgledy-piggledy. True, for both sides the water came only from Tajikistan, while the electricity came from Kyrgyzstan.

Because Chekbel was so far from the capitals of either country, it had preserved this state of chaos for many years. However, now that forty or fifty Chinese had arrived from Tajikistan to tunnel through a mountain that led back to Tajikistan, it became clear that the road-building had tipped the scales sharply to one side.

Suddenly realising this, Bekesh felt himself in a great state of anxiety, and everything in him was astir.

—

The people of Chekbel were swarming about like wasps in a nest that had been kicked. What with the Chinese construction workers casually arriving, turning up as if they were going to make themselves at home in Chekbel, and a road opening up in one direction, while there was none in the other direction, confusion arose. The matter was discussed once in the mosque and once at the market. In the streets, from morning to night, people were chatting to one another about this business.

Since Bekesh was a natural radio reporter, he had come to take a look at the Chinese with his own eyes. In a gully between two mountains, on both banks of the stream, three railway carriages had been installed, and Chinese men in orange clothes (one of whom Dapan had perhaps seen not so long ago) were brewing tea in a brazier that was hung from an outer door. Their quilts and mattresses were propped up against the carriages.

When these men were first spotted, they seemed to people's worried eyes like scurrying ants, unlike the serious, dignified villagers of Chekbel. Some of them were banging nails into old dried tables, another group took a length of wire from a sack and strung it between the tables to give themselves a radio signal, while a third group took spotless porcelain bowls, clean as a summer breeze, from their food store and laid them out on a sideboard: in short, not one of them waited for another to give an order. They were in complete thrall to their work, except for one person having trouble with his cooking pot. Bekesh stood there observing them: it all reminded him that the Chinese had at times been the most determined and vicious enemies of Manas.

> This Chinaman had come,
> So he said, to know him,
> He'd come apparently,
> Suddenly, to cause trouble,
> He was going, he said, to pull down
> The hero who had raised his head,
> He was going, he said, to bind
> A feeble, inept groom.
> When the black Chinaman came

Most of the nation ran away in fear,
Abandoning hope for their souls...

But when Bekesh's eye fell on any one of them, that person smiled gently in response to him, to soften Bekesh's sensitive heart. It was as if each one of them was saying to Bekesh in his own language, 'The goshawk perches on a beam, I'm ready to sacrifice myself for its tail.'

—

Bekesh stood there for a long time, watching the men. Without breaking off their work, one of them – a rather large man – was yelling out things in his abrupt language to somebody in the railway carriages. Then, limping out of a carriage, a man who didn't seem to be a Kyrgyz, but was definitely not a Tajik, and certainly could not have been a Chinaman, came out: in any case, he was good-looking. He was holding wire-cutters and a length of wire, and although he hadn't finished the job in hand, he approached Bekesh and greeted him in somewhat rough Kyrgyz, as if to say, 'Well, can I help you?' Then, so as to make acquaintance, he put the cutters and the wire in his left hand and offered his right hand, saying 'Mimtimin.'

At first Bekesh didn't understand the latter word, and replied only to the first question. 'Nothing really, I'm just hanging around.' Then, so as not to appear unfriendly, he spoke again, asking, 'What is it you just said?'

'My name is Mimtimin,' the young man repeated.

'Mimtimin?' Bekesh repeated. 'Are you Chinese?'

'No, I'm a Uighur,' came the slightly embarrassed reply. 'I'm the interpreter for them,' he added, pointing behind him.

Bekesh reacted adversely, showing he had his doubts about this young Uighur. Could his name really be a Uighur one? Or was it Chinese? he began by questioning.

'No,' said the interpreter, 'my real name is Muhammad Amin, but the Chinese written form is Mimtimin.'

Bekesh couldn't help laughing. This was exactly the opposite of Almambet in the *Manas*! When Almambet left his homeland, having adopted Islam, he renounced his father and mother's people and country and took the side of the Kyrgyz, and became Manas's closest friend and fellow warrior. Almambet went off into battle against China, whereas this young Muslim, despite his parentage, had changed his Muslim name and gone off to work for the Chinese. This was surely as senseless as a small fire which has neither a roof nor a cooking pot over it.

At this point Mimtimin's boss called for him in a harsh tone, and he froze as still as a driven pole by Bekesh's right side. If his boss shouted in the other direction, he would go back to wherever he was needed like a fresh breeze. Actually, the boss was now standing in the carriage doorway, turning his electric torch in its holder. Mimtimin turned back, without taking his leave of Bekesh.

For one more moment Bekesh stood watching this fuss over the breakfast that was cooking, gnashing his teeth at the men's indifference to humanity. Not one of them would stop mid-work and say: 'You're a human being with a head and four limbs, come here and talk.' Bekesh turned round and made for home. The ear will appear from wherever the cauldron master wishes, how true it was!

—

Bekesh left the dry ravine for the hill. Meanwhile Dapan and three or four boys of the same age had left school and were heading towards him.

'Where are you off to?' Bekesh asked them.

'To see the Chinese.'

'Who told you? Or was it the wind that brought the news to Chekbel?'

'No, my stepfather told me.' Dapan saw that Uncle Bekesh was amazed. 'Brother Adolat!' Dapan said, giving his stepfather's name. Yes, Adolat was the brother-in-law's name: Bekesh never had been able to remember it. How could the name Adolat (meaning justice) be assigned to that ninny? He was and always would be a pop-eyed hash smoker. And how had he known about the Chinese? Bekesh wondered.

'The Chinese came in a lorry,' Dapan continued. 'Joomart, who brought you here, was driving them, and he came to our house...'

'Were they talking about secrets with your stepfather again?' another boy piped up.

Dapan was beginning to get impatient and he shook his head at his friends. 'Mister Joomart brought a Chinaman who spoke Kyrgyz...'

Now Bekesh thought it best not to tarry with the children. Instead, he slyly followed them as they headed towards the dry ravine. Not approaching the railway carriages, he hid behind a poplar tree in the hillside and waited to see what would unfold. The schoolchildren, however, as if arriving at some spectacle, came and joined the Chinamen's camp, where they chattered away at the top of their voices.

The Chinese reacted to the children just as they had to Bekesh: not one of them stopped working. The children called for Mimtimin to join them. Mimtimin was now holding a paper and a pair of scissors; and when Dapan saw him rushed he towards him just as if Mimtimin were a friend he was saying hello to. Bekesh stood there observing. He guessed that yesterday this Uighur villain had been secretively exchanging words with Joomart and Adolat. Now Mimtimin, wiggling his mouth as if about to receive honey, was telling the children something, then asking them to wait at the entrance to the railway carriage, bringing out small objects like pens before sending them away. The young man's cunning tricks must be pretty nifty, Bekesh thought. He must have been given a task to do: 'Hang around, mix with people, take three or four months to find things out.'

—

When the boys went back home, Bekesh emerged from his hiding place, turning his gown inside out. On the way back from the Chinese camp he passed over the bridge, taking a slightly shorter way to the Tajik kishlak, and headed for Uncle Sattor's house. Sattor was not at home, having gone out to reassure the locals. 'He should be back any moment,' said Aunt Mutriba. And adding, 'The tea is brewing,' she spread a tablecloth over the garden mound, and brought out tea with three sticks of grape sugar. 'We've been drying apricots,' she said, pulling at one. She offered some bread. 'Have the Chinese arrived?' she asked.

'Yes,' said Bekesh, 'I've just come from seeing them.'

'Were there a lot of them?' Mutriba asked, as if she was fearful.

'Likely about a hundred or so,' Bekesh said.

He didn't know what attitude to take in this extraordinary situation: on the one hand, an incomprehensible regret had been aroused in him, as if he were in a city with no gates, but on the other hand, contemplating the contradictions in his mind, half of Chekbel's people were just like those Chinese, like himself, trying to make a living in foreign lands. If they had been at home, wouldn't they have managed to tunnel through a mountain and build a road with their own hands? So now they were sitting here, depending on the Chinese.

While Bekesh was apparently in thrall to these thoughts, Mutriba seemed to be pouring oil on the fire. 'They eat caterpillars and ants, don't they?' she remarked. Bekesh hadn't considered this. You couldn't feed them on the local people's horsemeat sausage, with a bit of mane in it, or add a splash of honey to the kumys. It was enough for them to have a lorry bring them noodles from the city as needed: like Soviet citizens, they would be happy with one hot meal a day. Or were they like hungry cattle who would graze on whatever was under their feet? Who knew?

While this conversation was in full flow, Uncle Sattor came into the yard. His face was a little flushed, and he embraced Bekesh when he saw him. 'When God wants to punish the khan, he makes him quarrel with his wife and then fight his people,' he said in Kyrgyz. Bekesh couldn't make much sense of this: he looked at his uncle with concern. Sattor waved his hand and ranted, 'I'm off to quell a popular revolt. Everyone's risen up, waving their pickaxes and scythes, saying "Let's chase the Chinese out of our land." "Hey, people, look at yourselves," I say, "from every household, from every yard one of you has gone to Russia! You can't become a Muslim until you've been a foreigner! Think for yourself, if your relatives and fellow clansmen were beaten up and driven out of Russia, how would you react to that?" I had trouble calming them down. Really, after taking their anger out on the Chinese, it's now directed at the Kyrgyz. Why? Well, thanks to this road, who's going to get the benefit? The Kyrgyz! They'll have an open road to Tajikistan, apparently. The Tajik government is not going to have any sympathy with us, they say. In short, a mother-in-law is as much trouble dead as alive.

'There's a story,' he said, calming down a little once he'd wetted his throat with a bowl of tea. 'In a certain city a sheikh was living. Every day he went out to a hill on the edge of this settlement and stood looking at the city beneath his feet. One day, when he was on the hill thinking his thoughts, a traveller came up to him. He greeted the sheikh and asked him, "What are the people like in that city? I'm looking for a place to settle." The sheikh then looked at him, and asked, "What are the people like in the country you've come from?" "Thieves and liars, robbers and traitors, no use to anyone else, they're brazen scoundrels," the traveller replied. "Thanks to them I've left the country." The sheikh observed him furtively. "In that case, continue with your journey," he said. "The inhabitants of this city are exactly the same."

'When he heard these words, the traveller continued on his journey.

'The next day the sheikh was again on the hill, standing pensively, when another traveller saw him and approached. This man asked, "What are the inhabitants of this city like? I'm searching for somewhere to settle." The sheikh asked him, "What are the people like in the land where you've been living?" The traveller praised his people sincerely, "A generous, hospitable, caring, gracious, child-loving people!" When he heard these words, the sheikh quietly laughed and said, "Welcome to our little city! Our people are just the same."

—

After listening to Sattor's stories, Bekesh felt a little tipsy, as if he'd been taking mouthfuls of kumys. 'Nobody can understand these stories nowadays,' said Sattor, then expressed himself in Kyrgyz: 'What's too heavy for the colt is too light for the horse.' Bekesh stood there quietly, but his uncle kept him waiting, while Mutriba cooked some plov. 'I feel uneasy at heart,' Sattor told his nephew. 'I hope it won't end badly. People have got fire in their blood. Everyone has turned grim and bestial. You might as well be talking to a brick wall. Just a tiny crackling, just a sidelong glance – nothing very big, something too small to notice – will push everything over the edge: the mob is ready to run riot! There used to be old men among us Tajiks, there used to be white-haired holy men among you Kyrgyz, with *Manas* reciters and storytellers. They would stop the rain if it rained, and the blizzard if it snowed, that's how it used to be. If anything happens, whom will your ayyl pay attention to now? To your so-called mullah with his broken religion? Or to you, who have worked in the city? I can see it all with my own eyes: throw a bone, it won't hit his tiny head, but yet he is drawing a sword against something as feeble as a locust.'

As Bekesh listened to Sattor, he thought that his uncle was afflicted with exactly the same anxiety and disquiet as he was, though he could not single out any remark of his in particular that rubbed down his heart. Had his uncle said something about a lump of rock? That made him remember again one or two *Manas* recitals in the summer pastures. Was it not about the Great Raid? About that conflict that flared up against China and the Kalmaks, when young men's eyes blazed and they applauded, so that Bekesh felt that the problem was one of unforrunate circumstances, rather than arrogance. He had an intuition, a feeling that in these reckless young shepherds and horse herders there was something dormant that was close to a feeling of nationalism, growing more and more acute.

'After all, just take a look at yourself!' said Sattor, getting heated. 'Whether you read them the *Shah-nama* or recite the *Manas* to them, what they are extracting from it, like hair from dough, is their superiority to the rest of the world. Apparently there were no people like them in the world, as if their wine and their beer, their way of getting drunk, set them apart. If you looked at their situation today – the monkey wept. 'He started clearing the snow, he went to bend his back in Russia,' but if you let them, they'll swallow the rest without chewing it.

'Yes, when I think of those people of yours, it makes my liver bleed, brother,' Uncle Sattor declared. But now the same thoughts were making Bekesh's ribs ache. What could he do?

—

When he was returning home, Mullah Shavvol and one or two young men were standing by the mosque, chatting. Bekesh greeted them, making out that he was just passing, but the mullah called him over with a wave of the hand. 'Did you see them?' he asked. 'Infidels have gone and penetrated our Islamic abode.' Then the mullah said a few things in Arabic, which he translated. 'Our prophet, peace be upon him, when he was asked "What is the best reason for migrating?" uttered this noble phrase, "It is to battle with infidels when encountering them!"' The words made Bekesh shudder. Mullah Shavvol evidently sensed this and shook his thin beard. 'I believe your Manas went to war with the Chinese infidels, didn't he?' he asked sarcastically. Bekesh suddenly swallowed his tongue, at a loss for a response.

'They say they will open a road, but the infidel government will turn us Muslims off the true path, God give us refuge,' Shavvol asserted, again gripping with reverence a handful of his beard. After working for long years in the city, Bekesh had absolutely no trust in the so-called 'crap government' and its affairs. Yet for some reason, when he heard such language here, as if he was getting involved in a conspiracy, he could only shudder. The cunning Shavvol sensed this, too. 'If you have a tooth, you can chew off a stone, our people say,' he said, passing from Arabic to Kyrgyz. 'Before the day passes as swift as a horse, like our forefather Manas we must be on our feet and ready to meet them,' Shavvol said, to counter Bekesh and to rouse those milksop youths against the newcomers. 'What if we set fire to their camp?' asked one of the boys. This exchange took Bekesh's breath away, it took the light from his eyes, the sound from his ears: there was no sense now in asking the idiot Shavvol any questions. 'Hellfire for infidels,' was the only thing he would hear this mullah say.

Bekesh felt he had some comeback: he had read in some booklets about Islam, which he'd come across in the city, extracts about peace and friendship, but he couldn't find the words to stand up against a dusty mullah. And so he headed home without pressing the matter, like a sparrowhawk with broken wings. Didn't they say, the path of a man who has chosen a path is clouded over?

—

Bekesh got to the house in a bad state. Dapan was sitting there, heated and excited, telling his mother various things. Bekesh's spirits rose when he saw Dapan and his Aunt Sairake. He came in and sat down beside them. Sairake was rolling sour milk curds into patties. Dapan seemed to know what he was talking about: what he'd seen and been puzzled by at the Chinese camp. 'The Chinese are a weird, rather odd people. When we went there the first time, they offered us pens and paper; then when we came as a group, they gave us a tour. There are ten of them sleeping in each carriage. The beds are double bunks, and every carriage has a television. Some of them were sitting watching Chinese television, some were playing cards, only their card games weren't like ours at all. None of them knows any Kyrgyz or Tajik. There was just one who spoke some broken Kyrgyz and Tajik. He hung around saying, "If you're hungry, I'm your food; if you're not, I'm just a stick to beat you with."

'They had their own cooking cauldron: they throw some stalks in the cauldron, then on top of that they put in five tench from our stream, they fried them without gutting them. The others were eating raw fish. We saw! There was a doctor there. He was caring for the ones who were bent double. He was really weird. One of them was chilled to the bone: the doctor stuck needles once in his hand and once into his heel.

'The music that came out of the television in one part of their carriage was just like beetles buzzing, you could see brand marks appearing, apparently the Chinese look at those marks when they sing.'

'That's called "karaoke",' explained Bekesh.

'Carry OK?' asked Dapan, bemused. 'What do you mean "carry OK"?'

'Not "carry OK",' said Bekesh, articulating each syllable separately. 'It's called that because someone plays a tune, and says what song he wants.'

'They don't need an ox to irrigate the land,' Dapan giggled slyly.

'Oh you devil!' said his mother, and both she and Bekesh suppressed a laugh.

Now Sairake took up the conversation. 'During the war,' she said, 'they brought a crowd of Germans to Chekbel. They built a corral on some waste land on the slopes, where the Chinese are now; as there weren't any shelters, they drove them all like cattle into it. Then we all lost our tempers and said, "The Germans have come, the Germans have come!" We were outraged. Really, our fathers and menfolk had been killed fighting the Germans, and now they'd brought Germans to stay with us, how could we say we wouldn't take out our anger and resentment against them.

'When we looked at them, these people were old men and old women, or mothers and infants, every one of them. There wasn't a single healthy young man fit to ride a horse, or a man in his prime. They were shaking and twitching when they looked at us. They were dressed in rags, in patchwork gowns, stumbling about, all moaning in pain, no more strength left. "The wind knows when I go, the spade knows when I've settled down," they said, as if they'd passed through seven hells to get here. Then we were terribly sorry for them, as if a sword had passed, barely grazing our ribs. We swallowed our resentment, we suppressed our desire for vengeance. The next morning quite a lot of them were chilled and frozen by the mountain cold. These Germans were not Germans from the war against Soviet power, they were our Germans, who'd been living around Saratov.

'God saved us then. To our shame, the hotheads were saying, "Let's pour kerosene all over them and exterminate them like lice!" When the blind man sees a white spot, he shakes his head till the skin comes off,' said Sairake, shaking her head in deep regret. 'We're all the children of our forefather Adam, aren't we,' she concluded as she went back to rolling out sour curd patties.

—

Then Bekesh began to talk about what he'd seen and found out in the street. Dapan unexpectedly came to life, coughed and suddenly started reciting from the *Manas*:

Jakyp's younger brother Közkaman,
Safely travelling a long way
with his son called Kökchököz,
Mounted his horse and went to see Manas.

Bekesh had always been frightened by this episode. Most *Manas* reciters omitted this part, it was not included even in the *Manas* printed in several volumes, but for Uncle Baisal it had been one of the most cutting and most loved episodes. Dapan now recited not like a small child, but grumpily, like an old man who'd seen plenty of things and was coming to the end of his life. Not with the usual precision, but in a dull, weary voice, he told of the journey of Manas's paternal uncle and his son to see Manas, the moment when Manas set off to visit the Afghan shah Tulki, how Kanikey waited for them, providing a thoroughbred charger to replace a tired horse, dressing them in golden gowns.

Kökchököz was in love with Kanikey. And now he began to contemplate killing Manas and making himself khan in his stead. 'The enemy who comes from your inner circle is the worst,' repeated Dapan three or four times at various points in his recitation. While he was relating the story of Kökchököz's plotting, Dapan was forgetting himself. He lost all sense of reality, as if his soul were in thrall to what had happened, and his voice were reaching his listeners from elsewhere.

When Manas came and conquered Tulki, Kökchököz organised a banquet and poured poisoned beer for Manas and his forty companions. Of those forty, thirty-nine collapsed: only one named Bozuul had drunk birch tree sap and sour milk soup instead of spirits and beer, and so he had survived. Manas was then in his yurt completely drunk, and couldn't even open his eyes. Taking no notice of his father Közkaman's pleas, Kökchököz tried to enter and raise his sword against Manas, intending to hack off his head. But Bozuul came to Manas's aid, so that Manas could vanish on his horse Akkula. Kökchököz chased after him and shot an arrow at Manas: Manas and his horse dropped into a ravine.

If anyone else were in Manas's place, they would have died immediately, but Manas survived. Kökchököz assumed he had died and went to declare himself khan, and make Manas's kith and kin bleed. He came to Kanikey. "If a heifer gives the wink, the bull will break its tether," he snapped. "I'm going to marry you." Kanikey refused. So Kökchököz drove Kanikey and Manas's other wives out of the house and took away all their possessions.

> Disconsolately calling out for Manas,
> Kanikey walked about screaming,
> Sad and grief-stricken,
> Having been deprived of everything,
> She could not stop howling,
> She went somehow from horde to horde,
> She sought some place to rest her head.

At this point Sairake began sobbing bitterly. Dapan joined in and his voice merged with his mother's weeping: he stopped reciting the *Manas*. As they both filled their lungs with weeping, Bekesh did not hesitate to pick up the poem from where Dapan had stopped. He was celebrating Manas's quiet recovery in a cave, gathering his forty companions, returning to his own country and wreaking his revenge on his cousin Kökchököz. Bekesh recited it as if he could see it with his own eyes, the total destruction of Manas's enemy.

—

Early next morning, after feeding Tumor meat and grain, and giving Topon oats and hay, Bekesh went outside to see how the kishlak and ayyl were getting on. At the start of his journey Adolat, his cousin's second husband, and another three or four local layabouts and thugs were standing around a tractor they'd stopped. As he came closer, it became clear that they'd surrounded a young Chinese man driving the tractor and were trying to make him talk, partly in Kyrgyz, partly in Tajik, making fun of him. 'Say "stream" then,' one said. They rolled about laughing. Say '*Nasha mikasham* – I smoke hashish,' asked another one. The young Chinese looked very awkward. 'Nasamikachambiki,' he said, wrinkling his brow and hunching with embarrassment. Again they all guffawed.

While Bekesh stood there looking on, they actually seemed to be trying to get him to smoke hash. Bekesh was overcome by pity for the wretched youth whom they were mocking. All he could think was not to meddle with these thugs, after all, not so long ago, they had nearly plunged all Chekbel into violence. But the lack of support or encouragement for this open-hearted young man was pushing Bekesh to intervene.

'Hey, you lot!' he said as he came up and mingled with the rabble. 'Let this young man go, let him do his job!' When Adolat spotted Bekesh, he gnashed his teeth without saying a word, but one of his sidekicks failed to recognise Bekesh. 'You with the big mouth, who do you think you are? Mind your own business, get the hell out of here,' he said, jostling Bekesh. Bekesh's face flushed bright red. Without hesitating, he punched the youth in the face, and with just a thump, the young man fell onto his arse.

Once again, family harmony was broken. Thinking that the rest were going to join in, Bekesh was getting ready to defend himself, when Adolat suddenly turned around and backed away. One other hothead followed him, but a couple of the sidekicks hung on and were now really rearing to go for Bekesh. Then that shy Chinese childlike arm flew in with a whish and, as if scything hay, knocked down one of the attackers where he stood. Another attacker shrugged and fled without looking back, not in Adolat's tracks, but in the opposite direction.

Bekesh looked at the young Chinese and said, for some reason in Kyrgyz, 'If you haven't got a wife, have a brother-in-law!' The Chinese youth furrowed his face and brow and said something like, 'No got wife, take boda in lo.' They both had a good laugh at that.

He should have known that this Chinese youth had a little bit of Russian. 'Where did you pick it up?' Bekesh asked.

'I used to work in Siberia,' came the answer.

'If you know some Russian, why were you letting those men torment you by making you speak Kyrgyz and Tajik?' Bekesh enquired, to which the young man opened his toothless mouth and laughed through his gums. 'Did you lose your teeth when you were in Siberia?'

'No, the police in China knocked them out,' he said.

'What for?' Bekesh asked, horrified. 'Do the Chinese beat up one of their own?'

'They certainly do, our police exist so they can beat up their own people!'

Then, as he wiped the tractor's oil and grease, he began to explain a few other things in his broken Russian. Bekesh may not have understood him properly, but to judge by what he did make sense of, this young man, whose name was Lin Ju, was a young 'illicit', in other words, a child who had an older sister. Given that China had a one-child policy, no additional child could be registered anywhere: not in the registry of births, not in kindergarten, not in school. If the child survived, he wasn't counted, there was no record of his birth, he was stuck among the 'living dead'.

'A lot of us here are of the same kind,' he said and went back to his tractor. 'Only when we are beaten and locked up by the police can we count as human beings, otherwise we don't exist!' He grinned again. 'That's why, in China, or here, wherever, nobody sees us as human.' Then he concentrated on his work again. 'So I am working over there,' he said and pointed to where the sun broke over the nearest mountain and lit up the side, revealing the sunny slopes.

—

After leaving the ayyl, Bekesh made for Dapan's family house: on his way, he saw the Chinese were very busy at work. There was a great din: the excavators were following the line of the hill, digging the earth to make a bridge over the stream, bulldozers were filling one place with the rocks and earth they had strewn about, some smaller excavators were standing in line, loading stones mixed with earth into enormous dump trucks. All this made the stream's water dirty; like a nervous horse it darted first in one direction, then in another, splashing about, roaring between the mounds that reached the heavens as it tried to make its voice heard through the construction. How could the stream be heard now! Everyone has to cope with his own burden, Bekesh thought.

It was all very well as he was striding over the ground, halfway to the village, and now at Adolat's place. Then he caught sight of something: a familiar truck by the clay wall. In fact Adolat was on the veranda mound, while Joomart was sitting there too, behind him Bekesh could see another of their blackguards. Adolat was confronting someone. Bekesh came up closer to the veranda, and Joomart's voice reached his ears: 'This is mare's sweet sausage meat: there's nothing better than that. A fair swap...'

He was handing Adolat something that looked like sausage, wrapped in cellophane, and in exchange he received something smaller. Then Adolat turned towards the street and saw Bekesh and, like a stubborn horse, came to a standstill and vigorously jerked his head back to the other men. The first to leap up was Joomart. He tucked whatever it was Adolat had just handed to him under his belt, and hurried towards Bekesh.

'Boss, how are you? Had a good journey?' he said, with an attempt at demureness in his face. But Bekesh spotted a man behind him: it was Mimtimin, the interpreter for the Chinese. With conspicuous politeness he came right up to Bekesh and greeted him respectfully. Bekesh responded in kind. But Adolat stayed where he had been sitting, not moving. Bekesh watched him as though he were a prancing, stamping horse: if he'd got any closer, he might have kicked him.

Sitting at the lower end of the mound, Bekesh made the Amen sign, and, pretending that he had not interrupted their conversation, he cast a glance at each one of them. Mimtimin and Joomart looked embarrassed, but Adolat was sitting pompously, looking like an idol, like a mullah, a sight that made Bekesh squirm. If he was a piece of filth ready to grab a cooking pot from a woman, then what was the point in him sitting here all puffed up?

It was now, however, that Bekesh understood something: those two idiots made Adolat look like a boss. Didn't the saying go like this: if a sledgehammer is strong, a felt stake will go in easily. But here the opposite applied: if the stake goes in easily, a felt sledgehammer will seem strong enough? But what was the secret behind their submissiveness to Adolat? Was it hashish? Other drugs? Opium?

—

Their secret wasn't going to be given away. The two sidekicks put on a welcoming act and kept the conversation entirely about Bekesh. These cronies of his brother-in-law's were the sort of crooks who'd cook a deer in a stone oven, Bekesh thought to himself, and turned the conversation back to them.

He looked at Mimtimin, 'All the Chinese are at work, so you can take a break,' he hinted ironically.

But Mimtimin did not object to this sarcasm in the middle of a straight conversation: 'You're quite right, that's how it is. When the Chinese are at work, they don't need us. So we sit around and have a chat. They need us when they go back home!'

'What about you?' Bekesh turned to face Joomart. 'You've garaged the lorry!'

'Lose a friend, and twist a bone. We've come to see our boss Adolat,' he said, trying to flatter Adolat. 'The Chinese can wait, we feed them enough soup to fill a lake and a mountain of meat!'

'Do you haul all that food for them?' Bekesh asked with interest.

'The God-forsaken Tajiks haven't given a thought to their food, their wages, or their entertainment, so our boss and Mimtimin are seeing to their needs.'

Bekesh was beginning to understand the conversation that they had been having among themselves, but his visit to his cousin's husband's house had a different purpose, and for that reason he addressed Adolat now: 'Talking about that young Chinaman driving the tractor, you shouldn't go and stir up the ayyl and kishlak. He's a pretty feeble lad: before anything happens, your sidekicks and I ought to come and sort things out,' he said. And without waiting for an answer, Bekesh took his leave and rose to his feet.

—

When he got back home before noon, he found a district official was waiting for him. 'The Tajiks have started building a road without telling us, so now we have to do something about it,' the man said. 'The authorities have telephoned. We have to organise some kind of entertainment for all our people, like a horse race or a wrestling match. They said you used to work at the radio station; apparently, you're a great expert at putting on such shows. Putting it crudely, money has been allocated to this job.'

Initially, Bekesh wondered why the man was buttering him up so much. But the 'big man's' words had some sort of effect. The fact of the matter was that the money Bekesh earned from work had been spent on a feast, a funeral wake, on clothes for Dapan and his young cousins: it was all gone. The idea that while he was here he might write something for the radio was no good: there had been no news in Chekbel worth mentioning.

But now that the Chinese had arrived and had begun to drill through the mountain, cutting through to the Tajik side, it would be odd to make a fuss on Kyrgyz radio. As the motto at his old workplace went, it's better to look bad by giving, than look bad by not giving at all. He didn't raise any objections with the district official, and arranged for Chekbel's Tajik kishlak to have a Sunday feast the day after tomorrow: they agreed to organise races and wrestling, tugs-of-war and *Manas* recitals.

'But I do have one condition,' he told the big man. Let's include the Chekbel Kyrgyz in this Bairam feast, and if they

want, the Chinese construction workers too!' At first the official dismissed the idea. 'In our view, we are responsible only for
Tajiks who are Kyrgyzstan citizens,' he sniffed, but then perhaps
he saw the advantages of Bekesh's proposal. 'When we have
wrestling matches with Tajiks, our bodies never touch the
ground!' he said. So he gave Bekesh permission to celebrate
Bairam for all nationalities. 'I won't say it's bad, but it's not
good,' he said, and remarked cryptically, 'The eye will see what
befalls the head.'

At this very moment Dapan came back home from school.
He gave the official a fleeting glance, but the official paid no
attention to Dapan: he'd done his job and his mind was now
elsewhere. He rose to his feet and, looking at Bekesh, recited
lines from the *Manas*, 'If you want to do good service, then
gather forty companions.'

Bekesh laughed, and pointed to Dapan. 'Just the two of us,
that lad and I, will do the job of the forty companions,' he said.
Bekesh could see that the official had no great confidence in
the pair and added, 'If someone isn't ready to risk his life helping this young man, nobody will be up to it.' The official now
understood the sarcasm, and matched Bekesh's tone: 'Until he's
old enough to be a real man, we shan't have a proper life.'
Then he went outside, heading towards his ancient Volga car.

—

That very day Bekesh and Dapan went from house to house,
inviting to Bairam anyone who hadn't left for Russia to make a
living. Everyone was invited to the races. Uncle Sattor would
spread the news to the Tajik kishlak at evening prayers. Actually, ever since the Soviet Union had collapsed, Chekbel had

not enjoyed Bairam nor any other celebration; people seemed to be so bored that they simply couldn't wait for Sunday, and anyone who had a trotter, or a colt, or even just a yak, would then mount it and start galloping up and down the streets.

The Chinese finished their work early on Saturday. Not wanting to be locked up in their camp, they instead hung about by the side of the mountains they had tunnelled, and watched rioting and fisticuffs going on below. The villagers' communication with them was now arranged through Mimtimin. This was how Bekesh got word that his new friend, Lin Ju, had found work. Once when Bekesh had decided to go and see Topon, Lin Ju turned up with a companion of his who was going to take part in the next day's races. In broken Russian, Lin Ju tried to broach the subject: 'We've got a skilled jockey. Could he take part in the races tomorrow?' he said, pointing to his friend, a man from Inner Mongolia. Bekesh saw so much palpable pleading and begging in this friend's eyes as he glanced at a crow flying overhead, perhaps remembering the lively horse he used to have somewhere else. But, as he said, he had no horse here. If he could borrow a horse, he could take part in the race tomorrow.

Since Bekesh was in charge of organising the celebrations, clearly, he himself couldn't take part in the races. The most he could propose now was to recite the lines about Kanikey's race from the *Semetey* epic. He had intended to give Topon to Dapan; then, on reflection, he had rightly given Dapan the job of reciting the *Manas*. On the one hand, this was a question of Kyrgyz magnanimity and generosity, wasn't it? It was obvious what he should say to this friend of Lin Ju's: 'So, here's my horse Topon for you: congratulations!' On the other hand, wasn't this the horse that Uncle Baisal had ridden? One glance would tell you this was not a run-of-the-mill horse, but a sacred animal, and for that reason he now felt reluctant. He decided he would think hard about this, to give himself time.

Then, just as he was about to tell his horse to gee up, at that moment like a mosquito in the Mongolian youth's eye Bekesh saw he was fixated by a hair in the lively Topon's tail. 'All right, your friend can get on him, then!' he said. When Lin Ju passed this on, the young lad leapt like a flea onto the horse, clinging tightly to Bekesh's waist as he rode bareback. Bekesh could feel the young man's heart pounding as they rode.

—

Early on Sunday morning an endless line of cars and lorries came from the district centre. One lorry had a loudspeaker, another bore light-hearted slogans in Kyrgyz; a third vehicle was carrying twenty kilos of rice to be cooked in a cauldron, which had been brought with a stove the same size; a fourth vehicle had all the equipment and trimmings for plov and sweets for the children. 'After all, you've had a road built, and we're having Bairam!' Bekesh passed on to all of them Uncle Sattor's advice. Wasn't he a radio man? So he picked up the loudspeaker and, speaking now in Kyrgyz, now in Tajik, he proclaimed the meaning and the procedures of Bairam up and down the roads and hills that led to Chekbel.

Dapan had brought his Bairam felt hat and gown to wear and had joined his uncle, going through the motions of announcing the meaning and procedures of the event, both in Kyrgyz and in Tajik: he was putting it in verse. He seemed to be announcing the race:

Today there is a mighty race,
After you've fought, come and see!

And while his Uncle Bekesh was announcing the wrestling matches, Dapan added lines of Firdousi to his Tajik version.

May you all live long and be merry,
Forget your terror and prepare for wrestling!

Thus he proclaimed to everyone on the square, regardless of nationality. The day was marked by yelling and uproar all round Chekbel. Further off, the Chinese, who had been intending to sleep in on Sunday, had now woken up, and had come out, half-naked, on tractors and excavators, to observe whatever was going on. Either Mimtimin or Lin Ju, apparently, told them about Bairam, and very soon they emerged, now dressed up, onto the streets and hills to make their first acquaintance with the kishlak and ayyl.

With his Mongolian friend, whose name was Ulankhu, Lin Ju came up and insisted that Bekesh accept two hundred dollars for lending them a horse. When he saw the money, Bekesh started to think. In Chekbel two hundred dollars was enough to keep a household going for two months. In any case, the 'big man' wouldn't have given him even half this much to pay for all the work required. But all the same, looking into the Mongolian's flashing eyes, Bekesh was unwilling to take his money.

'Let's begin the day now by putting on the trotters' leg straps for the hill. I'm only lending the horse for a trotting race, because in the free-for-all competition the horse will be raced by this young man,' he said, pointing out Dapan, who was by his side. Lin Ju gabbled away, explaining a few things to Ulankhu in his language. Ulankhu was a little hunched, and his brows broadened and his face beamed. He shook his head, said 'Dui! Dui!'[2] to Lin Ju. Then he really did fervently proffer his two hundred dollars to Bekesh. Now Bekesh felt offended and refused: he began to jerk his hands away. 'Taking his money goes against my gut,' he explained to Lin Ju. Whether Lin Ju's broken Russian was enough to understand this idiom, when he caught the word 'gut', he said a few things to Ulankhu, his tone softening. Then they decided to meet after an hour or so at the place by the start of the old Kyrgyz road.

Dapan and Bekesh went on with their work. Of course, if all Chekbel's population had been in the kishlak and ayyl, Bairam would have started with a game of goat-carcase polo. All the wrestlers and strongmen, however, had gone to work in Russia, and those who had stayed behind were either weak wretches or mere adolescents. That was why Bekesh proposed first of all to have a five-kilometre circular trotting race, and then a tug-of-war between the kishlak and the ayyl, after which there would be a *Manas* recital, followed by a free-for-all horse race.

In fact, the majority of those left in Chekbel were women and small children. What would putting on Bairam do for them, what contests could one organise?

—

By eleven o'clock, to the roar and rattle of the lorries and the clamour of the loudspeaker, nearly thirty elderly men and

2. Chinese, dui dui, 'yes, indeed'.

young boys had mounted their horses. Among the riders was the Mongolian youth Ulankhu on Topon. They gathered at the start of the Kyrgyz track leading to the district centre. The course was half a kilometre from a swamp, and lay between two hills, and most of the women watching were standing on those two hills. On one hill were mature Kyrgyz women dressed in colourful waistcoats and turbans, on the other hill, all dressed up in bright red embroidered headgear, were the Tajik ladies with their offspring, looking on at the spectacle below.

Bekesh had agreed with one or two officials who had come from the district centre, and were standing in their open-top lorry, blocking the road, that initially they'd distribute cloth numbers to the jockeys, and then use a loudspeaker to announce the rules for racing. 'First, you only let the horse trot! Second, the horse may only change its pace ten times in one kilometre! Third, a horse that jumps twelve times is excluded from the race! Fourth, there is to be no tripping up horses! Fifth, after two kilometres, the course is divided in two: trotting is on the right-hand side! Sixth, at the two-and-a-half kilometre bend you will be registered! Seventh, the winner of the race gets a fattened ram! There are track observers all along the route, so no tricks: are you all ready for the trotting race?' The jockeys were by now thoroughly worked up, their horses whinnied, and they said 'Ready!' as loud as they could. Bekesh made a sign to the driver in the lorry cab, and called through the loudspeaker, 'Once we've taken the vehicle off the track, the trotting race will start.' And with a roar of the engine, the truck left the track free.

Now the race was on! The horses had not taken part in a race for such a long time that some of them were scared of others, some were stimulated by the slappings and thumpings, one pushed ahead, one was so excited that it couldn't help looking around. Raising dust on the track, they began spreading out. Bekesh and Dapan had their eyes on Topon. They couldn't single out Topon among the other horses, but they kept their eyes on Ulankhu, who wore a Mongolian felt hat. It stood out clearly in contrast to the Kyrgyzs' white felt hats, and its red top was disappearing among the white hats so that Bekesh and Dapan realised Topon had put on a burst of speed. An old horse won't break away from the field, so went the saying: this horse knew where to place his feet among all the ruts and potholes, after all, Topon was trained on four districts of mountains and rocks. The colts and young stallions would be stronger in a free-for-all race, but it was hard for them to beat Topon at a trotting pace.

The horses were beginning to disappear from view, so Bekesh and Dapan turned their faces to the hills. It was over there that Aunt Rabiga was standing with her daughters-in-law. Uncle and nephew stared at them. Because the old woman and the young girls were making such a fuss, they realised that Topon was spurting ahead. Whether forced to, or of his own free will, Topon was not going to hold back! Dapan may have been a child, looking like a mare about to flee to the mountains, but he was impatient and felt it was time to recite his *Manas*.

A Karabayir steeplechaser,
Its lungs like a sieve, wings of brass,
Ears like reeds, thick hooves,
A pure thoroughbred, it gives a lot.
A Karabayir is a fast runner,
Never tired, galloping heavily,

Like stags, it gives a lot.
Covered in a special saddlecloth,
Protected by nine amulets,
How much an Argamak horse can give.
Men will be talking of it,
Making their horse sweat today,
Making it go as fast as it can…

'People, people, you're like an almond crop in an orchard! Don't say you haven't heard: Topon has come first in the trotting race, the race has been won not by a Kyrgyz hero, and certainly not by a Tajik champion, but by Ulankhu, a Mongolian from China! The sheep that has been fattened for slaughter goes to him!' Tears flowed from Ulankhu's eyes now he had to hand this sheep over to the owner of the horse, but Bekesh, who been the organiser and judge of the race, had to show he had no personal bias so as to protect himself from unwelcome gossip. He spoke to the whole crowd through the loudspeaker: 'Ulankhu wants to make the arrangements for the free-for-all prize race that follows. Whoever wins the free-for-all race will get a ewe, as well as a calf!'

Ulankhu wiped his face, aglow with both the heat and the cold, and said 'Dui! Dui!'

The sun had risen between the two mountains, the crowns of the poplar trees had stopped quivering, and now the time was ripe for the kishlak and ayyl to compete in a tug-of-war. Speaking now in Tajik, now in Kyrgyz, Bekesh went ahead with the announcement. On each side five or so young men, holding the rope but not wrapping it round their palms, joined hands and dug their heels into the ground. A line was drawn between the two teams. 'One – two – three!' Bekesh called as he signalled the start of the tug. Now a show of strength was underway. 'Hik! Hik!' cried the Kyrgyz youths, when the Tajik lads were tearing at the rope. 'One! One!' came the response as the Kyrgyz young men jerked the rope. Some were left sitting on their behinds by the strain, some were pulled forward by determined efforts, overexcited by the onlookers who were yelling, shrieking or whistling to encourage and support their own side. Then a burly Kyrgyz lad – who was used to setting up or taking down tents – exerted his entire bodily strength: with one bend, and then with two or three violent jerks, he split the Tajiks into two and, making a final effort, pulled their opponents across the line.

Bekesh took the loudspeaker to announce that the Kyrgyz ayyl had won, but there was no mistaking the fact that the 'big men' from the district centre were frowning and looking fed up. They were wondering why, with this second contest, after all the nit-picking and chopping and changing, the Tajik kishlak which was cared for by them should be left empty-handed!

So Bekesh unexpectedly picked up his loudspeaker and called on the women and girls to have a tug-of-war. In an instant, shaking their tassels, on one side were the Kyrgyz women, and on the other side the Tajik women gathered, tying up their hair under skull-caps. Once again Bekesh drew a line on the ground between them, then, as if to say he was going to declare the tug-of-war open, out of nowhere appeared Mullah Shavvol, wearing his turban. He came up to Bekesh and whispered into his ear, 'This does not conform to our faith, these practices are forbidden!'

But now the women on both sides were raising a cry of indignation: 'Come on! Come on, begin!' they clamoured. Bekesh made the announcement, using a Kyrgyz saying: 'Get on with the job you're doing, tie a thread in your hair: start tugging!' These young women whose husbands had gone to Russia really could tug. Their necks and arms bore the brunt of handling cattle and all the farm labour, their throats glistened like the moon, their forearms were bare and seemed to gleam with silver as they neatly tugged. The Kyrgyz women, used to tugging hard at a yak, seemed to be about to win, but the Tajik daughters, who were used to digging with mattocks, wouldn't succumb. At one moment the crowd supported one side, the next the other side was winning. Then Mullah Shavvol lost his patience entirely and shook Bekesh by the arm, saying, 'A corrupted people might as well have a dog as their mullah!' Clutching his thin beard with his fist, he forced his way through the crowd and vanished from sight.

Nobody won this particular contest. The two sides ended up in a draw, and the 'big man' came out and distributed Kyrgyz felt hats as awards to the participants in the two teams.

—

Next, perhaps thinking that they were as good as these people or as the womenfolk dressed to the nines, the Chinese started a tug-of-war among themselves. By now the plov, cooked by an Uzbek chef from the city, was ready. Bekesh summoned Dapan to come and taste the plov; others were preoccupied with eating plov and standing around drinking Coca-Cola and Fanta. 'Wherever wheat grows, there's a mill: so let's recite the *Manas*,' Bekesh said. As if they had already agreed, they would begin by telling the tale of Kanikey's race from the *Semetey* epic.

After Manas had made his Great Raid on China, he was wounded in battle and after he returned to his homeland, after his death, Kobesh-khan seized power and prepared to wipe Manas's kin and kith from the face of the earth. He intended to kill Manas's only son, Semetey; meanwhile, Manas's widow Kanikey, who refused to marry Kobesh, was left destitute, and his elderly mother Chiyirdi was thrown out into the street. Using a hundred different tricks, Kanikey and Chiyirdi, with the help of Bakay, manage to hold on to Semetey and set off to Bukhara, Kanikey's father's homeland. Here the infant Semetey, still a suckling, is entrusted to his grandfather Temir-khan and his uncle Ismail, unaware of true parentage. When he reaches the age of twelve, the boy's uncle Ismail lays a feast. If there's a feast, there has to be horse racing, and in this race, disguised as a man, Kanikey takes part, riding her horse Taytoru. This was the episode that Dapan began with:

Manas-khan laid on a feast and everyone knew it,
The celebration of Semetey was what nobody knew of.
The feast signalled galloping horses,
People from all over the world highly excited,
Heading for Bukhara's expanse,
Seven hundred households under the city's rule.
Kanikey sat there, bent double,
Closely studied by those who had come,
Firing up eight nations,
She was studied as she galloped.
When this news was digested,
His armour had a talisman
As colourful as Taytoru.
She fed him cockspur seed from the rice fields,
To calm him for the day.

When Dapan reached this part of the epic, he gave his Uncle Bekesh a sidelong glance and seemed to be carefully choosing a place to stop, as if to say now it was time for him. Bekesh picked up from the scene of the splendid race and started, with great pleasure and enthusiasm, at the beginning:

Do not feed to a sparrowhawk
My severed head, dried up from below.
Taytoru was in the thick of things,
This was close to Bukhara.
O God, don't let a woman be called a tramp!
Thinking so, she said.
Six hundred and forty spearheads to each charger
Was Torun's consignment,
They now stood together.
Ah, the dust that covered Bukhara,
The soul was stirred and fulfilled.
Old Eshon of Bukhara
With sixty heroes by his side
Went off to round up horses,
Scything them from ten heads,
Looking after dependents,
Caring for strongmen,
Sympathising with heroes,
As he travelled, his body raised dust,
He came galloping out.

The words were re-emerging from inside Bekesh, he was a little intoxicated by the poem. 'So, now I have turned into a famous *Manas* reciter,' he exclaimed in a flash of the imagination, looking all round him and for some reason his eye rested on the middle of the crowd, where he spotted Mullah Shavvol hiding behind a willow tree. In Bekesh's mind something seemed to click, as if he had suddenly forgotten he had to be somewhere or do something. So many words were on the tip of his tongue, but Bekesh couldn't make out their meaning or sense; he could hear them in his ear, but for some reason he kept repeating, as if he had a stammer: 'A man with a well-greased throat has a robe with a moth-eaten hem.' But why he was stumbling precisely with these words he could neither understand nor remember.

What was he doing here? Why was everyone staring at him? Where was he? Who were these people? Who was the child that had opened his mouth here, and waved his arm to the right and the left. Why were his eyes half-closed?

Suddenly all the questions, like seven snakes emerging from one nest, went slithering in all directions. Usually one thought on one occasion was like a thread, if it was a special idea, then it came in a sequence, stitch by stitch, each latching onto one: why were these inseparablejumbleduptangledthismuchclearly-turningcrazyinterruptedgodstrickenmanashorsegonesnortin-glotsofpapercome............

—

Bekesh didn't at first understand that he had now been disgraced and shamed in front of the entire gathering. His brain seemed to have been vomiting, he was sitting covered in his own vomit, his head hurt badly with a terrible pain. A few minutes passed, during which clapping and applause broke out on all sides, and then he seemed to be his old self again. He opened his eyes and looked: his nephew Dapan was thanking the audience by bowing to all four sides. Then Dapan came and stood next to him, and began whispering something. Bekesh couldn't understand, despite all his efforts, what the whispering was about. Some inexplicable frankness and calm spread through his veins. Once more he had a precise and clear conception of where he was and what had happened here. He was rid of the nightmare, and listening to Dapan's instructions, as if nothing had happened in the meantime, he returned to his normal state.

Meanwhile Kanikey's race had, as Dapan described it, come to a very satisfactory end, and the time was ripe for real action, for the Chekbel free-for-all race. Bekesh suppressed his inner feelings of embarrassment, like an old woman patching a hole in her clothes. He finally gathered his wits and rose to his feet; for some time Dapan, quite unconcerned, had been fussing around Topon, covering him again with a saddlecloth, tying up the horse's tail after the race so it looked like the others, taking a comb to his mane and grooming it. By now the 'big men' were perplexed. The reason for this was that since a television film crew had come from the capital city to Chekbel, they felt a need to hang about and keep their eyes peeled. 'Don't disgrace yourself, keep the people entertained!' the big man himself told Bekesh, articulating each word as he rode off to encounter the guests on his path.

Four men in black arrived in an open sort of jeep. As they say, next to the wearer of colourful gowns you will certainly find a mullah in a white turban. The big man was by now at their side, and after a brief intimate conversation with them, he gave Bekesh the order: 'Get on with it!'

This time, all of Chekbel seemed to be excited. Quite a few skilled riders (more than for the previous trotting race) were thinking about entering their horses for the free-for-all, among them five young ladies. After the incident of Bekesh's recital, he felt a bit dispirited, so he forced himself to say 'In the name of God,' and announce the race rules. This time the turning point was not two-and-a-half, but five kilometres. He made this fact clear. 'There's nothing wrong with your horse going at top speed and then all of a sudden trotting,' he said, glossing over not just the track's ruts and potholes, but at the same time his own state of mind, too.

While announcing the rules, Bekesh felt compelled to keep one eye fixed on Dapan and Topon. Topon was bellowing like a female camel coming into rut: Dapan had a lot of trouble bridling him. This was how natural strength came to the fore in the face of a challenge, Bekesh thought to himself with a touch of self-doubt. But the debate that he had initiated was now over; reluctant to hold back the excessive number of people and horses gathered round him, he realised it was time to begin the free-for-all race. Saying to himself that what happened would be the will of God, he signalled the start of the race by calling out, 'One – two – three!'

The moment he said 'Three!', the horses really did fly off. Scraggy old men, lumpen old women, people of all ages were enthusiastically cheering the horses on. One ragamuffin who had no horse to ride emitted an ear-piercing whistle. The Chinese contingent, too, exclaimed loudly and joyously in their language.

As the saying goes, if your guts hurt, your navel gets colic. Bekesh's thoughts were fixed on Dapan. Were horse and rider both firmly attached to the saddle? Had the other riders made Dapan's face bleed with a lash of the whip? Topon was a clever horse, he wouldn't play up, and surely he wouldn't stumble into any pothole. Dapan was capable of seeing things through! When the earlier trotting race had started and Topon could be seen ascending two hills, the aunt and her daughters-in-law had stamped the ground with their feet, and now they did the same. Sairake and Baisal had never let Dapan get dirt under his eyelids: the boy had been brought up nice and clean, that was why it was always someone else's horse that might get sweaty, some other boy's clothes that might get soiled. But Dapan would be worked up now by desperate enthusiasm.

So, the horses jostled and pushed, one trying to get ahead by ramming another with its chest as people applauded. Then, in the middle of the clouds of dust, Dapan and Topon could be seen gathering speed and forcing their way to the front! If Dapan were to be toppled from the saddle, this would be the fall not just of a child, but the end of Baisal's progeny. 'I've entrusted you to my God!' Bekesh said to himself: he hadn't slept for several days and he could feel his eyelashes heavy with fatigue. Worse, he had recently felt his mind was seething with worms and now it seemed as if black moths were attacking his brain, a pain that penetrated his temples. In this chaotic state of confusion, he cut through the crowd and made for the very edge, not looking for anywhere to sit, but trying merely to find a patch of fresh grass.

Because he was tired, or because of his recent embarrassment, one eye drooped a little. It was then that the big man came up to him and said: 'Hey, get up! Now we can see the first horses, let's film them.' Bekesh sensed that there was something sneering about the big man's remark: he jumped to his feet and, elbowing his way through the animated crowd, he emerged and took his place at the start of the course, at the line where the race was meant to begin and end.

When he looked, he found that the first horsemen were, in fact, now visible as hazy black figures, and somehow, judging by the snorting of the horses, there were signs that Topon was among them. But before them – as if you were splashing water onto hot ashes – raising a cloud of dust from the mountain track, the film-makers' truck was approaching. 'Well, they'll be showing your horse race to the whole country!' the big man said pompously. Bekesh couldn't take his eye off the lorry or the horsemen, now just about visible; in the cloud of dust the lorry raised some horsemen could be seen, and some could not, so that Bekesh began to feel anxious. He forced his sleepy eyes to focus, he tried hard to understand the cause of his anxiety, but couldn't put his finger on what was making him uneasy. Was it because he could not catch sight of Dapan in all that dust? Or because the lorry was getting in the way of the race? 'Hares get the plague only once in seven years, don't they? Who let that lorry get onto the course, couldn't they have parked it at the edge, on the hillside?'

The two clouds of dust approached: Bekesh and the crowd and the dust thrown up by the lorry, and the whirlwind of dirt thrown up by the riders. Then, as they got nearer, it was as if a dust cloud followed a typhoon, and raised something black.

The lorry was beginning to stall, no, not because of the zigzagging track, not even because of all the dust and dirt that had been raised, but because the riders behind were pushing and pressing and had no idea which direction to take as they left the course track. Some headed for the hill slope, others made for the dry riverbed. Apparently the lorry didn't have enough power to get out of the way: at one point the track was virtually bare and flat, and the lorry veered to the left, but too far, so that riders who clearly wanted to get away from the left smashed hard into the lorry. A howl of horror rose up all round.

'Dapan!' called Bekesh, as he ran as fast as he could towards that barren area.

'Dapan!' he yelled again, and the yell was echoed by the mountains and hills.

—

No, Dapan was still alive. Topon was a clever horse and, unlike the others, had not veered away from the left: until the very last moment he hadn't taken his eye off the lorry and the other horses, but had stayed on the course and, amid all the confusion and alarm, had come to a halt on the hill slope. Not one, but four riders, however, had fallen. It was clear that one horse had definitely been killed outright. Everyone ran towards the disaster scene. The first rider to have fallen was sprawled on the ground: he was lifted up by the other riders. When Bekesh saw that Dapan was alive, he rushed instead to the men lying on the ground. People were howling and lamenting, and Bekesh sensed that a nasty task lay ahead.

As if this recent accident were not enough, a vile trick was played on four or so members of the film crew, who were hiding, huddled in the lorry. One rider, still mounted, sent crew packing, not just with gestures and looks, but by lashing them with a whip. Other riders also attacked the men, and began hitting out and brawling. One of the film-makers in the lorry tried to shield his head with his camera. As he leapt out onto the ground and tried to make a run for it, two horsemen set a horse onto him; he and his camera were thrown under their hooves and crushed.

At the top of his voice Bekesh shrieked for them to stop, but even if he shouted through a loudspeaker the mob couldn't have been stopped now. One man was howling as he picked up a lifeless child; another, fearing that a horse lying on the ground in convulsions might die a godless death, proclaimed in God's name as he cut the animal's throat; another, taking vengeance on newcomers and outsiders, was inflicting bloody bruises on their faces and bodies; yet another man was calling out for help.

In an instant Bairam had turned into an apocalypse, creating a den of robbers, thieves and evildoers. Popular anger at the authorities seemed to have been on the boil for a long time: abandoning the bloodstained film crew, the horsemen started chasing after the big man and the judges. Meanwhile Bekesh did his duty: he called out loudly to the riders and men lying on the ground, and busied himself with loading them onto the open lorry; otherwise he too might have been trampled underfoot. Then he got in behind the wheel and, keeping his fingers on the horn, drove the dead and the injured to the kishlak's first-aid centre.

The rioting down below didn't stop: it got worse. News of a dead Kyrgyz child and Tajik father reached their families. They say if you hide an illness, death will be revealed: rage and anger infected the streets of Chekbel. People armed themselves with lumps of clay if they could; if not then with dry dung. The film crew's driver happened to be a Russian. 'You've killed our child, because you are such a cur,' the villagers said, and beat him almost to death. Things became even more muddled. When they started stoning a Kyrgyz official who had tried to protect the driver, someone felt sorry for his own people and provoked other Kyrgyz to attack the Tajiks. When the Tajiks

were told the Kyrgyz official was their representative, they tried
to take him under their wing. By now the Tajik kishlak and
the Kyrgyz ayyl were at daggers drawn. Houses were set on
fire; meanwhile fire broke out in the Chinese camp, though
the Chinese, besieged in their railway carriages, didn't know
which side to take, or what to do.

How people got through that night, God alone knew, and
Bekesh, fully awake, not sleeping a wink, was preoccupied by
thoughts that were as painful as an illness. By morning, when
young and old still had tears welling in their eyes, their throats
sore from shouting, Bekesh was desperately waiting for the authorities to show their power. Then Chekbel was greeted by
the sound of firing from the mountains and by goateed Islamists proclaiming 'Allahu akbar'.

Who should come with them, if not Adolat, who had disappeared just before Bairam? Who would be waiting to announce 'Allahu akbar' to them, if not Mullah Shavvol who had
cursed Bairam! Saying that the enemy's soul would be covered
in dirt, they surrounded the Chinese, and a gang of armed men
abducted them to the mountains. Then, going from house to
house, Adolat, Mullah Shavvol and their cronies rounded up
and beat those whom they had blacklisted, and locked them up
in the kishlak school. Despite Rabiga's curses and howls of
protest from her daughters-in-law, Bekesh, too, was struck and
beaten with their rifle butts and sent off to join the other prisoners.

Most of those arrested were men who had hunted with
Baisal, as well as Uncle Sattor and his associates. These clods
had got a pretty good haul, Bekesh thought to himself sarcastically, gnashing his broken teeth. Uncle Sattor embraced him affectionately and said, 'Our trusted leader and Hoja has been

swept away by the stream, so now you must stick one by one to the willow.' 'If a slave finds silver, he won't find anywhere to hide it,' came Bekesh's answer. Sattor laughed with bitter sarcasm.

Then he narrated the following story. 'One day,' he said, 'Harun al-Rashid met a dervish. "Where have you come from, wandering dervish?" Harun asked. "From hell itself," came the reply. When Harun asked what he was doing here the dervish replied, "I was hoping to smoke my hookah, but couldn't find any fire to light it from." "Well, did you find fire?" Harun al-Rashid persisted with his questions. "No," said the dervish. "We don't have fires in hell, the devil in charge there told me. How can that be, not having fire in hell? I asked the devil. His answer was: Everyone who comes to stay with us makes his own fire," So said the dervish.' Uncle Sattor concluded, 'So these vile criminals will light their own fires that they've brought with them.'

———

An hour later another five or six prisoners had been rounded up. The man in charge summoned Bekesh to the head teacher's room. Bekesh remembered his schoolchild feelings of fear, and the dread invoked by the headmaster's room. Some strange character was sprawled on a bench in the headmaster's room: his face was just a tiny patch in a black beard, he had an automatic gun hanging from his neck, and Mullah Shavvol was sitting by his side, running his eyes over a piece of paper.

As soon as Bekesh came in, this commandant asked, 'Is this the man who's been leading Muslims astray?' His question was addressed to nobody in particular, to Shavvol as much as to

Bekesh, or to the soldier on guard behind Bekesh. Bekesh was overcome by shame. Over the course of his life he, like them, had read not just one felt-covered book, but thousands. He had enjoyed the education of Uncle Baisal and of his Aunt Rabiga, he had crossed a lot of rivers in his lifetime, he knew who he was, he was familiar with Islam: how could this stupid oaf, who'd just about grown a beard, accuse him of being an infidel? He was about to tell all of them, his heart and mouth not holding him back, when for some reason he remembered the previous day's mishaps, his blackout. He'd better leave it, he told himself, feeling resigned.

But now a new bastard, perhaps a new governor, was getting hysterically worked up and sticking his index finger into the air. Looking at Mullah Shavvol he asked, 'Is this the renegade who's been leading Muslim ladies astray?' Shavvol, like a billy goat ready to come into the yard, shook his bearded head. 'So it is as they say, "Be cautious with married women, shy with little girls, and grab what you can from the brides." Is that how it is?' the commandant shouted menacingly at Bekesh, spraying spittle into his beard. Suddenly Bekesh could see this young man was a bandit through and through. He had blurted it all out, the swine!' 'I'm asking you a question!' the man with the goatee beard went on with the interrogation, as menacing as ever, and using the familiar form of address.

Bekesh said in a calm voice, as if he couldn't hurt a fly, but in an ironically conversational manner: 'I suppose there's nothing wrong with Muslims using a respectful tone when addressing their seniors, is there.'

The commandant raised his hackles, like a rabbit that's been grabbed. Lost for words, he stuttered and lost his temper. 'People like you should be shot!' he shrieked. 'Fifty lashes,' he ordered the guard.

—

They brought Bekesh out onto the street. They thrashed him in full view of everyone, then they threw him, barely alive, into the school detention room. But each stroke inflicted on his body seemed to cause not so much pain as satisfaction: every single stroke lashed the fake Bekesh out of him, forcing that ghost to vanish. As he lost consciousness, and finally his understanding and imagination, his body, covered in blood and bruises, became something that befitted him.

Uncle Sattor, saying he would wipe away the blood oozing from Bekesh's shoulder and neck, came up in turn to be interrogated and Bekesh was left in the care of the hunter Chokmor. Meanwhile Rabiga had come into the schoolyard and had heard Bekesh being thrashed. 'Give me my son back!' she wept. The guards blocked her passage, shots were fired into the air, but nothing was going to stop the old woman. 'I can't see any human beings here, call yourself a man?' Rabiga exclaimed, ready to ransack the house. Her bitterness turned into real rage: 'Haven't you got the strength to deal with one old woman?' she said, howling and wailing so that all Chekbel could hear.

In fact, all the women and girls from the kishlak and the ayyl began to gather. Bekesh, who had lost consciousness, was vaguely aware of a woman shrieking somewhere, but he didn't have the strength to comprehend what the cacophony was about. Rabiga, a woman who was afraid of nothing, was joined by others, and they reduced the school to chaos. That was when the rogues opened fire. Pandemonium broke out as bullets went whistling and crackling. Some were hit by bullets, others grazed: some fell, some bled, the people in the cell went mad, smashed the windows and broke the window frames with their bare hands. Some ran for it, some tried to protect the womenfolk, despite the firing. In a word, the schoolyard was turned into a slaughterhouse.

However much Chokmor the hunter might have been enraged, he didn't leave with the others. He stayed in the room as long as he could to protect Bekesh. Two armed men were now pushing and shoving into the room both Sattor and Rabiga, their faces scratched and bleeding; the men slammed the door behind them with a bang. The broken windows were hanging wide open, but not one of the people there threw themselves out to escape – whether because they were afraid of being shot at when they reached top of the yard, or because they saw Bekesh's wretched state, so that everyone clustered around him.

—

The shooting continued. Rabiga wetted a corner of her headscarf with spit and started wiping the blood off Bekesh's shoulder blades; then she tore off a piece of the scarf with her teeth and, with the help of the men, bound up the wounds on his shoulders and chest. Bekesh groaned and moaned: the pain made tears well up under his calflike eyelashes. They hadn't noticed that the shooting overhead had now come to an end. The window frames rattled: the men in beards were not going away, but coming in to see them. The old woman watched them from where she was sitting: 'You can cut off my head, but you can't cut off my tongue! Don't you know who I am?' she shrieked. The intimidators banged up two boards that had previously barred the window and attached them to the wall with seven-inch nails.

The shouting outside died down. Aunt Rabiga and the others sat around Bekesh, trying to bring him comfort. An hour passed, without them being beaten or hauled up for questioning. Meanwhile Bekesh had opened his slightly sunken eyes. When he saw those sitting over him, especially his aunt, he smiled gently. This brought Rabiga back to life: 'When the belly's empty, the eyes sink!' she said and stood up, went to the door – which was locked from the outside – and began knocking at it. 'Hey, you infidels, which one of you is there?' she yelled. But there was no answer. Once more she knocked, but there was still no answer.

'They've gone for a dip in the stream to wash themselves for evening prayers,' Uncle Sattor suggested with a laugh. Then he looked at Bekesh, who had opened his eyes. He told another story: 'As it says in *The Arguments of the Righteous,* just like these people, some ignoramuses were accusing Maulana Rumi of being irreligious. "You make jokes, you encourage people to dance, you recite poems," they said. Rumi refused to answer them. Then the Maulana's pupils asked him why he did not put those oafs in their place? Rumi replied as follows: "Just as you assess a chicken in the autumn, so rewards and shares, ours and theirs, will be given in the afterlife. Let time pass and show what will remain of anyone. It will know of every lion's existence and every jackal's. Today quite a few jackals go about claiming to be lions. But the flow of time will not depend on them. You must pay attention to fairy tales and to traditional stories. Once upon a time, in ancient days a certain lion passed: this is a phrase you have very often heard. But have you ever heard: Once upon a time, in bygone days a certain jackal lived?'"

This made Bekesh smile.

—

Another hour passed. Darkness was beginning to fall outside, it was obvious even through the boarded windows. This time Chokmor the hunter approached the door: 'Is anyone there?' he shouted. Again there was no reply. From the window opposite could be heard a woman's moan. So Chokmor went over to the window and banged the board with his shoulder. The board creaked and shifted. Uncle Sattor came to help. They combined their efforts and put their shoulders to both ends. With each blow, the boards began to come apart, creaking as they exerted pressure. In the end, banged to and fro, both thick boards fell to the ground with a loud noise. There was no trace of the guards.

As for Chokmor the hunter, holding on to the side of the window, he cast an eye over the schoolyard. Apparently, he couldn't see anything, so he poked his head out. Then he looked back at those in the room and said, 'Shoes made from a hare's skin will only last for a day.'

'Really, has the earth swallowed them up?' asked Rabiga.

'Nobody's there!' said Chokmor. 'The school gates are wide open.' He took a leap from the window into the yard. 'Well, strike me down!' he remarked.

Now Uncle Sattor had stuck his head through the window; not so far away, he saw several women's bodies lying on the ground. He and Chokmor rushed towards them: some were alive, either shot in the leg or badly knocked about; others lay moaning and groaning quietly. Another two bodies were cold:

Chokmor closed the eyes of one, and Sattor did the same for the second.

'I'll bring a horse or a cart,' said Chokmor. 'You stay here and look after these people!' It was certain that the tyrants had fled: they couldn't cope with the women's loud protests. But they must have taken away the horses and vehicles, Sattor thought to himself. One could expect all kinds of vileness from them.

First, Sattor cautiously carried the two dead women up onto the school veranda. He fashioned ribbons from their headscarves and tied their jaws, read a Qur'anic prayer over them, and then hurried back to the living. One by one, he asked the injured where they'd been wounded, bandaged heads, and gently laid to one side those whose legs had been broken. Meanwhile, leaving Bekesh in the room, Rabiga came tumbling out of the window. She caught her voluminous loose clothing on the nails and ripped them in two or three places, but she paid no attention to her garments and made herself useful. Having come to give help and support, she hastened to the aid of people she knew so well. She sent Sattor, as a man, to see to Bekesh, while she unbandaged wounds, cleaned them and re-bandaged them tightly, anointing blue bruises with clay slurry, and trying to cheer up a friend who had tripped by saying, 'You were running about like a child, you'll be more careful now.' So she brought everyone back to their senses and raised their spirits.

It was then that Dapan arrived in the schoolyard on a cart pulled by a donkey. 'Did Chokmor send you?' his granny chided him. 'Didn't I tell you not to stick your nose any further than the hunting room?'

'No,' replied Dapan, 'I came on my own initiative.'

—

No sooner had Dapan come than Chokmor harnessed a horse to the cart and came with his nephews. Dapan, Bekesh and Rabiga dealt with the women who were still alive and set off for the first-aid centre. As for Chokmor, he loaded up the two corpses and, together with Sattor the Tajik, they set off with one of them heading for the Kyrgyz ayyl and the other for the Tajik kishlak.

'I've slaughtered a calf in their memory, so please do come!' Chokmor told Bekesh's family. This time Rabiga made Dapan stop and get out of the cart, then went up to Chokmor.

'I can't possibly not go to see them,' Rabiga said and began to weep. 'However much we thought about it, your leaving was unavoidable,' she said, quoting a mourning verse.

Dapan's people entrusted Rabiga to the mourners, and they set off to the first-aid centre. Crossing the streets of Chekbel in the heavily laden cart, they looked around with dispirited hearts and tearful eyes at the aftermath of the stabbings from the night before. In one place, there was a half-demolished house; in another, windows had been smashed by stones. On the ground there were a woman's sandals, and on the wall bloodstains. So it was that married women, who the day before had enjoyed the taste of sheep's tail, with a turn of the wheel had a taste of the stick and were transformed into women without men. When Bekesh saw the traces left behind by the spray of bullets, he knew that those gunmen had left Chekbel after the shambles and slaughter in order to finish off those who hadn't already been killed.

'"When you see a black sheep, bury it deep in the grave,"

must have been the idea.' It was as if scenes from the *Manas* had come to life and the world of the dead had been recreated in Chekbel.

Beset by these thoughts of grief, they arrived at the first-aid centre. Fortunately, no waves of either rioting locals or of religious newcomers had been able to reach this place, situated as it was on a hill slope. Doctor Janish, Baisal's former hunting companion, came out to meet them. He hadn't slept a wink for two days now, having spent from first light to the depths of night taking in the wounded one by one, from yesterday's film crew to those who were injured in the mass slaughter. He began placing them next to a man from Chekbel.

'For us it's a matter of: "Better to die in convulsions than to die without moving,"' he said as he started work. Holding a large bowl each time, he washed off the dirt and the dung, then put iodine on the wounds, making the patients scream, before bandaging them.

He examined Bekesh and said, as he rubbed spirit into his shoulder blades: 'Brother, you know what they say: "I'd rather be alone, day and night, than be a liar." When you brought those people in,' he said, pointing to the film crew, 'you were as fit as a horse. Now what's happened to you?' Somehow these words affected Bekesh as if they had a hidden meaning. His skin had been shredded by the blows it suffered. Bits of skin stuck to the muslin, and as the doctor pulled at these bits, Bekesh couldn't help uttering a piercing shriek.

'That's over, it's over!' Doctor Janish reassured him. 'A carefully amputated arm doesn't hurt,' he said, and gave Bekesh some advice: 'There's a piece of flesh still hanging loose; if it goes gangrenous, your whole body will turn septic. We can't leave it on, we have to cut it off.'

Bekesh gave his assent, and the doctor took his lancet from the shiny metal bowl and cut off the still living flesh from Bekesh's back. Bekesh's whole mind became nothing but pain, and he bit his lips and groaned.

'I've turned down the rich man's daughter!' said Doctor Janish as he finished the job, pressing the wound hard and applying a cotton pad soaked in iodine. Bekesh fainted but the throbbing pain quickly brought him back to consciousness. The doctor unrolled some gauze and finished bandaging him.

'How did my father stand it in the war?' Bekesh wondered for a moment, and tears flowed from his eyes.

But there was some good in the pain his body felt: at least then a man can no longer feel his heart throbbing with pain.

—

Once Bekesh's body was bandaged, Doctor Janish moved him to a neighbouring room along with the others. Lin Ju and Ulankhu had been laid there on felt rugs. Bekesh looked at the doctor and asked: 'Clouds come out of the air, but how did these two heroes, friends of the whole world, end up as your prisoners?'

'Let's stop joking and I'll tell you the truth. These two weren't brought here with the other people, they got clubbed down in the fighting. One was beaten by the Kyrgyz, the other by the Tajiks; they were both hiding from the crowd and the militants. Today they were dropped off here at first light,' the doctor replied.

Suddenly Bekesh began to understand that this hadn't all been in vain and he was greatly relieved. 'Now you two have been left behind, together with me, we have not one but three guns in the house. If need be, we can defend ourselves,' he told Lin Ju in Russian. Lin Ju translated these words to Ulankhu. When Ulankhu heard the word 'gun', his eyes blazed; the things a descendant of Chingiz Khan could do!

After talking to one another, Ulankhu and Lin Ju had one question: 'What were you talking about yesterday so enthusiastically?' Bekesh was suddenly distressed. Very likely, all of them remembered his embarrassing blackout the previous day. 'And a child spoke, too,' Ulankhu added.

'Are you talking about the *Manas*?' asked Bekesh rather reluctantly.

'Manas is our hero, he's our Chingiz Khan! So we recite this poem.' Lin Ju repeated this in Chinese, and for some reason trembled and put his hand to his mouth. Ulankhu asked Bekesh through his interpreter, 'Is that poem about war and battles?'

Bekesh nodded slightly; Ulankhu's eyes were popping with anxiety and he pressed both hands to his mouth. 'You shouldn't have recited it, that's why the fighting started,' he said, and, without listening to Bekesh's pained mumbling to the end, he turned to Lin Ju: 'We never recall a single one of Chingiz Khan's wars. The people who know about them have been keeping them secret and haven't told ordinary people, who can't read or write,' he said, and began gabbling at length.

Obviously Bekesh had read about the secret tale of Chingiz Khan's life and, for that reason, in order either to reassure Ulankhu or to show himself in a favourable light, he said with a heavy heart: 'I know it, I do. It's the same with the *Manas*: not everyone can recite it. You have to have an epiphany to become a *Manas* reciter.'

'What do you mean "epiphany"?' Lin Ju enquired. Bekesh

began to talk about the dreams which come from other worlds to *Manas* reciters. 'Did you too have this kind of dream?' asked both Chinese men, as if rubbing salt into Bekesh's wounds.

'Yes, in a way,' Bekesh said, his tone flat. After the confusion of the day before he had no desire to talk about *that* dream again, and so he tried to switch the conversation to something else .

'Actually, I wasn't talking about war yesterday, but about the free-for-all horse race,' he said as if to clarify matters.

'And the young boy?' Ulankhu asked.

'Dapan? He was speaking about the race, too.'

Ulankhu shook his head. 'In our country, a young child would never under any circumstances be taught about such serious things. The burden of words can affect a child's life badly' Whether the words that Ulankhu spoke and Lin Ju translated into his broken Russian were rendered correctly or not, the conversation caused Bekesh real anxiety.

Gathering his thoughts from yesterday and reflecting on his sufferings, his suspicions and his doubts, all of which he had failed to find an answer for, he unexpectedly reached some kind of conclusion.

—

Meanwhile Dapan had come searching for news of his uncle. Bekesh suppressed his pain and embraced his nephew tightly. 'So this is the *true* youthful *Manas* reciter!' he said to Ulankhu, unburdening his heart. Ulankhu still wouldn't set aside his concerns, and instead he stood dumbstruck.

Dapan began to tell his uncle about the things he had seen and found out on the streets of Chekbel. 'My God!' he began, blurting out everything that was overwhelming him. 'The people down in our Chekbel have never been like this. They've had their flesh cut and slashed with knives.' At first Bekesh listened to the boy's story. But he began to feel awkward, and so he started to translate it for the two Chinese men. 'We were living our lives as young people do, and all of a sudden these things happened.' Dapan was talking just as an adult would, and for the first time Bekesh noticed that his voice was breaking. A month earlier, just before the end of spring, when the cattle were about to go to the mountains, the child still had a voice like bird song, Bekesh recalled. Had he grown up overnight?

Dapan talked, without hiding his tears, about his friend Jappar, the son of Jiparbek the hunter, who the day before at the horse race had been knocked down by a lorry and killed. 'Death is like a rich man. As they say, if a rich man can't find a lamb to slaughter, he'll ask a poor man for his only lamb. Jappar was Jiparbek's only son, a quiet boy. Jiparbek had neither a wife nor any other offspring. When they brought him his dead son, four Tajik labourers were working in Jiparbek's yard. Apparently, the people who brought Jiparbek's son said, "A Tajik killed your child, take your gun and have your revenge!" Jiparbek the hunter saw them off through the gates with a promise, but even before his son's funeral he hid the Tajik labourers in a pit. Then, when he was returning after burying his son in the cemetery, there was a Chinaman who had been beaten up and left lying on the road. Jiparbek loaded the Chinaman onto a cart, threw something over it to hide him, and took him home.'

Bekesh now interpreted these words to his companions, and Lin Ju began to sob. 'What is it?' Bekesh asked.

'That was me,' said Lin Ju.

At this point Dapan turned the story into verse, and made it part of the *Manas*...

Black enemy, unannounced, evil
When it came down our hill,
Smashed up everything in the street,
Scattered everything we had
Humiliating us like sheep,
Denying us our cattle
Desolately demanding your death,
Tying us hand and foot,
Seeing us humiliated, driving us,
Dispirited and grieving,
Parted from our relatives,
We are doomed to a pitch-dark night,
So will I ever see the daylight?

—

When they heard Dapan reciting the *Manas*, both Kyrgyz and Tajiks, their wounds bandaged, emerged from the next room. The Russian lorry-driver, who had been taken here the previous day by Bekesh, also came and joined them. The young lad gathered all around him so that the crowd was like that at the races the day before. Bairam had come back to the square; what seemed to be yogurt and milk were drunk, doughnuts and pea-flour bread were eaten. Jockeys on horseback raised the dust on the track then turned around and headed towards the public, while the lorry, as it took pictures of the men on horseback, quietly parked at the side of the road and observed the horses galloping past with a clatter of hooves. As if to say,

'There's no need for words which haven't forded a river,' Dapan was out in front, the first to arrive on horseback; he then made a dash to the finishing line. In the next section, the race became even faster, the horses jostled each other's necks as they galloped, their manes were tossed with each wave of the whip, under their hooves the clods of clay were reduced to crumbs of soil, the rocks were thrown aside, and then the Chinese man and the 'big man' and the womenfolk were all standing by the finishing line and rushing forward, filled with joy and pleasure. Bekesh now grabbed his loudspeaker; for some reason he had an eagle on his wrist repeating its loud call 'Killak, killak!'

Riding Topon, Dapan was first to cross the finishing line, and just a neck behind, Jiparbek's son Jappar managed to reach the finish followed by three or four other horsemen, one after the other. The evildoers' time was up, the good reached for the skies in their joy. That's how the festival in Chekbel ended!

It was at this point that Dapan seemed to ask, 'If your boots are too tight, what use is the wide world to you?' and returned them all to reality, bringing them back to the first-aid centre. Everyone was confused and disoriented: 'Was this a dream? Were we really dreaming it?' they wondered, disoriented.

Bekesh in particular was left dumbstruck and mute.

———

The next morning, as if planned, military forces from the two countries entered Chekbel from opposite directions and a barbed-wire boundary was set up along the line of the stream to mark off and separate the ayyl from the kishlak and the kishlak from the ayyl. In fact, the Tajik side brought in another fifty or so additional Chinese construction workers and new railway carriages which were set up in the same place, on both sides of the stream, while barbed wire was rolled out around the Chinese camp leaving just a few gaps on either side.

The population of Chekbel watched the soldiers of the two countries. 'Now war will break out,' people said as they were overcome with anxiety. In fact, the boundaries were being guarded, and both armies were encamped on either side. The Tajik forces were in the Kyrgyz ayyl, the Kyrgyz soldiers were in the Tajik kishlak, and so Chekbel's two parts seemed to have been forced into opposing and hostile zones. The Chinese came out to set out the boundary and lay the barbed-wire barriers under military supervision as if nothing had happened. The machinery which had been left behind by the previous Chinese contingent was put to work, and they went off to tunnel through the mountain and build the access road.

By then, Bekesh was still in bed in the first-aid centre, and it was Dapan who brought news of all this to him and to his local friends and the Chinese he had befriended. The injured Tajiks were dismayed: 'So are we going to be handed over to Kyrgyzstan now?' Dapan's mind was in utter confusion, and he had no answer. 'Shall I enquire?' he asked willingly. But Bekesh, distressed, snapped back at him: 'Sit down, don't mess around! You'd better go home and see to Topon and Tumor.'

'I rode here on Topon, and I've given Tumor a piece of felt today,' Dapan replied, and, with a frown, informed the men sitting around his uncle. 'Tumor is our eagle. Occasionally we give him a piece of felt, it cleans his guts.'

'Don't let him choke!' said Bekesh, who was once again behaving like a supervisor. The boy really had grown up to be more than a lanky milksop. It was though easier to direct him now. If he poked his head in every noose, he'd end up losing it.

'You can't hire out your camel if it's tethered to six geldings!' said Bekesh, quoting uncle Baisal's expression to criticise Dapan. 'For that reason, you should go home and sit and watch over your granny! Tomorrow, if I'm told I can, I'll come back home. Then we'll talk about all the rest.'

Dapan didn't understand such high-flown language from his uncle. He attributed it to the half-crazed state Bekesh's wounds had left him in, but he obeyed and, without further ado or more words, he set off home.

—

The latest development, although it seemed insignificant, turned Chekbel's life upside down. As soon as Dapan left, Bekesh lay there in the first-aid centre, preoccupied by his old and new pains, when suddenly he became aware that he could no longer go and see Uncle Sattor.

According to the passport he held he was a citizen of Kyrgyzstan, and so he might be able to move without trouble to Kyrgyz territory. But granny and Dapan who lived on Tajik territory wouldn't be able to go back to the Kyrgyz ayyl on the Tajik side. That's why, assuming there was no house-to-house search, he shouldn't show his passport to anyone.

What, in fact, would the injured Tajik brothers lying in the next room do? Or the Chinese, for that matter? There was no point making them anxious now, it would be better to discuss things first with Doctor Janish. There should have been a new Mimtimin for the new batch of Chinese; so it would be better not to show Lin Ju and Ulankhu to the Chinese, but rather to enquire about the general situation first. The Chinese were unpredictable: they might say 'You've betrayed your group by staying behind here and not following them,' and punish both men for that reason.

He wondered whether the armed forces had started a search for the Chinese and for the local girls who had been taken hostage? Or were they acting as the Russians would, 'Out of sight, out of mind!' Questions, questions, questions...

Both sides were now under military rule, but the locals' hunting rifles and eagles and hawks hadn't yet been confiscated. Would it still be possible to go hunting? Bekesh considered it, and suddenly recalled a story Uncle Baisal had once told him. Baisal had said something like: 'A man's path in life is like an arrow fired at a target. For the arrow to hit the mark you need at least a bow, and you also have to have an archer and a target.' At the time this seemed unintelligible to Bekesh; in the hasty years of his youth, he didn't even enquire about the words' meaning. But they had meant that, at the time, the flight of his arrow had been aimless.

What about now? Was Ulankhu, pressing both hands to his mouth, right to be so devious? Perhaps the arrow, once shot, had missed its target, perhaps it had flown and had hit, was hitting, would hit, quite a different target. And was the bow that shot it Bekesh's? Alas, just like a snotty child, had he used a twig instead of a bow? And had he shot a clod of clay thinking it was an arrow?

Now the weight of Uncle Baisal's remark fell on Bekesh's heart like a heavy burden.

—

The next morning Bekesh took note of Doctor Janish's comment. 'We need to wrap two hides round you so as to keep the chill off your flesh,' the Doctor had told him, so when Dapan rode in on Topon to bring the latest news, Bekesh, as if avoiding his heated thoughts, insisted on going back home. Both of them got on the horse, and there they returned. As they did, Bekesh thought about how Dapan was no longer going to the bilingual school, which was stranded in the Tajik kishlak; if he tried, nobody would let him cross the border. As for the Qur'anic lessons: 'There's nobody to drum them in,' he said, thinking of Mullah Shavvol who had run away with the Islamists. Since there was nothing to do as far as lessons were concerned, Dapan would have to go and spend all day looking after one horse, one eagle, one sheep and one yak. Dapan told him all this while they were riding back home, and both Bekesh and Dapan felt sorry about the school, its white walls visible on the distant mountain slope, but they had no regrets about Shavvol. On the contrary, when Dapan uttered a sort of vague mumbling on the subject, Bekesh said, speaking sarcastically, 'You've been deceived by smooth talking.'

As they rode by one of the two poplars growing at the roadside, they saw the ant-like Chinese hard at work on the river bank; for the Chinese, it seemed that nothing had happened, they put all their soul into their hands, in thrall only to work, never even looking aside. 'But they are working for us, after all,' Bekesh thought with inexplicable satisfaction. It was getting close to midday when they reached home.

According to her daughters-in-law, Rabiga wasn't there. This was the third day that she had been busy consoling the families of the women who'd died and the girls who had been abducted. The moment Bekesh dismounted, he was again struck by pain, not just in his neck, but all over his body. 'When this pain curses you, it's like fallen snow, when it blesses you, it's less than rain.' To put it out of his mind, he left Dapan and the horse and went straight in to see Tumor.

As Tumor hadn't seen Bekesh for a day or two, he was ill-tempered and gave Bekesh a mournful look, sat on his perch, his feathers ruffled, shuffling his feet. He was probably thinking something like: 'I've been wasting my life waiting for you.' Bekesh himself was thoughtless enough to go right up to the bird without any food to offer him. He forgot not just his mental agony, but his bodily pain too as he faced the offended eagle, and put his hands up to the bird's throat and the feathers on its wing. The eagle's eyes blazed with fire. Bekesh stroked him, and kept murmuring, as if to assuage Tumor's resentment, 'We've invited you respectfully to a feast, and you've come just to fight.'

The best of clever birds,
The eagle is majestic and great,
In all his winged glory
Tumor is a fine character...

Hearing his name being lauded, Tumor stuck his chest out, spread his talons, and displayed his tail feathers. At this glorious sight Bekesh blushed, his spirit overflowed, and suddenly he began to sob. 'They beat me up, Tumor.'

—

Taking advantage of the fact that there was nobody in the house, Bekesh pulled himself together and with a renewed energy called Dapan into the room. 'Come,' he said, 'it's such a long time since we last listened to our father, let's make sense of it together.' He inserted into the player a tape they hadn't yet listened to and pressed the button.

'Reciting the *Manas*,' a muffled voice began, 'is like setting off on a very narrow track in the mountains. It is very hard to cross the slope, the path is so narrow and runs along an abyss, there are forty ravines all round! I've seen a great number of those who fell. People went and risked their lives. The *Manas* turned out to be a burden to them. There's nothing easy about the *Manas*, there's no easy way of reciting it. A lot of people proceed by thinking that the *Manas* is about galloping horses and battles. They might as well try to thresh barley into hay. The *Manas* is like water flowing at an angle. The very word *Manas* means human significance. Manas's father Jakyp is the blue sky, his mother Chiyirdi is the mother earth, his horse Akkula is home, his wife Kanikey is water. Manas's gyrfalcon Ok is his desires and longings, his dog Kumayik is Manas's soul incarnate. If you recite his battles and gallops, what does this tell you about the war against Kökcha? The battle against destiny, and against Ayub-khan? Or Temir-khan?

'If you ask Sattor the Tajik, there is a poem in both Tajik and Uzbek called *Beauty and the Heart*. Looked at objectively, the whole thing is about human beings' inner struggles. We are a nomadic people. Today we pitch our yurts on one mountain pasture, tomorrow on another. Some people see their sense, their history, their fellow men as urban, and preserve all this in schools and medreses, books and manuals. But we get on our horses and carry everything on our persons, and we have to keep it like this, on the move, in our minds and hearts.

'Manas was a meat-eater in summer, and in winter he drank kumys and was always red-cheeked. His way of life was the Kyrgyz way, the prophet Hizr's way, relying on God, wisdom and luck. That's the essence of our language, our heart, our horseman's customs, our wisdom and knowledge, our past and our future.'

Bekesh was trembling all over with emotion. He looked at Dapan, not so much staring as accusing and askance. Dapan was repeating something and his lips moved in an inaudible whisper.

—

Dapan went out to see to some task or other, and Bekesh decided to use the solitude to think systematically over what had been happening and what he had heard. A vicious dog barks in the daytime, doesn't it? And like a dog barking at the wrong time, his heart had begun to torment his spirit. Was he thinking he was different, peculiar, special, just because the words he had extracted from other words at the radio station had then fallen into people's mouths? Or was he equating his superficial, shaky studies, which had cost him nothing and had been of no avail, with a recital of the *Manas* whose words are so redolent of meaning? Was he not aware of the process by which *Manas* reciters were selected by spirits? Hadn't he gone and very calmly offered hay to a mare, so as to win a charger's heart? What devil had led him astray? As he sat there, besieged by thoughts circling like moths, Dapan came in with his satchel full of textbooks and exercise book.

So, as night was about to fall, Bekesh, still in quite a state, sat down with Dapan to help him revise the lessons he had been doing, and it was then that Uncle Sattor unexpectedly entered the house. Bekesh asked in amazement: 'How did you get across the border?

'I was bringing a little bit of snuff for the Chinese, it was getting dark and they let me pass over from their camp,' said Sattor.

'Does that mean there are no border guards there, then?'

'Oh, they're just as likely to show a clean pair of heels. They seem to be frightened of bearded devils, so they all go and hide in any hole they can find.'

'I've been thinking about the future of Chekbel,' said Uncle Sattor, first reading the *Fatiha* sura of the Qur'an, before coming to the point. Dapan put his school books away and spread the tablecloth for tea. Meanwhile Bekesh listened to his uncle. 'You are someone who is well-known to the people in Kyrgyzstan, so you probably can write on behalf of us all a letter to the people in charge, can't you? If not, then our situation will go on being like that cat's...'

'What cat?' asked Bekesh.

'A man was expecting a guest, and he brought two pounds of meat for his wife. "Here you are, roast it for this evening," he said. His wife roasted the meat, and tasted a slice of the second piece. The meat was spring lamb, so soft that you could chew it with just your lips and then swallow it. She didn't notice how she ended up eating it all. Her husband came home and asked, "Wife, is the meat ready?" What could the wife do except sob and weep? "That damned cat of ours has eaten it!" she said and blamed it all on the cat, which was lying there stretched out. Her husband instantly picked up a set of scales and put the cat on the weighing bowl. When he looked, it weighed exactly two pounds. He was puzzled, and asked: "Wife, if the cat weighs this much, then where's the meat; and if there were two pounds of meat, where's the cat?" At the moment, we find ourselves in a position where there is neither cat, nor meat, don't we?'

When Bekesh heard this tale, he weighed it up silently and then laughed. Then Dapan brought in tea and bread, and Bekesh told him. He laughed, too. Over tea, Bekesh discussed the letter he might write, after which he changed the subject to what he was curious about. He said, 'You know, I believe, a poem called *Beauty and the Heart*. What is it about?'

'How do you know about it?' enquired Uncle Sattor.

'Baisal spoke about it.'

'Ah, your foster-father listened to this poem again and again,' said Uncle Sattor. 'In ancient times the Heart was born to the family of the Mind and the Soul. When he came of age, his father Mind gave him a fortress called the Body, and his mother made him the present of a book. In this book the Heart came across a turn of phrase, "the font of life", and he couldn't get over it. He made his servant Nazar, Sight, travel the world in search of this font of life. One by one, Nazar went to see King Afiyat (Health), the court of Salamat (Well-being), the city of Shuhrat (Fame), Shah Fakhr (Pride), Sheikh Zarq (Deceit), the river of Hayrat (Wonder), the city of Hidayat (Guidance), in short, all the faculties and features of a human being. He went and visited each one of them, but he couldn't find out the secret of eternal life – the 'font of life' – from any of them.

So Nazar, after a lot of wandering, found out that the font of life was to be found in the possession of Beauty, the daughter of the Shah of Love, and he passed on the news to Heart. Meanwhile, Mind made war on the king of Love; after various ups and downs, Heart and Beauty managed to meet, and by kissing Beauty, Heart drank of the font of life. Thus, the conclusion of this poem is about the nature of the self. Looked at

objectively, the whole thing is fundamentally about human beings' inner struggles.'

———

Oddly enough, to all appearances in Bekesh's life there were
two aspects, each separate from one another, pulling apart; but
inside him they were constantly approaching one another, even
unifying. 'You Kyrgyz are constantly setting one banner up
against another, sending clouds of dust up into the sky: you
have to be in constant motion, rushing about, and that's why
I've come to see you about something that needs doing,' said
Uncle Sattor, suddenly treating his nephew as a Kyrgyz. 'We
Tajiks are a people who like feasts and parties, we don't go further than just talking.'

But as soon as Bekesh started to think about what his uncle's
voice was uttering, he realised that the converse was equally
true. The Kyrgyz might have a saying 'Away is better than always', but did they know of anything better than just sitting
around chatting idly? If there was no lively talk, then story-
telling, or listening to the *Manas*; and if there was none of that,
then Bekesh, instead of working at the radio station, would
spend his time in the high mountain pastures, like a peaceful
shepherd occasionally listening to the radio while lying on his
side on the first spring grass.

So 'Tajiks don't go further than just talking,' was not really a
true saying, either. Then, weren't those bearded devils who abducted women and girls, who looted red gold, mostly yelling
in Tajik, after all? You can sum it up by saying: 'You were racing on a blind mare, and I was chasing after you on a blind
donkey...'

True, a Kyrgyz conversation is more frank and open, while a Tajik one is more roundabout. While Bekesh sat there thinking vaguely, Uncle Sattor seemed to be confirming his nephew's ideas, and began to tell Bekesh another one of his parables.

'So, nephew, say, as in a story, a young man in his prime, just like you, asks a religious Master: "Why is it that Europeans are a hundred times more powerful than us, but we are stronger than them in our faith?" The Master replies, "The fact of the matter is that in the times when these qualities were distributed, they were given the right to choose first."'

—

Whether Bekesh was a Kyrgyz or a Tajik, he couldn't have sat there enjoying the conversation very much for a thought kept flashing through his anxious mind: after this, Uncle Sattor had to get back to the Tajik kishlak as soon as possible. 'Could you stay the night with us?' he proposed, when he saw Dapan yawning behind Uncle Sattor.

'No, how could I? Your aunt is alone in the house. There's a state of alarm outside... All right, I'm off while the taste of the meal is still in my mouth!' Bekesh responded, 'I'll see you home' as he rose to his feet, but his uncle pressed him. 'You fell off the horse, but you're still clinging to the saddle, young man. How could you see people off in your state? Dear God, as if I were a stranger. What am I, a little child?' he said, looking at Dapan and screwing up his eyes. 'Do you think I can't find the way back, the way I came here?'

'No, but there's a border at every point. There are soldiers...'

'I'll go the same way as I got here, don't worry about it!' said uncle Sattor, and after embracing Bekesh and kissing Dapan's forehead, he vanished into the darkness.

'Uncle, should I go after him?' asked Dapan, ready to leave. 'Don't go!' said Bekesh, who was afraid, his lips covered in a touch of foam. Then he calmed down a little. 'Let's go and see Topon and give him something to eat,' he said, leaning on Dapan's shoulder. They went out into the pitch-dark yard, and there Topon caught the sound of their voices and the smell of their bodies and neighed, sticking out his heroic chest in the dark and standing proudly. Bekesh, leaning on Dapan's shoulder, stepped awkwardly and heavily until he reached the horse. Dapan helped Bekesh prop himself up against a pillar and himself offered the horse some hay. Topon didn't tuck in straight away, instead he stood still, making no sound and looking sideways at his master, and then pricked up his ears, which were like trimmed reeds, and quietly bent his head down to the hay.

It was then that fury broke out on the banks of the stream and gunfire could be heard. Although the voices were muffled in the darkness, the horse immediately jerked his head up and pounded the ground with his hooves. With his shoulder leaning against a pillar, Bekesh shuddered and Dapan cried out, 'Oh, my God!' and covered his mouth with his hand. Again, furious gunfire could be heard, this time the bullets leaving a trace of light in the air as they flew from mountain to mountain.

'Should we go down there?' asked Dapan, frightened by his own words.

'No,' Bekesh said in a hoarse voice, 'this is no time to go running through the streets!' He spoke lightly, but his chest was seized by pain, and suddenly a tear that tasted like lake water came to his eye.

—

That night Bekesh couldn't sleep: he went outside. He kept reciting a prayer: 'If you're a river, take me away; if you're a mountain pass, let me cross!' As the first of the Chinese tractors rattled past, he mounted Topon and set off for the Chinese camp. Once there, he couldn't find anyone who understood his language so he turned his horse back to the village and rode to the first-aid centre. When he arrived, he woke up Lin Ju and Ulankhu, who were both sleeping with the other wounded men, and they set off to the camp – he on horseback, they on foot, limping and stumbling. As they were reaching the Chinese camp, a pudgy man crossed their path. Once the man recognised Lin Ju and Ulankhu, he opened his mouth wide and began yelling at them. Bekesh was anxious and grieving: he had after all come to find out what had happened to uncle Sattor. He dismounted from the horse and, not understanding what was going on, stood bewildered among them. 'Give it enough space and a pig will come out to the hill!' he thought and looked at this craggy man shrieking hysterically. 'He may have a burden at home, but his nose is in the mountains!'

After a short time, Lin Ju turned to Bekesh. 'Our boss is saying we're traitors. If we can't find the others, we don't get any work!' he interpreted nervously what had been said. 'Can you help us at all?' Bekesh did not want to get involved with their work and the incident and he shook his head gently, intending to turn to the business in hand.

'But you ask him about the shooting that happened here last night: nobody got shot, did they, do you know about it?'

Lin Ju seemed to have understood all this, but couldn't make head or tail of the Russian word for 'shooting'. Again and again he tried to get his tongue around it, and all that came out was 'shooding' or 'chooting'. He asked what it meant, and Bekesh raised his arm like a rifle and went 'tak-tak' to demonstrate the firing of bullets.

So, may a pig dig up his grave, that Chinese man tossed his head back several times as if he had lost whatever knowledge of Kyrgyz he had acquired. Bekesh began repeating his questions, and with Lin Ju translating, put them in Chinese to Ulankhu. 'If we don't find the others, they'll shoot us dead,' said Lin Ju, who seemed to have utterly lost the knowledge he had acquired.

At first Bekesh couldn't understand why their answers didn't fit with his questions, then seeing how flustered the Chinese friends were, he suddenly grasped what they had inferred. They had thought that the question was about the two of them being shot. Then, when Bekesh was about to ask the Chinese foreman about those who were shot the night before, Topon's head rose and the reins shook. Bekesh looked first at his horse, then at what was frightening it and understood everything instantly: Tajik men, dressed in black gowns, on the distant hill slope – a whole ring of people – were reciting a ritual chant and *Allahu akbar*, and were moving off, lifting a coffin onto their shoulders. Bekesh's heart sank.

—

Now, Bekesh, his life hanging by a thread, took it into his hands and headed for the frontier and the border guards who were standing there, bent at the waist, and as he was leading

Topon by the reins, the two Chinese men for some reason followed behind him. As he approached the frontier, he saw the Tajik border guards standing there lazily. They were taking a break and looked exhausted. Bekesh said, pointing to the crowd that had climbed the hillside, 'My uncle has just died...' and the chief border guard waved his arm as a blessing, and the soldiers followed suit.

The rules were probably not yet laid down, otherwise surely a single Kyrgyz would not be allowed to cross over to the Tajik side. The chief neither asked for documents nor many questions. 'What about them?' he said, pointing to the Chinese.

'Those people aren't crossing,' Bekesh said to reassure the guards.

'We can't let your horse cross over, it's state property,' said the chief.

Bekesh suddenly trembled with fear: surely they wouldn't take Topon away from him? He was in a desperate state. 'The horse stays with him, then!' he said, passing the reins to Ulankhu who was behind him. The Mongolian grinned as he laid his hands on the whip and the horse's reins; his face turned bright red. 'Dapan, Dapan...' Bekesh whispered to Lin Ju from behind the horse and Lin Ju seemed to understand – although again, how could you tell?

But Bekesh didn't have time to think about them. Venturing onto the slope, he moved towards the Kyrgyz border guards. Guards began to appear from nowhere, raising hell: 'Where is your passport?' they asked all around.

'My passport is at home, my uncle has died, he's being taken to the cemetery up there,' replied Bekesh, his face pleading. This guard was the size of a gallows, whereas the younger guards were perhaps too callow to understand what was being said. 'Have I got any money in my pocket? they're simpleton Kyrgyz, aren't they?' thought Bekesh, poking about in his purses, from where, instead of money, he extracted his ID, with photograph, from the radio station. The word 'Press" was printed diagonally in big capitals over the photograph. And on one side, after Bekesh's full name, was the title of his well-known programme. When they'd had a look at this all the border guards became as affectionate as a white cat under heavy rain: one after the other they took Bekesh's hand in both their hands. 'Hey, no problems for a man like you!' they said, reproaching one another, and one of them fired a bullet into the sky, bringing the ceremonial procession to the cemetery to a halt.

'Stop!' yelled the commandant, who had just shot the bullet into the air. The procession was so terrified that they rushed about in all directions and began to shriek. Nobody actually ran off or dropped the coffin, but Bekesh saw that some of those at the back of the procession were hurriedly taking cover behind the coffin. 'Don't be afraid,' Bekesh yelled.

Limping and all alone, Bekesh began to climb towards the funeral procession. The people must have recognised him, for two young men separated out from the crowd and approached him. Both supported him under his arms, and began helping him to join the funeral procession. Bekesh didn't ask them who was in the coffin, but leaning on the young men and walking in step with them both he sensed their unspoken condolences.

The procession continued on its path and the mourners recited, with a ritual chant and expositions, one of Khayyam's quatrains, and one of Hafiz's, and one of Jami's ghazals over the coffin that they were carrying:

Alas, the capital has been taken from our hands,
Our hearts bleed because of the hand of death,
Who has ever had news of the other world,
Or ever told what happens to the departed.

—

The circle recited a prayer and memorial verses and buried Sattor the Tajik next to his younger sister, Bekesh's mother. When it was over, the mourners went back to the house of Mutriba, Bekesh's auntie-in-law. Once indoors, the women began to sob loudly, but no tears came to Bekesh's eyes, neither at the cemetery, nor here. Like a bush struck by lightning, he remained dumbstruck. It was as if he'd only just seen Uncle Sattor standing there, and then, with the spirit crushed out of him, as if he had vanished into the steppes. Bekesh tormented himself with these notions as he went into his uncle's yard, and so he didn't notice his Aunt Mutriba who had caught sight of him from under her white headscarf. Then she suddenly recited:

My fortress destroyed, oh, slipped from my grasp,
My friend has parted, oh, from my lonely flower,
Nobody expects anything, just laments and groans from death,

and came up to him. Then her weeping ceased and she said, 'He wanted to see you, and could find no peace. "Don't go," I told him, but he wouldn't listen to me. I should have clung to his leg, the wretch that I am.' She struck Bekesh's shoulder and neck, and Bekesh felt a shooting pain in his unhealed wounds, and then his heart throbbed with pain not because of the blows

but because of the guilt he felt. If only he had made his uncle
slaughter the dappled mare and put the meat in the big cauldron he would have survived, even though Bekesh wouldn't
have had even enough strength to see him all the way to the
Chinese camp. Bekesh was burning inwardly. He no longer
knew what to say to his Aunt Mutriba. If they'd been Kyrgyz,
he might have given them one of the laments from the *Manas*.
Now, using his sick kidneys as an excuse, he yelled out, but still
not a single tear came from his eyes. It was just as well that the
circle of men relieved him from this embarrassing situation by
taking him to the clay bench where they sat, and where it had
been the custom to sit with Uncle Sattor and listen to tales.

The unexpected death had knocked the spirit out of him.
'Which of the border guards killed uncle Sattor?' he kept wondering. 'Perhaps that slant-eyed guard who fired into the air?
Or was it the Tajik who prayed when he heard about the
death? Why didn't he beat the living daylights out of them?'

Had they observed the rule, 'If your enemy gives you water,
look on him as a friend'? But it was not too late yet to punish
them for slashing him in the side with their sword.

Bekesh sat down on the earth bench with the others.
Prayers were recited. Tea and bread was served. How many stories had he heard, sitting on this bench? Where were those stories now? If Uncle Sattor had been sitting there he would be
composing a story and a parable about death for them. However hard Bekesh might try, he couldn't think of a single story
about death that was fit to recite. Whatever he did, he wasn't a
Tajik. All he could remember was Kanikey's lament and
Kökötöy's feast, but he could not recall a single parable or com-
plicated narrative. All that came to mind were the jokes and
funny stories that his friend Yashka used to occasionally tell on

the radio.

'Once there were two brothers in a family. Each was as good and as clever as the other, although the elder brother was a little more pensive, and the younger more active.' (Just as Uncle Sattor had the night before been comparing Tajiks and Kyrgyz.) 'The brothers grew up. The elder pursued religion and was ordained as a monk. The younger turned to gambling and sport and devoted his life entirely to leisure, eating, drinking and womanising. When the elder brother found out about this, he prayed for him, hoping his younger brother would find a righteous life. But the younger brother, when he was dead drunk, was stabbed and died. The elder brother was by then living a long way away; he felt sorry about his brother's sins and spent his days and nights praying. Then he too died.'

'Then, which one went to heaven, and which to hell?' Yashka would ask at this point. Everyone gave different answers. The only reply that Yashka recognised was, 'The elder brother ended up in hell, and the younger one in heaven,' he said. 'Why, you ask? Because it was the elder brother's fate to be a great scholar. Yet it is written that a man who can save countless people from all sorts of diseases must devise treatments, but the elder brother was too haughty, and, being stuck up, neglected his duty, and decided instead to become a monk. In the book of fate of the second brother the despotic element was all-powerful, and the woe of countless people was pre-ordained. Because of the younger brother's irresponsibility, he let down just two or three women and himself. That is why he was assigned to be in heaven,' said Yashka, cunningly screwing up his eyes. In any case, Uncle Sattor's place ought to be in heaven, Bekesh hoped affectionately, and when he saw the others looking open-mouthed at the food, he began to weep bitterly.

—

After everyone had eaten, prayers were said and more ghazals were recited. As a Kyrgyz, Bekesh felt himself excluded, but when he listened to a ghazal that touched his heart it was enough to fix it permanently in his memory.

I saw an unfledged infant bird, I remembered my own heart,
I heard a barn owl complain, I remembered my journey's end.
Because of a broken promise I agreed to my death,
Night after night I remembered my killer's hand and blade.
In the clashes of the sea so many storms have wandered,
I remembered my towel that dried the lips of grief.
Let me not strike my head against a thick branch of juniper,
I was burning and there was sense in my fire – I remembered my barrenness.
O Sayid, I have seen this wretched earth's leaves and tulips,
I remembered the blessing said over game wrongly slaughtered by the blade.

Enthralled by the ghazals that these men recited, inspiration came back to Bekesh and, despite not being a Tajik and not knowing this circle of men, he suddenly exclaimed: 'In the name of God,' and began to recite, with a touch of penitence, not what had been sent to him as an epiphany, but what he had learnt by heart: the episode of the eagle White Gyrfalcon from the death of Manas:

White Gyrfalcon left Khan Manas

And circled, and hid,
Flew backwards, thrust out his chest,
White Gyrfalcon went and scattered
All the stinking food.
White Gyrfalcon fled,
Vanished, disappeared from sight.
White Gyrfalcon tore off
His short golden jesses.
White Gyrfalcon merged with the sky
Like an eye in the blue.

The guests were now getting to their feet and saying the final prayers while the women sat in the house, weeping and lamenting. Bekesh didn't want to bother aunt Mutriba and so he stood together with the circle of men and went towards the border. The Kyrgyz at the guard house were a new shift and because they didn't recognise him, the conversation was long and at cross purposes, questioning him at length about who he was and what he was about to do here. Once again, Bekesh showed them his identity card, clumsily, his heart not in it. Again, the soldiers and their commandant sighed, this time interrogating him: 'You're a Kyrgyz from our Kyrgyzstan, what are you doing going to Tajikistan?'

'My home, my horse, my eagle are in the Kyrgyz ayyl,' he replied, and only with difficulty could he get away from them. While he was being questioned, he forgot to ask 'Who shot my uncle?' As he was approaching the Tajik border guards, together with a greeting, he finally asked the question. It seemed to hit a nerve as, with their offended self-esteem, they suddenly burst out: 'Who do you think you are? Are you expecting a feast at the border?'

'If this goes on, it will bring on the final agony,' he thought. But he did not speak, for the border guard's wrath and fury was about to be unleashed. The guard yelled at Bekesh, 'I'm going to have you shot!' and butted Bekesh in the side with his rifle knocking him violently to the ground. 'He's going to fire!' Bekesh thought, the moment he collapsed face-down. The fall had opened the wounds on his waist and body, and blood-soaked strips were now visible. The commandant, who had been drinking Kyrgyz kumys and was both overexcited and drunk, switched from fury to curiosity. 'What's this?' he asked.

'The Islamists gave me a beating,' said Bekesh reluctantly. '

Why didn't you say so at the start?' asked the commandant, and lifted Bekesh by the armpits and propped him up. 'Did you hear the shooting last night? I reckon they were about again...' Bekesh kept his ears pricked, but the commandant didn't say any more.

—

By now people from the Kyrgyz ayyl had spotted him, and Doctor Janish came trotting up on his horse. 'Are things quiet now?', he asked and looked fearfully at Bekesh's pallid face. 'What has my patient been doing here, instead of staying in bed with his pillow and quilt?'

'When the groom comes, the girl gets ready,' joked the commandant with his bushy eyebrows, as he handed Bekesh over to the doctor. 'Your little brother seems to have caught a chill, he looks as if he's got a fever.' Doctor Janish put Bekesh on his horse and led him back to the Kyrgyz ayyl. While they were riding up the hill, Doctor Janish scolded Bekesh, 'If you were going to the border on business, I'd have told you to stay in bed and not move.'

'They shot my uncle Sattor,' Bekesh responded curtly. At that, Doctor Janish tumbled off his horse. 'Stop!' he said in disbelief. 'Stop!' he repeated. 'Stick a knife in yourself; if it doesn't hurt, stick it in someone else!' he added.

'I stuck it in myself!' Bekesh said wearily and as he got back into the saddle, doctor Janish waved his hand in an invocation to God. Feeling the pull of the reins, the horse stopped dead. 'Who shot him?' asked Janish. This time his voice cracked with repressed anger rather than curiosity. 'I don't know,' said Bekesh. 'The border guards are blaming the Islamists.'

'When did this happen?'

'Last night he came to see me. He was on his way back.'

Doctor Janish sighed with deep pain and said, 'There was a whole pack of pigs hiding behind the pine tree...'

Then, without prompting, a memory came to Janish. 'Do you know, once we all went hunting with Baisal. After the hunt, when we were sitting there recalling it, Sattor the Tajik entertained us with riddles and tales. It's one of those that I now recall. One day a lion took a wolf and a fox with him hunting. They went off sparing no efforts and got their quarry, catching a yak, a goat, and a hare. The lion joked about this, and said to the wolf, 'Look, wolfie, why don't you share out the catch?' The wolf shook and trembled. and said, 'You, lion, are probably the biggest of us all, so the yak is yours; the goat is mine and the fox gets the hare – that's fair.' The wolf's brazen arrogance angered the lion, and in one go he ripped the wolf apart, killing it. Then he looked at the fox and said, 'Now you, foxie, share it out fairly, will you!?' The fox replied, 'My dear lion, you eat all the yak you want, then have the goat for lunch, and for your evening meal you can swallow the hare. It would be right to leave the smallest for supper.' The lion gently asked the fox, 'Where did you, foxie, learn to be so clever?' The fox was unabashed, and answered, 'I found the incident with the wolf to be particularly instructive.'

By the time this tale was told, they had reached Baisal's household.

—

It was beginning to get dark by now, and Bekesh, astounded at the way he had spent these few days, pondered in silence, 'I've only just now gone down to the stream, and it's only been one day since I came to uncle Sattor's house.' There was then one thing that made him feel happy. Sensing another horse trotting alongside, Topon neighed.

Reluctant to break off his conversation with Janish the hunter, Bekesh, his chest thrust forward, dismounted and invited him into the house. Doctor Janish slowly dismounted, put all his possessions into his saddle-bag, tethered the horse to a pillar, and followed Bekesh into the house. There, they were greeted by a gathering of Auntie and the daughters-in-law, the odd guests Lin Ju and Ulankhu, and Dapan, acting as translator and servant for them all. 'Girls like anything that's red,' was the saying, and they were sitting with the two Chinese men, asking them all sorts of questions in broken Russian.

When she spotted Bekesh, Rabiga made everyone stop their chattering and asked: 'Is Sattor all right?' Now, Bekesh became conscious of her widowed state and childlike nature; he was, without wanting to, about to make her weep. Drawing a deep breath and feeling ashamed to be next to the womenfolk, the thought rose in him, 'I can't stop,' and he began to sob loudly.

Catching the sense of doom, Rabiga sat down and she too gave way to grief and sobbing. The Chinese men couldn't understand what was going on and sat as stiff as pieces of wood. 'I've come hoping for a feast, but none was ordered,' Janish reflected. He was lost for words and didn't know whether he should have come in or not. Still uttering sobs, Rabiga rose to her feet and approached Bekesh, who hadn't yet come to terms with his humiliation and bereavement.

> His light radiated brilliantly,
> His masterful work flourished,
> I shall never press against your side,
> How my brother-in-law is ashamed…

She tried to comfort herself, and holding Bekesh's shoulder and back, she started hitting out at him. His stitched wounds were throbbing after such a tiring day.

—

With her brother-in-law Sattor dead, Rabiga bent double, like an old woman: seeing this stopped Bekesh from weeping. Bekesh was feeling low and dispirited: he decided to tell them all what had happened. The Chinese men wept, the other men sat with their hands over their eyes. Now that darkness was falling outside as black as charcoal, Doctor Janish was preparing to stand up, but first looked at Bekesh and said: 'I was supposed to get this young man back on his feet; but he can't stand. I'll have to bandage his wounds again.' Leaving them sitting in the room, with Dapan's help, he led Bekesh, who was now so exhausted that he was barely able to move, into another room.

Dapan fetched the doctor's equipment from the yard. Doctor Janish was saying, 'Now try and get your strength back by walking about,' as he once again rubbed medicinal oil on Bekesh's wounds and then bandaged them tightly, especially round his shoulder blade and chest. While the doctor was busy treating Bekesh's injuries, Bekesh, exhausted by his recent fit of weeping, began trying to act courageously. He asked Doctor Janish, suddenly challenged him, 'What did my uncle Baisal die of?'

Doctor Janish was prepared for this question, though it came out of the blue: 'Your father died of something burning inside him,' he said. 'You should know that he'd stopped reciting the *Manas*. After that he spent a day tormenting his heart and tormenting his sleep; because the responsibility of the *Manas* had been entrusted to him, and if you've been chosen, you cannot simply stop reciting it by wrapping a gown around your head and saying, "No, now I shan't recite it." You can't do such a thing. Isn't it said somewhere in the *Manas*: "I came to the enemy, standing up straight; I came to the crowd, embellishing my tongue."?' Doctor Janish bandaged the last strip on Bekesh's chest.

'You mustn't play games with the *Manas*,' he concluded. 'You can't say, "Let me try, and if it's my destiny, then die." That's what made your father Baisal pass away.' Then he concluded, 'A chosen man refusing to recite is no better than a man not chosen deciding to recite: either way, it results in retribution!'

At first Bekesh didn't understand this statement, and so he asked, addressing the question to Janish the hunter, and to himself, and to Dapan: 'But why did he stop reciting the *Manas*?' Janish looked sternly at Bekesh.

'The boot has turned my foot into raw meat!' he said, pulling off his boot and flinging it into a corner. So Bekesh realised that this was not going to be a short conversation. This was how their talk became free, like a fruit with the stone removed, and suddenly he blushed.

'Once your father and I went to see the shepherds on the pastures of mount Özgön. We drank ladle after ladle of kumys from wineskins, I went to vaccinate the men and your father gathered a crowd around him to recite the *Manas*. We held session after session and went from one mountain pasture to another.

'One morning we came to a big village. As soon as the lark sang his song and with the sunrise spreading all over the sky, people said that the world-famous Baisal the *Manas* reciter had come, that there would be a recital for them, and they had already gathered round. Some came on a donkey cart, others on horseback, and some came down from the mountains on race horses. By then your father was quite decrepit. When he saw the gathering, he thought he'd raise everyone's spirit, and so he began reciting the story of young Manas's clash with the Kalmaks. Carried away, he remembered his own youth and the wars.

'As he was reciting, suddenly from down below three men on horseback came up the track on their way to the town of Özgön. There was no greeting from them, nor any response to a greeting. 'Do you know what's up? Have you ever seen anything like it?' they said. 'Uzbeks are slaughtering the Kyrgyz in Özgön, yet you are sitting around listening to a stinking old man's useless fairy tales. You share out a yearling's meat, until your tendons are showing, and you have an old man to help you!' one of them said pompously. 'Uzbeks are the same as

Kalmaks!' the people snorted. 'Death to the Uzbeks!' they said. 'Our father Manas killed the Kalmaks, we'll kill the Uzbeks!' they said, and that was the last we saw of them.

'All sorts of things, whatever Allah gets into his head, await a human being,' said Doctor Janish with a sigh. 'What the eye sees is enough to make you vomit. Baisal was yelling and shrieking, "Stop, you lot!" But why would a mob, all worked up, listen to anything he said. Then your foster-father took out something from under his belt and began to recite a prayer. I think it may have been an amulet, a bright green stone. I was amazed, wondering what it was. At the time those three wild horsemen were about to trample us down, and on they went to down. Just in time I just managed to push your foster-father against one of the donkey carts, and I managed save him. Something then cracked under the hooves of the race horses, and there was a flash of fire. "The stone... the stone," Baisal whispered despondently. Instinctively, I shoved the donkey cart aside.

'When your father recovered, we got as far away as we could from that accursed place. He opened his blackened eyes and said, weeping, "My face looks branded, as if soot's been poured over it! After moving house five times, my heart's not in any of them." Then he said, "Two men riding mares can save a nation, one man riding a mare can save a life." We had no mares, so that day we were lucky to have saved our lives.

'When we got back to Chekbel, Baisal said something which is still ringing in my ears: "If you see that it will end by killing you, then give your heart to the battle."'

—

The doctor went home, and Bekesh joined the others. Among the Kyrgyz, people were saying that 'You don't visit someone in the night for a heart-to-heart, tomorrow is the time for it.' This determined the direction the conversation took, and after discussing Sattor the Tajik's death it passed on to more cheerful subjects, but in the to and fro of the talk, Bekesh, like a bird with both wings tucked under its body, sat there soundless and aloof. Perhaps he felt this way because of the throbbing pain that had returned to his shoulder blade, or perhaps because of Baisal's stone, or of the silent reminder of Sattor the Tajik's memory – how could he tell?

Then Auntie Rabiga came out and looked at them all one by one, and somehow, her eyes singled out Bekesh. Rabiga said, 'If you don't take it too close to heart, let me say something. After the war, Baisal was arrested, then he was freed, and we left Chekbel to go to the mountain pastures. "The reputation of a pure heart doesn't fade," he said. Anyone dear to us came up to the pastures to visit us, despite the distance. One day Sattor the Tajik came to our yurt. By then your real father had married your mother, so Sattor was a new member of the family, he drank kumys, and used to go hunting with Baisal. I overheard him once telling Baisal that "Someone came to Chekbel to see you." I was afraid it might be more of that interrogation stuff, but he said no, that business is definitely over, and he reassured me. But Baisal was worried. "Let me go back to Chekbel on my own," he said, and he left me in the mountains with my younger brother. He stuck close to Sattor, and went to the village. I didn't like him going at all.

'After two days, Baisal came back. Although he didn't show it, I noticed that he was feeling very happy. He discussed many things and then he said that we should go back to the village.

We folded our tent, packed our things, loaded a horse and a yak, and returned. As soon as we arrived, Baisal felt as though he was in heaven: the land of milk and honey. I was trying to work out why, and discovered that a green-eyed Russian lady had come to the village where she was teaching Russian language at the school. Baisal got very cosy with her.

'Everyone sticks to what they have, don't they? I was very hurt. On the other hand, Baisal was always happy. Whenever he came or left home he was laughing. "Agreeing to my hell is better than disagreeing with your paradise," is not something I would say, so instead I got on the horse and went down the three roads to see the 'big man'. I asked to see whoever was in charge, and went into his office, blocking the doorway. A young woman came out and said, "No, I'm not going to let you in." But I paid her no attention. The boss was a man who fought everything, even to protect a dog. I told him: "You're supposed to be in control of your people: do you know what's going on? You appoint a teacher, and you let a blue-eyed bitch teach children; she's broken up my family. What habits are the children going to learn from her?" I made his desk shake with my hammering and my tears.

'He tried to calm me down: "Your eyes are coming out of their sockets, you're getting ahead of yourself!"' he said. "I understand you. Now you go back to your village, and let me take official action! You should leave it to me to sort out, go home and do the housework!" I went back home the same day. I didn't feel like doing any work, and I turned the cooking pot upside down. At the end of the day, Baisal was used to stuffing his mouth with my cooking. One evening he came in, with his boots soaking wet like a wineskin and as he strode about, he shouted: "Where have you been?" I responded, "I went to fetch water. Have you been cuddling up to that green-eyed Russian bitch of yours?" I asked. "Where have you and I left our hearts?" I said. He didn't make a sound, just left the house and went out into the dark night. By morning he had a black eye and the end of his nose was as blue as a frozen onion. He was drunk. Then I went off to stay with my mother's family.

'After three days, I heard that the blue-eyed Russian woman had turned into something like the Moon Lantern swan: she'd flown off to Russia. After a few days the door opened and Baisal came in. He was barely alive, he was the shadow of a screech owl and shedding a lakeful of tears. But I wasn't going to give in. "You can't blame a wormy sheep, can you? You spread your dung and burnt my dry grass!" I said. "Or does this clever boy come to his senses only in the afternoon?" I went on at him. "What is this, your face or just soot?" He was crying: "Forgive me!", he said. "That green-eyed woman saved my life in the war." Then he told me the whole story.

'There was a whole legion of them who fought in the Ukraine on the Germans' side, they ended up at a village, which they call a *khutor*, a ranch. They spread the soldiers out to search house-to-house. Baisal was billeted at a sick woman's. The woman had a little girl in plaits. Although it was the depths of winter, the girl had to walk eleven kilometres every day to reach another settlement where she could get bread and noodles from a friend in the military who lived there. She did all this to look after her mother. That winter there were wolves all round, but the girl wasn't afraid to make these trips. When Baisal saw this, he felt sorry for her, and shared his own food with the girl and her mother, and when the time came, not letting anyone know about it, he put the girl on the back of a horse, and took her all the way to the enemy settlement where he tethered the horse so it couldn't be seen, and hung about in the forest waiting for the girl.

'Winter was now passing into spring and the woman was getting her appetite back. She could now stand on her own feet. Then the Reds suddenly attacked, routing the legion's soldiers. Fighting was hand-to-hand, with daggers. Baisal's horse was shot from under him; the little girl said 'I'll see to the horse for you.' She herself came under fire, and Baisal himself was wounded, but a woman took pity on him and hid him in the straw barn. Baisal survived but the girl died of her wounds. As soon as the soldiers left the ranch, Baisal was on his feet, and dressed himself in the clothes of the green-eyed woman's husband who'd never gone to war, and off he ran, not caring where to.

'But he held an urge to see the beloved saviour again, didn't he?' Auntie concluded her tale, and everyone was silent.

—

Early next morning, out of nowhere, a thick fog fell over Chekbel. Despite the dense fog all around, Bekesh saddled and loaded Topon. He filled both sides of the saddlebag with provisions and equipment, put Baisal's leather coat over his shoulders, attached his two guns to his shoulders and put on his Chinese gauntlets, and he then perched Tumor, who had by now been well fed, on his wrist. Dapan, fussing about, offered to help, but what he really wanted was to go out to the mountains with his uncle. Bekesh refused, saying: 'You must stay at home! You are just a schoolboy in our eyes, and if something happens to me, who is going to keep an eye on Auntie and the others?' Ignoring the boy's weeping, Bekesh took the two Chinese with him as he set off for Askarkaya.

The fog wouldn't stop Bekesh, who was used to finding the track during the pitch-black nights. Once he left Chekbel, he crossed to the sunny side of the mountain and set his horse at a trot, the two Chinese men walking by his side. The horse filled its lungs with the air that was heated by the morning sun, and it snorted as it went along, while Tumor, on Bekesh's shoulder, had his eyes covered by the leather hood over his head. On reaching an open area, the eagle became excited and wouldn't calm, and it got so unsettled that it began panting. Its sharp claws dug into Bekesh's wounds even through his thick gown, so that Bekesh, deep in thought as he rode along, was suddenly unsettled.

As they turned off the mountain slope, they could see Askarkaya, their destination, and they tried to follow the paths where those bearded men had gone. In the clumps of tamarisk, the birds had started to sing with silvery voices making Tumor quiver, and he began again to shuffle his feet on Bekesh's shoulder. With one hand Bekesh stroked his crop to calm him down. 'If you shut a bird's eye when it's seen something, he'll hear it from all sides anyway,' thought Bekesh: Tumor seemed to have heard something, for he was shrieking.

The path was getting narrower and they were slowly coming face-to-face with both the sunny and shaded sides of the mountains. The two Chinese, where they were once jostling one another with a lot of fuss and discussion, now fell silent. 'If a mountain where deer go is big, their eyes will turn red,' they wanted to say. Both of them became cautious, stretching out to their full height.

When they turned around the hill below the stream on the mountain's slope, the fog began to lift and the whole area became visible. Now they were keeping to the sunny side, but the freezing temperature of the cold mountains and the snow on their summits hit them. The fog, which Topon had recently sniffed, now began to come out of his nostrils like the feather on a bird's wings. On the mountain, thoughts seemed to fly into the heavens, upward like the mist. Sensitive to everything, Bekesh's thoughts had been seething in his mind: Baisal, Auntie, he himself, Dapan were Kyrgyz, after all, and at every step they were comparable with Manas, whether acting or prevaricating, they took their example and model from the *Manas*, they adapted to it, and they interpreted their every move according to the *Manas*, from which they sought their answers.

But here, like a bullet fired from his mind, another thought came to him. Didn't the Kyrgyz say, 'If a thief comes from a good family, the head of the family is sinful too?' His brain was filled with contradictory thoughts. Bekesh realised, as he abruptly halted, that it wasn't the people following the *Manas* in their everyday lives; on the contrary, it was the epic itself running and guiding their destinies, entering their blood and their bones, dictating one thing, forbidding another. Suddenly Topon was standing with one hoof on the rocky path, and rearing back onto his hind legs, his loud neighing making everyone quiver and forget.

—

Looking carefully to his right, Bekesh saw a dignified-looking old man sitting on a donkey. Bekesh felt he knew him, and, getting off his horse and tethering the bird to the saddle cantle while keeping hold of the reins, headed towards him. 'Salam aleykum!' he said, and he and the old man looked at one another. The old man did not dismount from his donkey, instead he smiled a toothless smile and he spoke.

'You're still a striking young man. You must be Bekesh, the foster-son of Baisal the *Manas* reciter, am I right?' he asked.

'You've got a sharp eye, what you say is right!' Bekesh responded, and he realised that this must be Shapak the *Manas* reciter, whom Dapan had one day visited in his cave.

'Guests come from God; my eye was roaming, that must be why!' he said.

Shapak the *Manas* reciter was a man of few words, and he led everyone in single file along a mountain path to his cave. When they reached it, he lead them inside and, in the time it would have taken to brew tea, they reached his house which was built into the cave. The cave was buried in the junipers, on steps carved into the mountain, but once inside they saw it was a house. Next to the house was a broad stone area where five or six sheep and goats were munching hay. Old Shapak nimbly jumped from his donkey and tethered the animal to a rock in the corner. He showed Bekesh another corner rock so he too could tether his horse. The sheep and goats were alarmed at the sight of the horse and the eagle until they saw the guests, and they began to bleat, which perturbed Tumor. So Bekesh made a sign to Ulankhu, who took the horse's reins, while Bekesh pressed the eagle to his chest and stroked and soothed it, and, following after the old man, hurriedly took it inside.

Because he'd come from the bright light into the darkness, his eyesight was blurred, but when the old man said to his elderly wife, 'Woman, we've got guests, let's receive them!' he saw not only an old woman inside, but he also sensed the silhouettes of others hastily scrambling about. If he hadn't been holding the bird, Bekesh would have been frightened. As his eyes got used to the dark, he saw Mullah Shavvol and Adolat sitting discreetly on his right. Bekesh felt like setting the eagle on them or picking up his gun, but the old man was no fool and sensed the tension between them, and said, 'No! A house guest is more precious than your own father!' Meanwhile Lin Ju and Ulankhu had come. Bekesh calmed down once he saw that, other than Shavvol and Adolat, there was nobody else in the house. 'Even if I didn't have a gun, there are more of us than of them,' he thought, 'but it has to stay like this.' He unstrapped one of his five-shot rifles from his shoulder and held it in his free hand.

The two men, who were frightened by their own shadows, were scared and trembling now, and they buried themselves in the corner. Did they think that Bekesh would shoot them? Adolat said, without so much as a greeting or acknowledgement, 'They flogged me!' and he pulled his shirt over his head to show everyone the wounds on his shoulder blades. 'If Mullah Shavvol hadn't intervened, they would have killed me.' His croaking voice was submissive and humble. Shaking his beard like a billy-goat, Mullah Shavvol joined in, the two of them showing their pathetic state instead of justifying themselves or apologising.

Shapak the *Manas* reciter could see the awkward situation. 'I've slaughtered a goat for them, do I have to slaughter my ram for you lot? If not, a hungry man's eye is swallowed for want of food,' he said, while clapping his guests on their shoulders. He left them to the old woman, who was stroking her forehead, and went out to the stone yard to slit the ram's throat.

———

After slaughtering the black ram, he put the meat in the cauldron. Tumor calmed down after being handed the ram's innards and he went to sleep on his perch in the corner. The two men were still sitting hunched over, huddling together in the corner of the room, looking warily on but not taking part in the conversation. On the other side, the cauldron was quietly coming to the boil. Shapak asked about Bekesh, and about his two friends. Bekesh at first spoke very curtly about himself: 'When my father died, I came back to the ayyl. At one point, before then, I had been sleeping with the sheep in the yard, and at another time I went and lay down with a dog in its kennel,' he said, describing his city life. 'Then these two friends of mine had problems at work. A frog was competing with an ox in drinking water: the frog drank so much that it nearly died of a burst belly. So they joined us Kyrgyz. At our celebrations, those bastards' evil eye – the pickaxe beards,' at this point Bekesh, for some reason, pointed at Mullah Shavvol, 'attacked our ayyl, and about fifty Chinese were driven out in to the mountains. The very next day the government replaced them with another fifty Chinamen, and claimed that these two were traitors. As they say, we couldn't even convince a goat, so we became the carcase in a game of polo. These two aren't allowed to return unless they get their friends to come back.'

Shapak the *Manas* reciter sat and nodded, biting his tongue. Lin Ju and Ulankhu understood nothing. They eyed first one, then the other speaker, not knowing what to say.

Then Mullah Shavvol, from the corner, suddenly broke into the conversation. 'God willing, I now know where the Chinese are. They wouldn't be any use to the militants. When they found out that their batch was being replaced by another one they left and took two Japanese with them as hostages, that was all. Nobody would give a penny for this Chinese lot: "We'll take a ransom for the Japanese," they said...'

Mullah Shavvol was gabbling away, perhaps feeling a little guilty, as if saying, 'Forgive me, everyone.' Bekesh wanted to tell him, 'If you irrigate the rice, you irrigate the weeds, too!' but somehow felt as if it was Almambet speaking to Chubak, or Manas to Kungirbay. He was a little apprehensive. Then suddenly Shapak the *Manas* reciter said 'If you irrigate the rice, you irrigate the weeds, too!' and continued the conversation by telling Bekesh, with a sidelong glance, 'If one man is saved, then the others are saved, too: that's what I want to say.' Bekesh instantly found himself lost for words: he suspected that the tea he was drinking had one or two herbs added to it. But no, it was the usual saiga grass tea.

'Our tea is pure saiga grass,' said the old man hurriedly, which made Bekesh's eyes goggle, rather like the eyes of the ram that had been slaughtered.

The old man had noticed that Bekesh was on bad terms with the men in the corner, and he continued to speak.

'Thanks to water, the land becomes green; thanks to the nation, a man grows strong. You, my child,' he said, turning to Mullah Shavvol, 'when you see a mare, don't say, "I haven't seen anything!" Instead, give your help to these poor people. What is beautiful about being a Muslim is helping. When you meet those boneheads, talk them round, get them to free all the hostages.'

Here the hidden dislike Bekesh had for Mullah Shavvol became visible, and he said to himself, working up his sarcasm, 'Only an oaf tries to smash a bull's nose with his fist.'

Shapak took another look at the corner and the old man said out aloud: 'Only an oaf tries to smash a bull's nose with his fist, so don't be like that, make things flourish, and flourish in return!' Bekesh and Mullah Shavvol nodded in unison, as if coming to terms with one another.

Waiting for the mutton in the cauldron to come to the boil, Bekesh found that he had nothing more to say. His ears were still ringing with Shapak the *Manas* reciter's words: 'We have no children: my old woman and I are just the two of us, what with one thing and another, our strength has gone.'

—

The mutton had boiled and half the food was eaten, but apart from the old man and his wife, all those who remained were hostile and alien to each other. Bekesh was tight-lipped, in thrall to his thoughts; the meat he was chewing wouldn't go down his throat. Lin Ju, who was used to eating bits of grass and silkworm, was lost, eating the soft flesh hanging from the bones, while the Mongolian Ulankhu seemed to feel as if he was back in his yurt, deaf to anything anyone was saying. Mullah Shavvol was embarrassed at sharing a meal with men who hadn't made Muslim ablutions, while Adolat, who was clutching a piece of dark meat, could not avert his eyes from Tumor, who was perched in the corner. The conversation faltered. The old man tried to talk about his wife, saying, 'The strength has gone from my wife, as she's aged, she's following my example.' The woman grinned with her toothless mouth; that was all. They went on chewing meat, drinking the fatty gravy with it.

Outside, the daylight was taking on various shades of red. Then suddenly it became dark. Bringing the meal to an end, the old woman gathered up the crockery, while the old man, after a failed effort to get the conversation going again, made up beds from furs and leather coats in a corner for everyone, next to his two earlier guests. The Chinese men went outside for a short while, and then, without uttering a word, came back and lay down.

Bekesh followed Shapak the *Manas* reciter outside and gave the horse and donkey hay. Then the old man slowly made a bonfire in one corner and lit it, and on a rock next to it he sat down and pointed to another rock for Bekesh to sit on. Bekesh sat to the right of the fire. The red sun was still burning one section of the sky, and the sparks that were flung out as it moved down seemed to be thrown into the heavens and turned into stars.

'There was something you were trying to say,' Shapak the *Manas* reciter said, inviting Bekesh to speak, the flames from the fire reflected on his face.

Bekesh shrugged his shoulder that the rifle still hung from. The old man went on regardless.

'A while ago you said that it felt as if Almambet or Chubak or Bakay or Manas were speaking from within you...'

Bekesh was astounded. Had this thought come from inside him, or had he really spoken it out loud?

The old man delved deeper: 'It's not us reciting the *Manas*, but the *Manas* reciting us, you were saying. The words guide our life onto its path, they manage us, you said. There's a story I heard from some old men. You can call the word a moth. It flies and it's off. But nothing deprives us of all the words we have thought or spoken in the course of our life. It may not be visible to the human eye, but the black and white in the water is removed when it hits the rocks, it may even be turned to dust. In the same way, these moths are all around us, invisible, they move around like the souls of the dead.'

As if to confirm what the old man had said, tiny moths, attracted by the fire, began flying out of the dark. 'A good word is a white moth, a bad word is a black moth,' Shapak the *Manas* reciter summarised. 'Some people can't sleep at night, can't find peace in the daytime, and will live a life of fever and anxiety: they drink kumys all day, and have a girl at night. So, when their days are over, hordes of those invisible black and white moths come back inside a man, and among them a great and deadly battle begins:

> The white ones glistening like daylight,
> Smoke swirls from its mouth
> Quivering from head to toe at the sight,
> A roaring fountain like burnt snow.
> The black ones are as silent as the night,
> Thick clouds of dust are raised,
> The fire belched out soot,
> And covered those who'd come...

'War here, war there!' said Shapak the *Manas* reciter, closing his eyes, surrendering to the words inside him. Over their fire a moth brushed its wing, which turned into a spark.

> Those in front
> Lashing their horses with their whips,
> Pierced in the face
> By steel-tipped lances,
> Were taken in the fire, and taken by the neck
> To be strangled and piled up.

The old man was bringing scenes of a horrid and brutal war

to life; then, when he got his breath back, he said: 'If a white moth gets into a man's chest, it takes his soul to a white wing, and flies to the pure white mountain tops. But if the horde of black moths should triumph, then they lay wandering worms in his innards, and they will be there, eating him up inside...'

—

Bekesh had no idea if he slept that night. He may have been dazed by Shapak the *Manas* reciter's bewildering words and his silent skills; or he may have been preparing for the enemy attack. He held onto his gun, and he had remained alert and watchful: how could he not have? He woke up in the morning on guard. 'Your day has come!' said Shapak the *Manas* reciter, who encountered him after bringing firewood and grass down from the mountain. In the early morning light his small house, nothing much to look at, seemed even smaller, and it astounded Bekesh that so many people could have been squeezed into it. Once more, Shapak seemed to be reading his thoughts: 'If you dig a grave, dig it wide, they say, and if nobody lies in it, then surely you will,' he said.

Reviving yesterday's bonfire, the old man put the new wood onto it and over the fire placed a brass ewer. By the time he'd given hay to the cattle and the herd, the tea was already brewed.

'Has your heart, so depressed by grief, calmed down now?' Shapak asked as he offered Bekesh tea. 'If we act like that, with my old guest as a middleman, we can send him together with your friends. If need be, I can go myself, only I feel sorry for your vicious bird,' he said. 'It's the eagle to end all eagles. He's got a head like a snake, he's full of pride and dignity. He moves his wings, his tail and the rest of his body gracefully. He sits beautifully, that's a pretty hefty eagle. Why don't we take it out hunting?'

Bekesh was in agreement, but he wasn't at all pleased about his two friends being left in the hands of Mullah Shavvol.

'So in that case,' Shapak said, 'if you go with your gun ready, together with your friends, then won't your enemies say to you, "Come any time, take what you want!" Otherwise, even if you survive, you'll lose your two guns, and your eagle as well.'

Bekesh had already heard from Baisal and from Uncle Sattor about this elderly hermit's extraordinary powers; he had forgotten that Shapak had also found Dapan's calf. Bekesh himself was now witnessing how the old man could see his thoughts as though through a glass. There was no point of boasting to the old man about those enemies. He wouldn't say about them, 'While you're looking wide-eyed, I'll wipe you out.' The old man cast a glance at Chekbel far below where smoke had begun to rise.

'You wouldn't say to them, "While you're looking wide-eyed, I'll wipe you out."' he said. Bekesh, not trusting his own ears, sipped his tea. Let everything be as the old man said!

—

While the other guests were waking up, Bekesh took Tumor out into the air and fed him the heart of the ram that had been slaughtered the night before. After tea, only Adolat and the old woman were left inside the house, all the others gathered in the stone yard. Following a consultation, they intended to send Mullah Shavvol with the two Chinese men to see *those people* and come to terms with them. This gave Mullah Shavvol a chance to whisper into Bekesh's ear: 'You and I are like milk-brothers, but the marijuana and the drugs of that husband of your niece was the reason he got a thorough beating, so you'll have to be careful!' He spoke as if he was revealing a secret. Then he spoke so everyone could hear. 'As for the Chinese, we can probably cope with the issue of them, God willing, but negotiating with the Islamists about the Japanese will be a bit trickier,' he said before reciting the first surah of the Qur'an. His gestures pointed to Lin Ju and to Ulankhu, who were moving in single file towards the pass which could be seen in the distance. An instant later, they had disappeared between the mountains.

Shapak went indoors to get ready for the hunt. Bekesh saw behind him two white moths fluttering and this reminded him, somewhat painfully, of the story he'd been told the night before. If he thought about it, the years he'd spent working at the state radio station were spent producing so many meaningless words, talking nonsense, so that if they didn't return inside him as black moths, they would certainly come back as colourless moths, neither one thing nor the other. What would Bekesh's soul do in this case? Or as Mullah Shavvol had said, should he revert as quickly as possible to piety and start saying his prayers?

Remembering the story of the moths and the radio, Bekesh recalled an earlier conversation. When he had been recording Baisal's stories for the radio, the old man had also spoken of black moths. In fact, Baisal's story was somewhat different, starting with Adam and Eve arguing about whose seed would produce the human race. So Adam collected his seed in a cotton capsule, while Eve collected her seed in the cotton itself. After a short time, caterpillars appeared in both of them and moths came flying out. That was how white moths turned into angels and black ones into demons, Baisal had said at the time.

But he continued his parable: 'Every white moth will encounter a black one on its path.' Black moths will be wearing a black wild boar's felt gown and leading a black hunting dog, according to Baisal the *Manas* reciter. At that time, Bekesh was thinking about Karlygach, a young woman he used to work with at the radio station. It was then that Bekesh said, 'Pretty or not, loving you was pretty,' for he was in love with the slim-waisted Karlygach, with her deep-set eyes, and he hoped every day at work to catch sight of her, while on Saturdays and Sundays he would go to the town park where he would sit for a while and watch out for Karlygach in her black coat with long black leather tassels, taking her tiny black lap-dog for a walk among the trees and people. He buried his first love deep in his heart, and just when he had plucked up the courage to reveal it to Karlygach, she met her death, together with three drunken colleagues, when their car tumbled off a bridge. 'You're a man who's collected silver; six bastards have enjoyed it.' Ever since then, Bekesh had been like a man badly burnt. Now he understood: this was his black moth.

Shapak the *Manas* reciter invited Bekesh to come back inside the house, but Bekesh still felt that his heart was reduced to dust and ashes. Could Baisal's story of black moths actually have been preserved on those tapes?

—

'Did you ever record your father's parables?' Shapak asked Bekesh. By now Bekesh was not in the least surprised by this question.

'Yes!' he replied.

'Why haven't you had any children?'

Bekesh was ready to mention Karlygach, but the old man said, 'Take off your rifle, and lie down here! I'll pray and it will heal!' and he pointed to the fur coat next to Adolat.

'Whoever burns your soul, is a soul mate; how can someone who doesn't burn you ever be a friend?' he asked with a giggle.

Bekesh looked at Adolat, who was lying face down in the corner, then he unstrapped the guns from his shoulders, put them down and pressed them underfoot as he began to undress. Lying face down on the fur coat, he shifted the rifles closer and kept his hands on them. 'Don't be afraid,' said Shapak, 'I've put your enemy, your niece's husband, to sleep, he won't catch sight of your gun in seven dreams.' Bekesh took his hand off his guns, and felt his chest. His heart seemed to ache because of what he had been imagining, or it may have been his injuries: there was no knowing.

'If one tooth aches, the other teeth will start hurting, too,' said Shapak and, as if to explain these unexpected words, said 'If we go out hunting together, you'll be the hunter and I'll be the beater. While you feel the pain, I don't have to endure the suffering.'

Shapak then quietened down and recited a few things in a whisper, after which he tapped Bekesh's spine with a whip, as if trying to tickle him. Finally, he picked up a wooden ladle that was behind Bekesh and sprinkled what seemed to be drinking water or something, before whispering some more. When he finished he struck Bekesh's shoulders with his calloused palms. 'You used to be like a horse, stand still, young man!' This made Bekesh feel a lightness all over his body, a lightness that he'd felt as a child when he mounted a colt with a stick or a riding crop and made it break into a canter. From a standstill, he would leap and mount a horse, then trot off to the mountains and steppes.

Now he leapt to his feet. There was no trace of the strip of flesh that had been so painful for some days, and he moved his hands to his shoulder blades: no rough places, no scar scabs, instead his skin was as smooth as silk. He put his shirt on, then his gown and he hung his guns upside down over his shoulders, all with not the slightest sign of pain. He glanced at the old man, who said, 'Old age is a house which has its superstitions,' and when he had put on a gown and a felt hat, he showed Bekesh out.

—

With Bekesh on horseback and Shapak on a donkey, they headed for Ko'sh-urkuch mountain. By now the sun had risen from the dark side of the mountain and was lighting up the gorge. They climbed two passes and reached the old man's destination. Between two mountains, on a broad square, was a dense growth of grass and bushes and to judge by the birdsong, there was plenty of animal life. Tumor, perched on Bekesh's arm, couldn't see his surroundings because of his felt hood, but with his entire body he could sense it. He quivered and his feathers rustled. When Shapak saw this, he stopped next to a boulder and dismounted from his donkey.

'Before the hunt starts, let your bird fly, let him stretch his wings!' he said.

Bekesh stood there thinking the same thing. He took the hood off Tumor's head, dropped the jess from his hand and sent the eagle flying into the open sky, applauding it with an excited shriek. The bird gave two flaps of its enormous wings, found a current of air and without further movement once more began to soar to great heights, propelled by gusts of wind. At one point the bird entered the sunny circle of the sky and became lost to their sight. Trying to see by putting their hands over their eyes, Bekesh and Shapak found their vision blurred, but in an instant Tumor, although diminished, became visible once again. Then he shot upward, as hard as a nail, flying out to check the boundaries of this oasis in the air with his sharp eyes and then he emerged from the heavens and headed back to them.

Tumor's shriek began to ring in their ears as the eagle spotted something over by the rocks, but even though they were unable to see the sharp protrusions of the eagle's talons, Bekesh sensed something there out of reach. Tumor made one circuit, then another around the boulder. Then, what sounded like two shots were fired from behind the boulder and two hawks rose into the heavens. 'Did you spot their quarry, Tumor?' the thought flashed through Bekesh's mind. Suddenly, the peace and quiet of that perfectly clear blue sky was disrupted, and the sound of shrieking and burbling rose up.

Like a flash of lightning, the shrieking hawks flew over Tumor; undeterred by the eagle's grandeur and bravery, they attacked him. One flew like a bullet, trying to stick its iron beak into the eagle's serpentine head from below. Any bird other than Tumor would have been killed by the first attack that drew splashes of blood from the eagle's head. But Tumor veered left, and plunged down again, shadowing the hawk which had dropped beneath it. Seeing this made Bekesh's heart quiver, and he gripped his rifle hard and raised it intending to shoot one of the hawks, but the speed of the sky battle had become so great that there was a danger of hitting the circling eagle instead.

Tumor reached the low-flying hawk, intending to dig his sharp talons into it, but at that moment the hawk flying above closed in on the eagle, aiming for his eyes. Tumor sensed the threat from above and performed a somersault, sticking his talons into the hawk. The hawk was no match for the eagle's skill and, skewered like a piece of meat, was wedged sharply on the eagle's talons. In an instant its innards and guts were ripped open.

When the second hawk saw this, it tried to hit out at the eagle, and then soared up into the sky and attacked. But with one shake of his leg Tumor threw aside the hawk he was holding and prepared to attack once more. Soaring up now, the second hawk lunged its beak toward the eagle's throat, but was slashed by its claws, and, convulsing, gave up the ghost. Dead, it fell to the ground.

'If you think you're a man, then you must think the other is a lion,' said Shapak pensively and went to collect the hawks.

—

This was a lucky day for hunting. The men took two fledglings from the nest of the now dead hawks, and they killed two foxes and bagged an antelope. Following the custom, hunter and beater shared equally.

Towards the end of the day, when the sun was about to set, they returned home. The old woman said, 'Share it out!' and took charge of what they'd caught.

Bekesh replied, 'So be it!' and offered the old woman the fox. 'You can make a fur coat and a cap!' he said. The old woman made them a good meal and recited a blessing, when a noise down below announced the arrival of Lin Ju and Ulankhu. They made signs to Bekesh from a distance to say that he was the only person that they could trust and that they had something important to communicate to him. Bekesh was glad to see them back, alive and well.

'Until she gets to the bridegroom, the girl won't find peace,' said Shapak. 'Go down to them, go...'

'My white dog kept running about until it got pregnant,' Bekesh replied, matching the old man's saying, and tethered his horse to a boulder before making his way towards the two men.

Once they could catch the sound of his voice, Lin Ju began a conversation in his loud, broken Russian: 'We've taken the *Zhōnghuá*,!' he seemed to be saying, and pointed towards the hill below them. What was that? Bekesh staggered to his feet. 'By putting a hand on the colt, you get an idea of the mare,' wasn't that what they were saying? He should at least have taken Shapak's donkey to get down. Nonetheless, the two excited Chinese were hurrying closer towards him.

When he approached, Lin Ju – an illegitimate child – did not explain any further what he had just said, nor did he try to make it clear. Instead, he put his arms around Bekesh then he fell at his feet and began wiping the dust off him with his moist lips and his flowing tears. 'What's happened?' Bekesh asked, astonished.

'*Zhōnghuá, Zhōnghuá,*...' Lin Ju repeated what he had just said. Bekesh looked at Ulankhu, who pointed to the road which wound along in the distance. Bekesh's blue eyes peered into the blue sky and saw on that road a tiny little black lorry.

When all three of them went down to see what was happening, they saw in the back of the lorry driven by Joomart, whose long beard was now like a shovel, about fifty emaciated and dishevelled Chinese, while in the cab, next to Joomart, sat Mullah Shavvol and the interpreter Mimtimin.

PART THREE

Autumn came early that year. By then, since Bekesh had so generously brought back those fifty Chinese, their number had doubled and the volume of work and the results were now more than double too. Never stopping or relaxing, the Chinese tunnelled through the mountain ahead of schedule, and perhaps that was why the cold dark breath of the Pamirs on the other side was now blowing in, the poplar trees were turning yellow, and the apricot leaves were reddening. Human hearts were also cooling. Like two scabby nags meeting in the reed beds, if anyone was having the time of their life – in the reed beds on the banks of the stream – it was the Chinese camp. They could do as they liked. They could get to know the people in the Kyrgyz ayyl, have a day off and ride foals and drink beer straight from the brewers' cauldrons. If they preferred, they could go to the Tajik kishlak and chase after girls whose skirt hems were well above the knee, or smoke hookahs filled with hashish, or play a game of cards. The soldiers, once they got the Chinese hostages back, no longer manhandled them but made the border into a home and were busy getting both meat and the wherewithal to cook it. When the day was over, you counted your blessings.

In fact, after the Japanese hostages had gone, all sorts of people turned up. Then soldiers would make an appearance, and their guns rang out, or they went clattering through Chekbel's streets.

Dapan kept close relations with Ulankhu and was learning to chatter away in Chinese. His school had started again, and Mullah Shavvol had come back, shadowing the Chinese, and had once again begun to give Qu'ran lessons, without leaving his house in the Kyrgyz ayyl.

Bekesh almost never left the house now; looking after Topon or Tumor, he was busy working at home. He did sometimes go out hunting out on his own to the terrace on the reed banks that Shapak had shown him, and for some reason he made a detour to Shapak's house, and often returned from there. Shapak was nowhere to be seen on Bekesh's trips, and nobody knew what was happening to him. People used to say: 'When you have a horse, know the land; when you have a father, know the people.' But now nobody seemed to care a straw. Everyone was getting ready for a long winter.

But Bekesh had a secret reason to rarely leave his house. He'd taken one of the fledgling hawks he had taken with Shapak as a beater, and he was busy caring for and training it.

—

'A newly caught hawk has enough qualities for two fates,' they say. Bekesh gave the fledgling the nickname 'Barchin (Big Eagle)' and the bird's secrets and skills were innumerable. Had he seen its parents' stubbornness and fearlessness? When he first brought it, it wouldn't take food, not even quail flesh, from your hand. Bekesh skewered tiny pieces and fed the fledgling from the skewer. He kept the young Barchin well out of Tumor's sight, in his own room, and put some felt in a wickerwork basket. The person that the fledgling got used to quickest was Dapan.

On the basket its feathers, still soft, were rubbing against each other, as if it was trying to fly, and it still couldn't stretch out its wings and tail. Then it put its wings together and, as it gathered strength, rose up on its legs to the edge of the basket. To stop it falling, Dapan put out his hand and the fledgling tried to flap its wings again, now perched on Dapan's bare arm and leaving marks with its talons. Dapan stroked the fledgling's chest affectionately with his finger, and the bird, still unused to humans, pecked back as hard as it could. A tiny drop of blood came from his finger and Dapan held the bloodied finger to Barchin's beak, as if to say 'Shame on you': the bird opened its beak to swallow this drop of blood.

'Aha, so you and Barchin are going to be blood brothers!' said Bekesh, who was standing behind Dapan. As he quietly tried to remove the bird from off Barchin, the fledgling flapped its wings into the air, hitting one side then the other, and it started to circle the room. The bird was confused and seemed to tire, and it struck the edge of the basket once more. As it spread out its little wings, the bird flopped down and fell onto the felt laid out for it.

'It's time we tied jesses to its legs,' Bekesh then said, and he tied a length of leather strap to Barchin's leg.

Later, Bekesh and Dapan wasted no time in sewing a hood for the bird's head, covering its leather surface with silver to make it shine, and decorating it with patterns of multi-coloured silk.

By autumn, fed on a diet of pure minced meat and quail
flesh, Barchin's wings and tail had grown, and his talons and
beak had become bigger and harder. He was turning into a real
gyrfalcon, his body was as black as soot and just a few white
spots on his tail. His chest feathers were like a stone grouse's
and his stance was upright, elegant and majestic. By this time,
he had become used to Bekesh and Dapan and he would perch
on a gauntlet for food and water. His refuge was no longer a
basket, but a roost built in a corner.

—

Whether because of the bird calls made by Bekesh and Dapan,
or perhaps the feathers stuck to their shoulders — or God
knows how — Tumor sensed, even if he couldn't see, the presence of a new bird in the house. Even if Dapan wasn't, Bekesh
was still visiting him as before, and, if not every week, then
every other week taking him out hunting. This much was clear
to the eagle: they were treating him like a second wife, or like
a child after a new-born baby appears.

Dapan was a young child: they say, 'the twisted blackbird
may be sweet, but there's no meat on it, in the end its body is
all fat,' but Bekesh could sense what was happening: 'when a
foal turns into a horse, the horse retires.' Now, when his master
came into the hunting room, Tumor did not shriek, nor did he
communicate his pleasure by ruffling his feathers. Instead, his
eyes were fixed on a single point and he perched as old men do
when they sit with their hands clasped behind their backs.
Even when out hunting, he did not overexcite himself; he did
his job in cold blood and, when Bekesh called him back, he
much preferred to perch on his bosom friend Topon's saddle,

rather than Bekesh's arm or shoulder.

Had Bekesh got it wrong? Perhaps he should have fed Barchin in the hunting room where Tumor could see him. As the saying goes, 'If you're shoeing a horse, the donkey will lift its leg.' Maybe Barchin would then have learnt everything from Tumor. Even if Tumor had killed the fledgling, would it have been less tragic than the situation now? There was now no way of making them get on. He would have to launch the hawk from bare ground. What should Bekesh have done, then? Who could give him advice? Perhaps Doctor Janish? But he'd never looked after birds. Shapak the *Manas* reciter? But like Bekesh he would be frightened of going near Tumor, and anyway Bekesh was scared of going to see Shapak.

'If your innards are on fire, lick salt!' Bekesh told himself, as he sat there, fired by his own thoughts.

—

Meanwhile autumn really had begun. The Kyrgyz were bringing their cattle and sheep and their calves and lambs down home from the summer pastures. Large groups of Tajiks and Kyrgyz were returning from Russia. Both sides of Chekbel were filling up. The Chinese now seemed to be a little wary, and their behaviour was increasingly guarded. Chekbel's young men, their pockets bulging with money from distant lands, now hired the indigent Chinese as labourers, or built themselves houses, or at least rebuilt the crumbling clay walls.

Lin Ju and Ulankhu were now frequent visitors at Bekesh's house. Ulankhu in particular found time to indulge his interest in learning how to rear the new bird, and he always brought Lin Ju with him. True, while Dapan was there, with his ability to speak Chinese, Bekesh didn't need Lin Ju, but, when school and the Qur'an left Dapan with more work on his hands, he would be away from home all day unlike during summer. At those times Lin Ju acted as interpreter between Bekesh and Ulankhu.

'Look, your Chubak and Almambet are at odds,' Auntie used to say, either teasing or giving Bekesh a warning, as was her wont. Repressing his laughter, Bekesh had secretly got used to them being called by these names and looked forward to the two friends' visits. They were orientals, too: they never came empty-handed, once they brought a box of Chinese soap, on another occasion a small portion of dried Chinese noodles, but what Bekesh most appreciated was the duck meat that was given to the camp. Even if Tumor wasn't very fond of duck, Barchin loved it, not diced, but in whole pieces, and would only stop pecking when there was none left at the bottom of the dish.

If not for the other household members, for Bekesh the birds were a pleasure and joy. Dapan spent most of his time studying; separated from Uncle Sattor's conversation, Bekesh spent his evenings at home listening to what the Chinaman or the Mongolian had to say. There he sat, fully entertained. In particular, Ulankhu's parables, taken from the history of the dreaded Genghis Khan, evoked for Bekesh scenes from the *Manas*. The struggle between the brothers Temuchin and Jamukha, when the latter's deep love turned to the most embittered enmity, aroused a feeling of reserve: thank God, the relationship between Manas and Almambet hadn't taken the same form. Manas had gone to meet and welcome Almambet, and he had offered him a choice of horse and then given him a gift of some of his property, and in response:

The man Almambet thought thus,
then spoke as follows:
'Taking the measure of your black soul,
Akkula was Manas's horse,
he was mounted on his personal charger
he was a man who came out openly.
Akkuba was Manas's gown,
Beloved even now,
The road was opened for me.
Manas's property was in Oqqalta,
If I stand and single out my horse Sarala
The herd of horses is worthy of me.
By setting aside the horse from its gown,
Let the rule not be broken.
If an evil soul is not allowed to prosper,
Let that soul be for the good.'

Among these great names and stories, Bekesh sensed something clearer and more definite: the petty trivia of his life seemed to be guided as foretold by the great names in that great poem.

One day Bekesh tried to bring Barchin outside for the first time, taking him out from his room into the yard in case he become too much of a pet. Dapan had gone off to his Qur'an lesson, but Ulankhu and Lin Ju were at Bekesh's house for the weekend. Normally, birds captured when they were fledglings would not fly away. But as with Barchin, if a bird had inherited a stubborn streak, anything was possible.

Now that it was autumn, meat wasn't so hard to find. Bekesh stocked up, then, cautiously, he tied Barchin's leg jesses to the end of a fishing line which was wound to a reel, through the hole in which he passed a long shaft. When the bird flew, it turned the reel on the shaft, and the fishing line would unroll, but it would stop the bird after around fifty metres. Admittedly, Bekesh was not particularly happy with this line. If the bird got caught up in it, it could be hurt. On the other hand, just as a horse's hooves warm up while galloping, a bird's wings were worked up in flight. If the bird launched into the air like a shot, it might even break its leg. And once a target was found, a lethal outcome was inevitable. What then was the use of the line?

Bekesh reached a decision. Closing the door behind him, he would put a piece of meat on a wall ten yards away and, removing Barchin's hood, let him fly on his fishing line towards the wall. Then, he would call him from the wall to his wrist to see if the gyrfalcon would come back or not. If it came back, then he'd try once, maybe even twice again, then he would let him fly free. If it didn't, there'd be no free flying today. If the cat can't reach the meat, let the cat say the meat was off!

Bekesh explained all this to Lin Ju and Ulankhu, and he familiarised them both with the workings of the fishing line. During their discussion, Bekesh whistled to make Barchin, who was straining at his jesses, perch on his wrist, then he covered his head with the hood. But the bird was clever and it seemed to sense something was up and its heart began pounding. Then Ulankhu went out and placed a piece of fresh meat on the clay wall and, with Lin Ju holding the reel, Bekesh went out as well with Barchin perched on his wrist.

When the gyrfalcon felt the fresh air, it began to quiver. Its wings trembled and it shook its head under its hood. Bekesh stroked the bird with his free hand and tried to calm it with his breath and his voice. But, because of the wind, or the heat, or the noise, or the smells, all the bird's feathers and every one of its muscles were affected by its emergence into the open air and its wild blood was aroused. Bekesh's heart was in tune with Barchin's: it too was pounding, and his arms were trembling with excitement.

You'll do what you have seen, the way the poker's waved about, they say. When he was a child, Bekesh went to Baisal to see how he looked after a bird: had he remembered or had he forgotten? He took the reel from Lin Ju and with his free hand tried to remove the hood from Barchin's head, but he stopped in case the excited bird became tangled in the fishing line.

'In my mind I can pull the earth's seven measuring tapes, but in reality I can't even sort out one reel,' he said, and he reluctantly handed the reel back to Lin Ju and called for everyone to be ready.

Ulankhu was standing in the middle of the yard, all eyes and ears, as Bekesh took the hood from off Barchin's head. Now, with its eyes opene to the world, the gyrfalcon seemed to lose itself for a moment and looked from left to right. Bekesh then launched the bird towards the wall, yelling 'Fetch! Fetch!' and with two flaps of its wings the hawk perched upon the wall. It first spread then folded its wings. When it set eyes on the meat, it didn't peck at it. It didn't show any voraciousness at all. Instead it averted its eyes and seemed to be familiarising itself with its surroundings. Then it pecked once at the flesh, then twice, as if savouring it. Bekesh called, his voice first affectionate, then strong: 'Barchin! Barchin!' Then he whistled. Barchin pondered before he turned his head right round. Then, with two leaps from the wall, he flew back to Bekesh's wrist.

—

After a couple of practice runs, the bird would fly and return from other walls as well. By now Barchin was comfortable perched on a hand, and he would rest there without incident. Bekesh thought that the bird must be so filled with meat by now that it must taste of earth, and so he stopped the practice. But as the bird was not completely sated, he detached it from the fishing line and let it fly free, shouting 'Now, sir!' as he launched the gyrfalcon into the air. The bird rose up, and in an instant, he crossed three walls and was out of sight. When the bird couldn't see anything to eat, he soared even higher and after finding a draught of air, began to glide. Bekesh felt both pride in the beautiful hawk's first flight, and a fear that he would fly too far and an urge to call him back. Not knowing what to do, he stood, his gaze fixed to the sky. Then Barchin rose, bending to one side, and suddenly he rolled over and plunged headlong down away from Bekesh's yard. For a moment Bekesh froze. What had Barchin seen? Perhaps a scurrying mouse, or a frog that had jumped out of the water? On one side, Bekesh could hear a knocking and he was about to answer the call and open the door with both hands when, from the side wall, he saw the silhouette of the goshawk and heard its chirrup. Bekesh was so surprised that he slumped to the ground, and a tiny hare was dropped from the sky. The bird was aiming for Bekesh's wrist, but as Bekesh hadn't stretched out his arm, it sank its claws into the hare's flesh and perched over its quarry.

'Fine bird!' said Bekesh. 'Strong lad!' The first words felt as though they could have been evoked from deep within him by the spirit of Baisal, the second by Sattor. He didn't remove Barchin from the hare, as the bird wasn't simply spilling blood but was calmly eating its prey. This made the bird's belly swell; it then stepped back from the hare and wiped its beak on its chest feathers. Bekesh picked the bird up and launched it into the sky: 'Now you can fly just for fun while you digest your quarry,' he told it. The bird flew free. There was nothing to fear from the voice of a gyrfalcon flying in the open air!

All of the men stood, their eyes enthralled, looking up at the bird as it soared in the wind-swept spaces. But the scenes made the neighbour Irisqul march hot-foot into the yard. The neighbour said the first thing that came into his mind: 'You can smash that bird of yours on your father's grave!' emitting fire from his nose like a black devil.

'You can find shit for any shovel,' Bekesh thought, unable at first to make any sense of the yelling and fuss. Then he realised, Irisqul's enormous finger was pointing at the hare lying on the ground, torn to pieces.

'Your bird has gone and caught my pet rabbit in my own yard: I want blood money!', he shrieked menacingly. Bekesh was looking at the sky again, imploring 'Keep flying, my Barchin, keep flying, but don't land too far away!'

Then he interrupted Irisqul's outburst. 'What's the going price for a rabbit?' he asked.

Irisqul had worked himself up and forced himself to laugh, 'I'll help myself to whatever you've got on your plate!' he said sarcastically.

'The lost knife's handle was made of gold!' Bekesh retorted sarcastically, then he bent down to Lin Ju's ear and whispered something. Lin Ju and Ulankhu both rummaged in their pockets and each brought out a hundred dollars. They offered the money to Irisqul and his eyes goggled. At first he put on an act, before getting off his horse and clinging to the saddle.

'Make sure you keep your bird's ugly face as far away as you can!' he said and, pocketing the money, he banged his camel-like heels and, walking bow-legged, left the yard.

After he left, Bekesh looked heavenwards and whistled...

——

When he was a boy, Bekesh saw a hawk that had been caught in a trap bent over a piece of pigeon flesh. The hawk wouldn't let go of its quarry, it was sinking its steel claws into it and hanging on to its beauty, while, sitting on a distant rock, Baisal and Bekesh were skilfully pulling threads tied to sticks to form a net. Entangled in the net, the bird was fluttering, trying to wriggle its feathers free from the trap. Seeing this, ravens and crows flew over the net cawing. The time had come for 'A lot of dogs against the blue dog' as they say, and they planned to stick their talons into both the hawk and its prey.

For some reason Bekesh couldn't stop himself from imagining this scene; he thought of it happening to Barchin, but he also applied it to himself: as if words had woven nets all around him and however much he struggled a flock of black ravens would rob him of the prey he had felled but not yet torn to pieces. Before, coming from a pile of rocks, Baisal and uncle Sattor would be there to free him from the trap, but no one else was sympathetic to him.

It was for this reason that he was so very afraid of travelling to see Shapak the *Manas* reciter: didn't Bekesh feel as if Shapak was setting the same traps for him? But as soon as he came through the door, he thought that the trap was set for somebody else. Maybe he did need to go in and see the old man Shapak. Wouldn't the person who had set the trap know how to free him from it?

While pondering all this, Bekesh looked at Barchin, who, after flying happily into the sky, had come to rest on Bekesh's wrist. After putting the hood over his head, Bekesh offered him to the excited Ulankhu. Exhilarated, the podgy youth stroked the bird, while Bekesh spoke in Russian to Lin Ju, who was standing like a Russian who's dropped his axe in the water, not knowing what to do: 'The next time we get a moment, we'll take a day off and go hunting with Ulankhu: tell him!' Lin Ju translated this for Ulankhu. As the saying goes, 'If a bald man is happy, he'll throw his skull-cap into the air,' Ulankhu for some reason then thrust a hand into his pocket and took out another 100-dollar note. Bekesh refused it outright and withdrew his hand, and turned to Lin Ju, mixing Kyrgyz and Russian: 'Badly ploughed land won't fill a sack!' Then he added, 'Translate that!'

—

Now, Adolat, Bekesh's brother-in-law, became hyperactive. According to Dapan, he had been leaving the house every week, or every other day over two weeks, to a mountain, apparently to gather grass, then under cover of night either the shaggy-bearded driver Joomart or the smart-arse Mimtimin, the Chinese interpreter, would come and after a quick exchange of words would plunge into the darkness and disappear. Adolat hired a dozen or so workers to rebuild his house completely, both roof and walls, and lay the foundations for a luxurious new building, but Dapan knew there was a snake burrowing under all this: he'd heard Joomart's remark, like Satan spitting blood out of his mouth: 'One day I'll come and bring you a new car.' Perhaps this was why Dapan's mother was content to have him share her bed.

For this reason, Adolat was going about snorting, using Dapan as an intermediary, and sent Bekesh a message: 'You're rearing a new bird these days. Sell Tumor to me. Whatever you're asking, I'll pay double.'

With heavy heart, Dapan passed on this message, staring at the two sides and he bit his lower lip and shook his head twice.

'No!' Bekesh retorted without the slightest hesitation. 'Even if I became a beggar without a thread to his name, would I give Tumor away? He should know his father's place!'

Dapan nodded in agreement, secretly pleased at what was said. By then he hadn't sat down for some time, so he returned home. But, as he said some time later, when Adolat heard these words, his face fell. He screwed up his eyes, put his fist to his orphaned head, as if to eat it, and said, 'A bastard son killed the eagle my father found.' This would be a grudge he would nurture in secret.

—

As the Kyrgyz say, the white camel had given birth. It was a fruitful and gracious autumn. As agreed, Bekesh, when the next free days came, got Ulankhu and made preparations to take Barchin out hunting for the first time. But Dapan threw a tantrum: 'Let me come, let me come,' he pleaded. Bekesh responded by asking, 'Who's going to look after Tumor?' and found something else for him to do first. To counter any underhand tricks from Adolat, Lin Ju was going to sleep over at

Bekesh's house, but as far as the hunting trip was concerned, there was plenty of cause for concern for Bekesh. Since Ulankhu's homeland was on the foothills of the Altai mountains, he chatted away freely with Dapan, and just as Dapan had a certain level of Chinese, albeit fairly low, Ulankhu had acquired a small amount of Kyrgyz, so he did not see much point in taking his friend Lin Ju and he began to fantasize about what he would do in preparation for the hunt with Bekesh. 'Could I become a Kyrgyz?' was a provocative question but obsessed Ulankhu, and, pretending he was making fun of a deaf person, he kept asking Bekesh this same question.

When he left work and had washed he came to Bekesh's house to see if he could lend a hand, and here he confronted his host. Again, he put this same question to him, and threw everything he could at Bekesh. 'I look like a Kyrgyz, and if I spare no effort learning Kyrgyz, I shan't be an outsider. I will be a perfect Kyrgyz...'

'Why do you want to become a Kyrgyz?' Bekesh asked heatedly.

'I'll get on a horse, I'll drink beer, I'll go hunting, I'll marry a beautiful Kyrgyz girl; if you teach me, I'll recite the *Manas*...'

'Oh no, you won't!' said Bekesh. 'For that you need to have been born a Kyrgyz. You have to have a black spot on your waist!'

'But, what do you mean?' asked Ulankhu, puzzled.

Bekesh lifted his shirt and showed his birthmark. 'I've got exactly the same thing,' Ulankhu said in broken Kyrgyz, and he untucked his shirt from his trousers to reveal the birthmark on his waist.

'Don't you actually want to be Mongolian?' asked Bekesh, hoping to end their argument. 'You've got your Genghis Khan:

you have the same way with horses and beer...'

'No,' said Ulankhu, turning serious. 'In China everyone has to be a Han Chinese. I want to stay here!'

'Yes, but this place is Tajikistan!' said Bekesh, his cup now overflowing. 'Here you have to be a Tajik!'

For a moment Ulankhu was lost for words, he groaned as if he'd been swallowed up by the ground and said, 'No! I want to be a Kyrgyz like you, with a horse, with a bird and with parables to tell.'

Bekesh was dumbstruck: 'Where did you learn the word "parable" from?'

Surely, Dapan must have told him. Could it be Dapan who filled this fat Mongolian youth's head with all these phrases?

'My mother was a Tajik,' said Bekesh. 'Horse, bird, stories are things that the Tajiks have a lot of, too...' He spoke along these lines, but inwardly he was thinking with regret that the horse and bird were inherited from Uncle Baisal, while only the stories and sayings had come from Uncle Sattor.

'How about the birthmark, the birthmark?' Ulankhu said, showing off the word that he had just learnt and screwing up his eyes cunningly, eyes that seemed to Bekesh to have been carved out with a razor.

———

This left Bekesh wondering: who had appointed him as the supreme judge with the right to accept or reject people as Kyrgyz? At one point he thought that 'your garden doesn't stretch as far as Talas'[3], you shouldn't be so conceited. Why did you

3. Talas, a mountain on the border of Uzbekistan and Kazakhstan, is the extreme point of Manas's empire and, supposedly, his burial site.

react so vehemently, why were you so hostile to Ulankhu saying he wanted to be a Kyrgyz? Baisal might have said such things, Dapan might have as well, but who made you do it? You yourself are a mongrel, half Kyrgyz, half Tajik. Didn't the saying go, 'A roof you can climb onto is better than a yurt cobbled together?' Ulankhu might turn into a better Kyrgyz than you.

As a Kyrgyz, you alway set a high bar for yourself – as a genuine Kyrgyz to the core, you made yourself a *Manas* reciter. If you don't know the secrets that Shapak knows, if instead of plunging from the summit down to the very depths of life like Uncle Baisal you simply go to the city and talk a lot of rubbish, can you hold your wrinkled head up so high? At this point, like a camel beginning to rut, Bekesh began to foam at the mouth. His thoughts were probably affecting his nerves, and he couldn't settle down in one spot, but wriggled in his seat.

Willingly or not, the solution to Bekesh's problems depended on one man: on Shapak the *Manas* reciter, a man who could see through his soul as through shining glass. However much he tried to stop thinking about him, his image, constantly smiling, was imprinted in a corner of Bekesh's brain.

Here was someone who could provide the answers that Ulankhu and Bekesh needed. He might not even be withholding his approval and blessing from Barchin, either. With this in mind, Bekesh took the tape recorder, inserted one of the tapes that he had not heard yet, and listened. The silence in the room was disturbed by a childish radio voice that he didn't recognise: 'Father Baisal, what does being Kyrgyz mean?' it seemed to ask. Baisal cleared his throat: 'To answer your question, I'll recite from the *Manas*,' he said, picking up his three-stringed komuz.

'When Yrchuul turned Chubak towards Almambet, he spoke as follows:

If he comes and says, equal to your father,
You open your palm, equal to your hand,
Two clans of the Kipchak nation,
Five clans will come from Khiva,
There is disorder with the Mongols,
There is silence with the Charqov,
There are so many Kyrgyz from the high steppes.
If your white sheepskin shoots it will be covered in salt,
It's on the son of six fathers, Juz.
A damned girl of the Kalmaks,
Are you beneath Almambet the slave?
He took your sovereignty from your hand,
He took your place from your path,
He took account of your people,
The cunning Kalmak went off in a rage,
Your power he took from your waist...

Chubak said in response:

My regret was as great as a mountain,
For standing watching and not dying,
A man did not die
From work that was demeaning.
To come from the Kalmaks not finding a husband.
To come from the Kazakhs not finding a place,
Who knew how low it was?
A wanderer who can't find a single stream,
Having left the salts of China,

In these hardships what comes out
Of the Kyrgyz's oppressed traces?

But let me give Baqay's reply to Chuvoq about Almambet:

If you have a clear understanding,
Of the antiquity of my words,
You go about disturbing the people,
What is this work of yours?
When you see Almambet,
Whoever says he is a Kalmak,
Is a man who has lost his mind.
He will sacrifice his life for us,
He has done great service for you.
For a man who has served the Kyrgyz
What's the point of galloping about shrieking?

—

The Kyrgyz have a proverb: 'If a man on foot sees a horse, his legs get tired.' Stopping the tape, Bekesh was plunged deep in thought. Rather than saying 'I'll be a Kyrgyz', if Ulankhu had said 'I'll be a Tajik', would Bekesh have got so agitated? Or would he have said: 'No, you don't know the *Shah-nama* or the *Masnawi*. I'll recite them for you.' Would he then recite the tale of *Rustam and Sukhrab*, or the poem of Siyavush, so close to the *Manas*?

Kaykavus's son teaches Siyavush all the skills of Rustam the hero. But Siyavush's stepmother Rudaba leads him astray. As Siyavush won't let her do this, she uses every underhand trick to make him. Meanwhile the Shah of Turan, Afrasiyab, is drawing up a peace treaty with the Shah of Iran, Kaykavus. Kaykavus uses this to attack Turan, and he chooses Siyavush to undertake this. But Siyavush does not agree to this rather treacherous action and switches to the side of Turan and Afrasiyab. Afrasiyab embraces him, takes him in and marries him off to his daughter.

But just as Chubak turned against Almambet, so Afrasiyab's brother Gersivarz slanders Siyavush, and makes him seem a traitor in Afrasiyab's eyes. This was exactly how Chubak and Almambet explain things to one another and make peace: Gersivarz whispered to Siyavush about the danger he was in and suggested to him that he should flee. Siyavush trusted him and thought that he would be safe if he fled, but on his journey one of the Turanian guards detained him and Gersivarz personally beheaded Siyavush.

By telling this story, he would make Ulankhu give up any idea of becoming a Tajik. Was this precisely what Bekesh had in mind? In fact, could Ulankhu select a single thread from the bundle that had entangled Bekesh's mind over the years? Bekesh had never shown the end of this thread to anyone but hadn't the tangle of his identity had become even more mixed-up in the process? The Kyrgyz have a saying: 'The mouse couldn't get into its nest, so it tied a sieve to its tail.' And the Tajiks seem to say: 'Love looks easy at first, the difficulties come later.'

—

While he was preparing for the hunting trip with Barchin, Bekesh spent most of his time with Tumor. But Tumor seemed to sense that his master's affections had grown cold, and Bekesh started to feel guilty. He had now made new jesses and new hoods for Tumor, and he was feeding him hare meat and cleaning out the guts with soot. But Bekesh began to notice something: if he stared hard at Tumor, Tumor was his past, just like his Uncle Baisal and his aunt, and just like his childhood and the *Manas*. If he said goodbye to all that, then Barchin appeared to be an unknown future. Just like his Dapan... Good luck to the child, the world was his oyster. But before any time had passed, he became amazed at his own thoughts and the conclusions he drew. If Baisal were still alive, would he not say, 'A lamb deprived of milk becomes the ram that attacks everyone.'

He recalled Baisal just as much as he attended to Tumor. He could not get rid of the feeling of his indebtedness, and, for several months, he thought about the documents that he had hidden in the wall cupboard. He had run his eye over them, but hadn't actually touched them. He now retrieved them, the sheets of paper rolled up in muslin between the mattress and the animal-hide under-blanket. Now he began to read the criminal case papers, taking his time over every word. Here was the issue of an arrest warrant, here was the first interrogation paper.

Question: After you came back from the war, did you take part in counter-revolutionary propaganda when you were present in the kishlak tea-house?

Answer: No, I was never involved in counter-revolutionary propaganda in the tea-house.

Question: Did you talk about overthrowing Soviet power, slandering it, in the homes of Imonaliev and Rysbekov?

Answer: No, I never slandered Soviet power in the homes of Imonaliev or Rysbekov or anywhere else.

Question: On the day of Eid al-Fitr, when you left the

mosque, did you not go about with religious propaganda, telling people that they had to believe in God or else they would end up going to hell?

Answer: No, on the day of Eid al-Fitr I did not go about making any kind of religious propaganda.

Question: When you were reciting the reactionary *Manas* poem, were you not undermining people's trust in Soviet power and the collective farms?

Answer: I never said anything against them, at no time have I undermined Soviet power and the collective farms.

Bekesh picked up the next piece of paper. This was witness Sarimsoq Jeenov's evidence.

Question: Do you know that Baisal Jakypov who is sitting facing you? How long and in what capacity have you known him?

Answer: I have known Baisal Jakypov, who is facing me, since 1933, as a mullah, an exploiter and a counter-revolutionary. I didn't go to war, but when he got back from the war he continued his activities against Soviet power.

Question: What examples can you cite of this?

Answer: For example, when he left the mosque on Eid al-Fitr, he told people that they must fear God and, if they didn't, they would go to hell. He was making counter-revolutionary religious propaganda...

Bekesh clenched his fists. Without reading the document to the end, he picked up the next one. It was another record of confrontation. This time it was with someone called Tukumbay Karasayev.

Question: Did you see Baisal Jakypov recite the reactionary poem *Manas* to people?

Answer: I did. He recited this reactionary, counter-revolutionary poem to hundreds of Soviet people. He expressed opposition to the Soviet peoples' friendship with the Chinese People's Republic.

Bekesh's sight began to blur. The image of Shapak the *Manas* reciter was stamped in his brain, screwing up his eyes. 'If you rely on saying "Oh, I'm a Kyrgyz," then tomorrow you perish,' was his Kyrgyz saying.

—

Finally, the day had dawned when Barchin would hunt at the location which Shapak had indicated. Aunt Rabiga had taken her daughters-in-law off to celebrate a baby's first cradle. Bekesh had Barchin perched on his wrist as he left Lin Ju, together with Dapan, who was now becoming upset. Seating Ulankhu behind him on Topon, Bekesh set off towards Askarkaya. They followed the banks of the stream as it ran downhill. When the black uniforms of the border guards and soldiers were no longer visible, and struggling not to tire out the horse, they began moving out towards the mountains. They first stopped at a piece of flat ground, then followed a steep path.

Friendly and at ease with Bekesh, Ulankhu was asking about various things in a mix of Kyrgyz and his own language. But Bekesh, instead of responding with any old nonsense, was thinking about the order of their journey: should he go hunting straight away, or should he get Shapak's blessing first? Unable to decide, he began weighing up the pros and cons of either choice. Finally, he made the horse walk slower; wherever the horse goes will be my choice, he thought, and he stopped dithering.

When they came to a fork in the road, Ulankhu, who was mounted behind Bekesh, became alert as the horse chose the path that went downhill. 'I'm the hunter, you're the beater!' said Bekesh, as if to establish his status, even though Ulankhu didn't understand most of what he was saying. Ulankhu was still gabbling away behind him, but Bekesh was now free of those awkward thoughts and instead he concentrated on the prospects for the hunt.

Within an hour or so they had reached the tamarisk and spiraea scrub by the reed beds. Ulankhu dismounted and walked alongside the horse, and Bekesh could see his eyes taking in this the lush landscape. He halted the horse as it stood at a high point, and he looked around readying Barchin for the hunt. Barchin was now behind his master, turning his head and looking in all directions, his cherry-like eyes revolving in their sockets, its gaze piercing the landscape. Suddenly, fifty paces away, between a rock and the sand, something moved, and then began to run in panic, and Bekesh released Barchin from his gauntlet and launched him into the air. The hawk flapped its wings loudly and flew towards the fleeing hare. Topon pricked his sharp-tipped ears. Bekesh did not call out, and Ulankhu burbled in Mongolian. Barchin wasn't chasing the hare for long. Perhaps he had drawn a line from the start, and once the hare crossed it, he dived to the ground with his wings drawn-back, as if saluting his quarry.

Bekesh set his horse at a gallop towards the hawk. Keeping up with the horse, Ulankhu went on, filled with joy. When they reached the spot where it had landed there was no need to slit the hare's throat, for Barchin had ripped the hare's innards open with his claws, and his beak was pecking at its heart. Bekesh let the bloodthirsty bird sate itself on the carcass.

Ulankhu said something in Mongolian, and added the Kyrgyz for 'no mercy', while the tears of joy from his eyes could have flooded ten fields.

—

If you're really sleepy, you're not fussy about the state of your bedding. Perhaps because they'd gone hunting at first light, or because they had bagged a good haul, it was time for sweet dreams after they'd had bread and tea and untied the five hares they had caught and hung them by their chests from a branch of a beautiful willow. Next, they perched Barchin in his jesses, before spreading out a wide horse-hide groundsheet that had served Ulankhu as a saddle on a nearby patch of grass. Then they dozed for a while. The air was autumnal, and the frequent gusts from the mountains made the men alert as soon as they awoke. When the horse whinnied, both of them woke up and went to take a look. On the other side of the willow two eyes were staring at the hares hanging from the tree: it was a fox. 'Sh-sh-sh!' Bekesh whispered to Ulankhu, and held him back with an abrupt wave of his arm. A fox is crafty: it watched the hawk that had been put on guard, but, as if sensing what had been tied to the willow, was trying to work out: if I run off with one hare out of the many there, perhaps that hunting bird won't be able to get me.

Bekesh knew only too well that foxes were not only crafty, but stubborn. In fact, stubbornness was part and parcel of their cunning. This was a brazen statement, saying: 'I'm going to grab anything you have.' Not only was it unafraid of the horse, it had no fear of the two men lying nearby either. 'Just you wait!' Bekesh said to himself. Yet there was no question of using his gun since the fox hadn't run far from the willow tree and had only a point where Barchin could not reach from the jesses. 'So we have to wait and see: your cunning against the bird's powers...'

The fox seemed now to be aware of the men and kept half an eye on them. Even this watchfulness had an element of arrogance about it.

'It won't move nearer to where we are lying, because its mountain lairs are behind it, and if it goes into one of them, neither bird nor human being will be able to get at it,' Bekesh thought as he read the fox's expression. But the fox was the ideal fox: it would make a wonderful hat... He waited and watched out for the animal to retreat back to the willow-tree, and, without turning round, told Ulankhu, 'One... two... three!' then leapt three paces towards the tree and, taking advantage of the fox's astonishment, cut Barchin's jesses.

At this point, Ulankhu leapt into action, throwing himself at the fox to make it run to the opposite side as it dashed towards the tamarisk bushes. Barchin, who by now felt as though he had been teased and ridiculed by the fox, swept in pursuit of the animal. Because the fox was about four times bigger than the hawk, Bekesh picked up his gun, mounted Topon, and hurried after them. The horse's hooves thundered as the bird flapped its wings, and Ulankhu shrieked in Mongolian.

'A fox's most vulnerable part is its black muzzle,' experts say: the first strike of Barchin's talons and the first stab of his beak would show whether he could deal with a fox or not. This thought struck Bekesh, and flashed through his brain before fading. All this time he didn't take his eye off the fox, which by now had run many yards away, and when Barchin reached the fox, and was about to sink his steel claws into it, the cunning fox leapt aside, span round and hit out at the bird with its legs. The bird's wings were twisted and Bekesh saw the fox open its jaws as wide as it could; unable to endure any more, Bekesh unleashed a volley from his gun. The fox and Barchin, closely embraced, convulsed and then lay still. Whipping his horse mercilessly, Bekesh rode up to them and dismounted.

Both of them, sprawled on the ground, were bleeding badly, and both were dead…

—

When lightning struck Bekesh,
The fledgling hawk in your view
Was struck in the beak by death,
Your wing broke on your mountain.

If you gallop and race in the moonlight,
Your charger will stay at pasture.
Suffering and in agony,
Your Bekesh is left with his loss.

He grieved, and he wept, and he howled – if only these words had any meaning! Bekesh was utterly heart-broken. Hadn't he told himself that he should have reared Barchin next to Tumor? At this point he imagined Baisal was Tumor and that he himself was Barchin. Yes, that's how it was.

Ulankhu loaded Topon with the quarry and the corpses, and as he urged the horse on, Bekesh, thoroughly weakened, had no more idea than the dead Barchin where he was going or why. Topon was taking them uphill on a path that led to the bare summit. Ulankhu's fire had by now gone out, and as he walked, without exchanging a word with Bekesh, he was thinking in his native Mongolian about the disaster that seemed to have struck. They had lost all sense of how much time and distance had passed and only when a rectangular house could be seen tucked in between mountains a short distance away did Bekesh, who seemed to be in a dream, realise that they had reached Shapak the *Manas* reciter's hovel.

As usual, there were three or four sheep in the stone yard and some distance away was Shapak's donkey, which had already seen plenty of disasters in its long life. Yet however patiently they waited, the old man failed to appear. Finally, like a heavenly bird hoping for food, Bekesh made a dive for the old man's doorstep, finally he had reached it. Summoning what little sense he had left, Bekesh tied the horse's reins to a boulder and took a little hay from the donkey nearby and put it down in front of Topon. He held on tightly now to the two biggest hares. Bekesh went to take a look inside and Ulankhu followed. When Bekesh went to greet his hosts, steeping into the darkness that no candle or torch lightened, he heard a muffled greeting from the old lady of the house, and when his eyes finally grew accustomed to the darkness, Bekesh could make out the old woman sitting, bent down over the old man who was lying on a quilted mattress.

He approached the man who had been lying for some time in this dark corner. A barely visible light came from the door, and as he was focusing his eyes, Bekesh saw that the old man lying down was Shapak in his white silk skull-cap, his lips murmuring something or other. Bekesh sat down next to the old woman and kissed the old man's hands.

'I knew you were coming...' said Shapak, gasping for breath. 'We're close friends, you and I...' He seemed to read

Bekesh's regretful thoughts. 'If only you had come earlier... I wouldn't be able to be your beater, yet my help might have been of some use to you... Then we'd have saved the bird you loved...' he said and fell silent for a long time.

The old woman sitting next to Bekesh was sobbing hopelessly. Bekesh's heart was overflowing. How good it would be if he could do as he had last time, getting Shapak off his quilt and on to his feet like a horse. If only he could this time find something to heal the old man...

'I've brought a hare we hunted, why don't I make you a nice thick stew?' Bekesh offered.

Shapak smiled gently and said, 'When your mouth tries to get to the plov, your face will hit a rock. There's a lot you're keeping to yourself, don't add salt and oil to your words, just let it all out.' Bekesh pondered. Which of his problems and which of his dilemmas should he begin with? Should he start with the dream that prompted him to return to his ayyl, now that he could talk about it? Once Shapak got his breath back, he turned towards Bekesh and without lifting his head from the pillow, said, 'Enemies will say anything, you can dream of anything...'

Perhaps he was talking about Ulankhu, who was squatting some way behind them, and his longing to be Kyrgyz? Or should the words that Shapak had whispered be some kind of hint? Bekesh had been thinking of questions to ask him, as enormous as looming mountains, in preparation for this encounter. But now he couldn't find a thought, not even one as small as a sheep's dropping! Should he talk about the magnificence of Baisal and of Tumor, or of his own and Barchin's uselessness? Just as there was nowhere left to go, and no mountains left to climb, he may as well be like pauper and ride a dog.

Shapak was now mumbling something else. Bekesh pricked his ear, but ended up hearing only the last part of what was said: 'If the water only comes up to its nose, a dog will float.' Weren't Bekesh's questions about the full weight of the *Manas*, and who would take it up?

———

'I keep thinking about the mountains,' sighed Shapak. 'Men and countries are like them, too: their beauty doesn't lie so much in striking and annihilating others, but in standing shoulder to shoulder.'

Then he said to Bekesh, 'Please help yourself to the food, Auntie already feels like a widow, she's lost her place...' and he pointed to his wife by the cauldron. Bekesh felt like a bird that had been freed from a net, and he led Ulankhu towards the cooking pot.

'As the Kyrgyz, say, "Don't be difficult, don't lose your temper, give it all you've got!"' So they very quickly skinned not just two, but all five hares, gutted them and put the meat in the cooking pot that was standing on the fire, and the steam and the fire quickly warmed up the house. Bekesh thought about the saying that if you wait for the sun, you might die of cold, thinking that just by looking at the well-off you could die as well. He thought on those words as he watched the fire, and he sensed also a different meaning, one that he hadn't felt before. The last time, when Topon had dug his hooves into the ground, he launched Tumor into the sky; when they had come here, he was in a wretched state. But now, when coming here as a good-looking young man, he seemed like an immature child: where was Barchin, and how was Topon?

Nothing could be hidden from Shapak, but if ignorant people knew, they'd be laughing through their backsides. They would say that instead of Tumor he had used an immature bird to try and get a fox. Wasn't that just the same as saying that Baisal's heritage had fallen into an idiot's hands? He stood, fixed on this thought. Bekesh was utterly disheartened. Yet he forced himself to turn his attention to the food. He took a mountain onion from a bag that hung over the hearth, crumbled it into the cooking pot, then added five or six carrots that hadn't frozen to the boiling stew.

A nightingale is famed for its singing, a parrot for its fine feathers. Ulankhu now cleared his bag of Chinese salt and black pepper and, with a grin, offered them to Bekesh.

'What can you ask of a man on his death bed?' Bekesh was thinking to himself. 'In the face of death all questions are so trivial; when darkness covers you, when you're around a burning hearth, it will distract your eyes from what you see...'

Bekesh looked again sternly at the juniper on the fire. The dying fire that he had seen flared up, like a dead man's soul coming back to life. He remembered the day he'd returned to the village, in the snow and the darkness. When had that been, in what life?

As he was turning these disordered thoughts over in his mind, the stew had finished cooking, and so Bekesh poured the boiling hot liquid into bowls. If it had been horsemeat or beef, he would have known very well which cut to offer Shapak. But what could he do with the old man in his present state? It's a man's job to slaughter a hare, and a dog's job to pull off its chest, is that what's he'd say? With that in mind, he took the biggest hare and tore it to pieces. He then placed the tenderest part, felt whole, on a broad dish, and then thrust it at

Ulankhu. The first portion of stew he offered to Shapak, the second he passed on to Shapak's wife. Then he propped up Shapak, who was now leaning against the wall, with several pillows and raising the old man's body which was as light as a bird's chest, he passed the stew to him.

'Tether the baby camel to the bride, chew the tail for the old woman, and then what have you cooked for an old man like me?' Shapak asked with a smile.

'Game stew,' Bekesh replied.

'Whose son might you be, what race do you come from?' the old man asked, looking at Ulankhu as he served the old man a giant plate of hare meat. Ulankhu was lost for words.

'He's a Mongolian,' Bekesh explained, but Shapak appeared not to hear.

'You must be one of our flat-faced Kyrgyz...' he said.

Ulankhu's jaw dropped when he realised what had been said, and, radiating with joy, he replied: 'Oh yes, I'm Kyrgyz, I'm a Kyrgyz!'

—

They drank the gravy and they ate the tender hare meat. Shapak the *Manas* reciter joked, 'I have a long way to go, I have to see that my legs are solid and strong,' then he tried a piece of the soft hare haunch and, giving it a blessing, began to recite what must have been a poem: 'But I have unfulfilled wishes: there's no obstacle arising from what I have taken, there's no exile arising from my goings, no hero from stabbing – I came as a free bird, I go as a free bird.' He then lay down on his back. His eyes became moist. Looking at the ceiling, he whispered: 'You can bury me now as you'd bury salt, or you can bury me with a rock to protect me, as you like. But don't leave my old woman on her own...' Then he fell silent for a long time.

Bekesh gathered up the bowls and stacked thick lumps of wood on the hearth. He went outside and put the cows and sheep out to graze. He wanted to distract himself with work. Outside everything was partly frozen, they were after all in the highlands, but there didn't seem to be any snow although there was a hint of it in the air. Ulankhu followed him outside. In the cold air his breath seemed to condense and freeze as ice on his thin moustache. They were soon hunched with cold and both came back inside, and they took a saddlecloth and a horse-hide under-blanket outside, spreading the bigger item over the horse, and the smaller over the donkey.

Bekesh was worried. His guts were churning and he couldn't sit comfortably. Again, he went to the hearth and took a poker to re-arrange the burning coals. Ulankhu was by his side, and he told him, with nothing else to do: 'If the poker is long, your hand won't get burnt.' He didn't care whether Ulankhu understood this or not.

Lying on his mattress, Shapak the *Manas* reciter was recalling something, or perhaps he was starting to have nightmares: 'If you get smallpox, people will call it a bad cold; out of superstition they'll call it black deer, when serving bear meat... A bird flew... A bird's attack is more interesting than its catch... A good dog won't show its corpse... How about a child?'

These words resounded in Bekesh's ear, but he couldn't make sense of them. Yet they felt familiar and they clung heavily on his chest.

'Up to a hundred, it's called a squad; up to a thousand it's a flank, over a thousand, it's called an army...'

In the old man's piling one thing on another, making variations on a theme, his voice was sometimes audible; sometimes his words were unspoken thoughts.

'Oddly enough, he's had the cream from three goats, not for nourishment, but for his heart's content...' At this point the old woman began to howl and sob:

> Oh, the moon is on my threshold,
> Oh, my old man is as handsome as the moon,
> Do not leave me alone in the world,
> God has separated us, alas!

Then a cacophonous noise started. The door, which earlier had been shut without a sound, opened with a bang, and thousands of white moths like sparkling snowflakes streamed inside, chilling the air and turning earth and sky inside and out into one single grave. During the blizzard Bekesh's eye fell on the old woman as she was tearing out her hair. As she howled, the steel dentures in her toothless mouth made her look like a horrible tin woman. Bekesh saw the face of death, not in dreams, but in reality...

At first light, Bekesh loaded Shapak's sparrow-like body that was wrapped in white cloth on to Topon, lying on the horse behind its saddle. The old woman discarded all of her worldly possessions and mounted her donkey as Ulankhu herded their sheep, now without a shepherd. They were all, birds as early as larks, following the frozen path. They now had to take care not to slip on the ice as they steadily made their way to Chekbel.

The snow must have shifted in the night, or there had been a blizzard, for in several places piles of rocks had come down from the mountain top and blocked the path, and it took all

Ulankhu's and Bekesh's strength to roll them down. Where they didn't have the strength, they had to find a way round them. In fact, before leaving the rock-strewn slope, they had to lead, hand to hand, first the horse, then the donkey, then the old woman, then the sheep, tying a lasso to them as they edged along the precipice.

If the old man's death had not filled everybody's breast with hot tears, flooding them all with grief, they may have frozen on the journey. The old woman couldn't come to terms with his death, all she could do was to recall her old man: 'When he walked, he kept his nose straight, and his eyes looking up,' she said as she wept, desperately anxious to commit him to the ground as soon as possible. 'It's not as if we're going to a place where we didn't grow up, is it?' she told the donkey as she urged it on with a kick of her heels.

Around noon they came to the outskirts of Chekbel. When they saw the old woman and the shroud, a few people approached, blocking her path with their questions, saying a prayer, or joining the procession for the old man. It was then that Bekesh understood what Shapak had meant when he joked the night before that 'You can bury me now as you'd bury salt, or you can bury me with a rock to protect me, as you like.'

The Chekbel cemetery was in the Tajik kishlak, whereas they were on their way to the Kyrgyz ayyl. So how would they now get to the cemetery on the Kyrgyzstan side? Neither Shapak nor the old woman had a passport, all their lives they never had any papers, except for a talisman. Suppose they entrusted the task to the Chinese? While Bekesh was pondering all of this, he cursed himself: 'I must be blind, may a wolf bite my arse! How could one entrust a sacred father of the Kyrgyz to the care of the Chinese?'

As they approached the ayyl, the old woman's weeping grew stronger.

> The burning coals turned red,
> What's gulped down won't come back.
> The tiger is lurking in the high steppes, they say,
> The Kyrgyz heart is pounding...

When they heard the weeping, girls and old women came out of their houses and joined in their lament. There was uproar in Chekbel. As they approached the frontier, the Tajik border guards met the crowd: 'Who's died? Who's died?' they asked, as they began to recite the first sura of the Qur'an. Somewhere or other, a coffin was found. Shapak's corpse, wrapped in its white shroud, was taken off the horse and put in to the coffin and some young men passed it over to the Tajik border guards who were be take it to the Kyrgyz guards.

Bekesh left his horse in Ulankhu's care and sent him home. In fact, he didn't send the old woman off with Ulankhu because the Kyrgyz border guards dug their heels in and insisted that she hand over the old man's death certificate.

'Hey, you crowing arseholes, what certificate? This is the body of a Kyrgyz *Manas* reciter, his ghost will strike at you!' Bekesh said. He had never used such rough language before, but if ever there was a time for it, it was now. Unfortunately, he didn't have his radio ID on him. Now the old woman, still sitting on her donkey, was calling out to the chief in charge of the border guards. She then whispered something in his ear, he seemed to have taken a liking to her. The commandant softened, took a look at the old woman's sheep and pointed to the fattest black sheep: 'That's enough,' he proclaimed. 'You can pass with twenty. All the women wearing widow's headgear, go back to your houses!'

Before any time had passed, the men who were holding up the coffin went one way and the sobbing women another – and the fat sheep became a sacrifice to the border guards who hadn't seen meat for some time.

> The cattle will graze in the reed beds,
> Water will gather in the filled flower.
> Father Shapak's eye has passed,
> Who will come and ask after wretched me...

—

In the Tajik kishlak, men and youths gathered around to help lift the coffin. The situation in Chekbel had made people miss each other's company, and they took turns to silently carry the coffin. Those left behind were crowded together, everyone asking after one another, all quietly grieving as they walked. People from all sides were moved. If you were ill, the doctor was on one side; if you were dead, the cemetery was on the other side, everything and everyone was in chaos. But it was not the people of Chekbel, but the garish Chinese who were strolling calmly about.

'A goat that has twin kids still doesn't become a sheep,' said a Kyrgyz, to which a Tajik added a couplet by Hafiz:

> Though a friend does not buy us a thing,
> For the world I would not sell a hair of a friend's head...

Bekesh listened, unable to focus either body or spirit. He wiped the tears from his eyes as he walked, and just as there were two unrecognised tears on the outside, inwardly he felt as if there were two companions on the final journey of Shapak the *Manas* reciter – Baisal and Uncle Sattor. Thick flakes of snow began to fall.

There had never been gravediggers in the cemetery, and spades and pickaxes had been left at the entrance. Dropping the coffin, the young men began to dig, and one of those who had witnessed such things before began to recite a burial prayer. Taking the corpse from the coffin, they laid it in the ground. A rock was placed over the open grave, and with Bekesh at the grave's head, earth was shaken from the pickaxes. Everyone kneeled down again, and the mullah began a reading from the Qur'an. The appearance of Ulankhu silenced the noise of the crowd as he trampled the earth beneath his feet, yelling unintelligible words at the cemetery.

Everyone was listening to the reading and nobody, except Bekesh, had been alarmed by Ulankhu. 'This Mongolian thinks he's a Kyrgyz now, I wouldn't be surprised if he starts sobbing so he can throw in a handful of earth,' Bekesh thought. But in spite of the silence and the Qur'anic breaking through, Ulankhu didn't stop his awkward pacing or his yelling. When the reading finished, and all who were gathered said Amen to the first sura of the Qur'an, Ulankhu sought out Bekesh in the crowd. He pulled him aside and, his eyes wet with tears, said 'Tumo! Tumo!', waving his arms in the air as if they were wings.

'Is a fog falling, is that what he's trying to tell me?' Bekesh wondered at first, thinking he heard *tuman*, the Kyrgyz and Russian word for mist. But was a father's grave a suitable court-

house for a mist to fall? Bekesh was deep in thought and pic-
tured Shapak standing and laughing.

'Tumor... Tumor...' the incoherent Mongolian said as he
tugged once more at Bekesh. Then Bekesh's heart sank. Tumor! Yes, Tumor...

—

On the return journey, when the border guards began to in-
spect passports, Ulankhu tugged at Bekesh's sleeve and led him
back to the Tajik kishlak. As was proper, Bekesh had told the
young men that they'd be gathering at the house for a meal,
and Ulankhu decided to take him along with him in his
zigzagging route to the Chinese encampment, before leading
the way to a Tajik family's yard. Bekesh tried politely to refuse
as it was already getting dark and he tried to say that it would
be shameful to enter someone else's house, but Ulankhu took
him by the hand into the yard, and then from the yard to the
well. Opening the well's trap-door, he lead him then down a
juniper-wood ladder and, standing precariously at two paces
above water level, took him through a door on a slope to an
underground pit. Passing through this pit, they emerged into
the Chinese encampment.

As twilight fell, all the workers had come back to their railway carriages ready for supper. Nobody there had yet seen
them, and certainly nobody found anything to say to them.
Both Ulankhu and Bekesh got out to the Kyrgyz ayyl by a legal
gate, not an underground one, and, gasping for breath, they ran
off uphill following the border stream towards the poplar trees
in the direction of Bekesh's family fortress.

There was the sound of weeping coming from the house,

but this did not astound Bekesh in the least: hadn't he, before anything else, despatched the old lady to see his Aunt Rabiga? But it was this weeping from as many as the fifty or sixty young people crowded around that made him quicken his pace. 'They've heard about Shapak's death and have come for the funeral feast, or else...'

Pushing through the mob, Ulankhu led Bekesh inside. The womenfolk inside forced themselves to sob, despite the other mourners. Children whispering like Ili-valley Uighurs eager for the manger took Bekesh aside and dragged him towards his room and the hunting room, the Mongolian being too mute to say why.

When Bekesh entered the room, having taken off his felt cap, he saw that his animal hide had been worn off against a rock, and then he felt his heart snap and break. The tapes were scattered all over the room, with blood everywhere. The tapes with Baisal's voice were covered in spider's webs from corner to corner, while on the opposite wall in fresh bright red blood someone had written two large Chinese characters:

上天

'Read it!' Bekesh shouted to Ulankhu.

Ulankhu didn't understand what it could mean, but he could reproduce the sound: 'Shàngtiān.'[4]

'What's that?' asked Bekesh, his eyes goggling. Ulankhu had heard this asked a hundred times and knew very well what it meant but couldn't find the words he needed to answer in Kyrgyz. Instead, he pointed his index finger at the sky and imitated the flapping of wings. Then he shut one eye and stuck his

4. 'shàng tiān', meaning 'heaven God'.

tongue out, pretending to lie down with his hands clasped.

'Has Tumor died?' Bekesh asked, enfeebled, suddenly exhausted. Ulankhu apparently remembered the words he needed when he interpreted the two characters written in blood on the wall, words that he had repeatedly heard Shapak say in his cave: 'He's died... he's died... he's died...'

—

After he saw the hunting room ransacked and ravaged, Bekesh's eyes lost their sight. Nothing was left untouched; it could have been Mamay's army passing through the two rooms. Bekesh was overcome when his eye once more fell on the word 'heaven' written in Chinese. Where might he have seen anything like this? What had Ulankhu just said, 'shàngtiān' was it? Ah! Only that was in a way the opposite of Tien-Shan! That Chinaman had in fact turned the Kyrgyz's Ola Mountains into death! The words from the *Manas* surfaced in Bekesh's brain:

> A great force has come from the Kalmaks, alas!
> If I think, strong in hand, alas!
> Will the Kyrgyz, locked up, now die, alas?
> Will every one of our people become a Chinaman, alas?
> Will it put fear in the heart, alas?
> Will the ugly-faced dark Chinese
> Enjoy trampling us down, alas?
> Will that nation, as numerous as ants,
> Come down from our hills and crush us, alas?

Perhaps he shouted these words, his mouth and nose streaming, as he emerged to join the young people. If God could strike a man, he would become a teenager, even if he was fifty. Bekesh told himself he that would take revenge on that treacherous fool Lin Ju, and in that he turned back into a fifteen-year-old boy. The old woman hadn't been able to stop him with the sight of her toothless mumbling, nor, for some reason, had the despair that ensued: 'He is her child who softened her breast of stone, he is her first-born who opened her eyes, leave them in peace!' said his shrieking aunt, but he was leading the crowd now, burning with anger, towards the Chinese encampment.

Holding guns, daggers at their waists, raising hell and not knowing what to say in their fury regardless of the clouded sky and frozen ground, came the ominous procession. Some carried lighted torches and flares, some carried pickaxes, others wielded scythes and sickles fit to behead a man. As they marched, they collected stones along the way.

'If you spit enough, you get a lake,' was the saying, and every one of them harboured his own particular grudge against the Chinese. Some were cursing them: 'They've led my child astray'. Others said, 'We say hello to them, they don't answer.' One man, working himself up, shouted: 'They've come to stink out the village.'

Others, with spittle dribbling from their mouths, let out their wrath with: 'They've come to eat dogs and lice everywhere they find them, now they've started hunting donkey foals.'

What followed sickened Bekesh to the core and curdled his blood. That bastard called Lin Ju had gone and fried his Tumor in his big frying pan: Bekesh had noticed his perfidious skills! Why had he entrusted Lin Ju with his Tumor and with Dapan? Why?

—

That night, flames from the two mountain slopes engulfed the Chinese construction workers' camp on the banks of the stream. When the Tajik riff-raff saw the riot, they attacked the encampment and they too joined the brawl. It was then that the knife-fights began. Before that, the Chinese who were in the railway carriages at the edge of the camp came out half naked, and once they were in the snow-chilled air, fear made them waggle their ears in all directions as if they were hares. Then under the hail of rocks, and the screams and shouts, they began to defend themselves. One demonstrated his martial art skills, another man leapt onto a bulldozer and drove it at the crowd. And so began the deadly and bloody hand-to-hand battle.

The bitches stuffed themselves at a feast,
Swallowing what they could,
They were carried away
By easily killed booty!
If the Chinese arrogance
Be put down like this,
Why should we spare the souls
Of a people who are now besieged?
It will be a judgement on the Chinese,
Let's burst in on all of them,
Afterwards see the battle
Send them back to their roots!

Bekesh was searching everywhere for Lin Ju, and for Tumor

and Dapan, shouting: 'Nobody can find a remedy for my pain!' He would have been glad to find just a shadow of them in this hell. The bullets he had saved for his gun would be used on that devil Lin Ju.

But the first person he came across was the diabolical Mimtimin. He struck him with his rifle butt, knocking him to the ground, and straight away jumped on him and wrapped his hands around his throat.

'Millions of Uighurs are going through hell in concentration camps, but you, you bastard, are up to your foul tricks. Where are Lin Ju and Dapan? Tell me!' he snorted. The strangled Mimtimin mumbled something, but in the uproar and confusion Bekesh couldn't hear what he was saying and relaxed his grip. 'Tell me, you bitch. You're dead meat! If you don't then I'll kill you!'

'Last night they took his corpse from your place. I didn't kill the boy! His father shot him, his father... His drug addict father was trying to find the eagle and some magic green stone... That was after your bird killed Lin Ju when it was flying away...'

At that moment, a heavy cudgel struck Bekesh on the head.

—

Why did every poem in the *Manas* end with a death? 'Death is a comrade, the quest is casual,' goes the saying, doesn't it? Just as poem after poem might conceal life's pain, death seems to proclaim its true nature. When Manas himself was wounded in the Great Raid he made on Beijing, it was at his wife Kanikey's hand that he gave up the ghost. His son, the destitute Semetey, however much his mother Kanikey and wife Aychurek tried to mediate, placed his trust in his treacherous comrade Kanchoro, and would be killed by his own army. Semetey's son Seytek, Seytek's son Kenenim, Kenenim's son Seyit, trying to be as manly as they could, would all die in vain.

Seyit's son Bekbacha had all his life tirelessly charged off to war to protect the peaceful life of the Kyrgyz. When he was nearing ninety he got together with a beautiful Kalmak girl and from her he had a son called Sömbilek. The unfaithful wife then put drops of poison into Bekbacha's kumys and murdered him. If only to make up for this, So'mbilek lived a prosperous life; in the middle of life's labours and ordeals enemies mercilessly speared him. The very last, the eighth hero of the *Manas*, Sömbilek's son Chigitey, tied a kerchief round his head and went relentlessly into battle, but the horse he had mounted was entangled in string and fell; he falls off his horse, is wounded by an enemy and gives up the ghost... Death after death, death after death...

So the enormous black stone of death is thrown into life's reservoir, and ripple after ripple spreads in every direction... What is this sequence of poems trying to teach us? About death's sentence, or about the force of life that follows it? Ultimately, when Manas dies, close behind him comes Semetey, after Semetey Seytek, and after him Kenenim takes his father's place... Perhaps it wasn't a smeared spear that time threw at your plans, but the so-called 'cycle of time'. And there is a ripple coming after this ripple, sending a moth flying into the sky, burying a caterpillar in the black earth...

... A violent blizzard on all sides... White snow and a black sky have covered up all that exists. Tearing off his jesses with a steel beak, a black eagle will fly, after it has seized someone's head in its talons. 'Beating is for the winged, pecking for the

beaked...' a voice seemed to say. A child's voice... Once more
a freezing wind was rousing all. 'A dying ox won't escape the
axe,' said another voice. Whose voice was it? Who was talking
to whom? It wasn't the snow so much as an evil drug that had
flooded the entire world: the thought, the thought was elusive.
'Who killed the boy?' people called out in Tajik. A whirlwind
of snow rose up to the black sky like a dragon. Was it white
kumys, or an overturned chalice contaminated with drugs,
pouring its poison onto the ground? Drip-drip-drip... Or, is
someone speaking Chinese? What did he say? He didn't hit a
lot in the fields at home? Soldier, fire, knife-fight... Sparks flying against the snow. Again, someone's Farsi words:

Now he who was unemployed has become a worker,
When he looks at his son, humbled in his father's presence...

The wind, which had turned everything into a blizzard, left
no one's possessions on the ground. The earth's face seemed to
have been shaved with a razor and left utterly bare... Clothes
without their wearers were flying about, together with bread
covered in mould. There was a bitter smell of juniper... You
couldn't get about if you bent double, if you didn't writhe like
an emaciated sheep... Moth after moth, the quantity of snow
was so great that the black earth could barely stop everything
swaying... Your white flesh's heat would fade like a juniper
fire... Far away, a tiny silhouette, probably a boy, joining a
group of about forty men in a yurt, all with completely white
eyebrows and bears... Their eyes as piercing as an eagle's...
And words without a master, weeping...

They cut the head off

The boy that was burning.
They made a donkey
Of Topon in his old age.
The lady, grief-stricken,
Said, 'Let me not be left alone,'
Said, 'Let me not die covered in dirt.
Let me not see from this world
Blindness alive and walking.'
She said, 'Let me see a dagger and take it.'
She was able to find comfort and say, 'Let me die!'

At that time,
shedding hidden blood and tears
Over his face, scratched by his nails,
Dark-red blood dripping,
And in despair he said a word,
And the word he said was this...

tiltedaxispress.com

The rights of Hamid Ismailov to be identified as the author and Donald Rayfield as the translator of this work have been asserted in accordance with Section 77 of the Copyright, Designs and Patent Act 1988.

ISBN (paperback) 9781911284574

ISBN (ebook) 9781911284567

A catalogue record for this book is available from the British Library.

Cover design by Soraya Gilanni Viljoen

Edited by Saba Ahmed and John Merrick

Typesetting and ebook production by Simon Collinson

Made with Hederis

Printed and bound by Clays Ltd, Elcograf S.p.A.

Supported using public funding by
**ARTS COUNCIL
ENGLAND**

ABOUT TILTED AXIS PRESS

Tilted Axis is a non-profit press publishing mainly work by Asian writers, translated into a variety of Englishes. This is an artistic project, for the benefit of readers who would not otherwise have access to the work – including ourselves. We publish what we find personally compelling.

Founded in 2015, we are based in the UK, a state whose former and current imperialism severely impacts writers in the majority world. This position, and those of our individual members, informs our practice, which is also an ongoing exploration into alternatives – to the hierarchisation of certain languages and forms, including forms of translation; to the monoculture of globalisation; to cultural, narrative, and visual stereotypes; to the commercialisation and celebrification of literature and literary translation.

We value the work of translation and translators through fair, transparent pay, public acknowledgement, and respectful communication. We are dedicated to improving access to the industry, through translator mentorships, paid publishing internships, open calls and guest curation.

Our publishing is a work in progress – we are always open to feedback, including constructive criticism, and suggestions for collaborations. We are particularly keen to connect with Black and indigenous translators of Asian languages.

tiltedaxispress.com
@TiltedAxisPress